"You wouldn't believe the number of people who want a piece of me."

Most of them female. Even before Miss Georgia, the newspapers had reported his dating exploits so comprehensively Bethany wondered how he found time to make it into the office. But evidently he did, because lately the press had been covering the foundation's charitable activities, and in that sphere at least it seemed Tyler was a saint. Albeit one untroubled by anything so pesky as a vow of celibacy.

"I want a piece of you, too," she said. Tyler raised his eyebrows, and she stuttered, "I–I want you to guarantee me that appointment to talk about my funding. Please."

"I like a woman who knows what she wants." Before she could decide if he was being provocative, he turned to his assistant. "Give Bethany some time next week. And when I tell you to fob her off, don't let me."

Dear Reader,

This is the first book I've written that features a baby—in this case, a little boy who's been abandoned at the office of charming-but-shallow philanthropist Tyler Warrington. Tyler has no idea what to do with a baby—beyond using it to promote his own public image! But someone has to change the diapers, and Tyler has no intention of performing that messy job himself. He needs a sitter.

Unfortunately for him, tenderhearted, determined pediatrician Bethany Hart decides she's the woman for the job. She has a score to settle with Tyler, and she sees right through his charming facade. As you'll discover when you read *The Diaper Diaries*, Tyler has a lot to learn about babies, about life and about love. But so, it turns out, does Bethany…

I hope you enjoy this story—please e-mail me at abby@abbygaines.com and let me know what you think.

Many readers of my last Harlequin Superromance book, *Married by Mistake*, e-mailed to say how much they enjoyed the extra scenes for that book, which I made available on my Web site. So I've done it again. If you'd like to read some After the End scenes for *The Diaper Diaries*, including Tyler and Bethany's wedding, and more news of minor characters Silas and Olivia, visit the For Readers page at www.abbygaines.com.

Sincerely,

Abby Gaines

THE DIAPER DIARIES
Abby Gaines

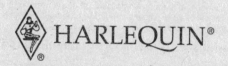

HARLEQUIN®

TORONTO • NEW YORK • LONDON
AMSTERDAM • PARIS • SYDNEY • HAMBURG
STOCKHOLM • ATHENS • TOKYO • MILAN • MADRID
PRAGUE • WARSAW • BUDAPEST • AUCKLAND

ISBN-13: 978-0-373-78225-3
ISBN-10: 0-373-78225-X

THE DIAPER DIARIES

ABOUT THE AUTHOR

Mrs. Brady or Mrs. Cleaver? Carol Brady is my fantasy...never yelling at her kids and, um, a husband with permed hair. **Cloth or disposable?** Less time washing diapers means more time with the baby. **Favorite bedtime story?** *Beauty and the Beast*–I was a romance reader from a young age. **Keeper quote from your mom?** "What you do and what I do are twenty-five different things." It's one of those lines I always swore I'd never say to my own kids...so far, I've managed to restrain myself. **I wish my baby could've stayed forever at age...** I've adored them all at every age. **Most poignant moment?** My son–my first child–was born with an enormous hematoma (a big, bloody bump) on his head. It lasted for weeks, but I thought he was gorgeous. I have to admit, though, I chuckle when I look at the photos now! **What makes a mom?** Loving your kids despite, even because of, their flaws and imperfections. Knowing them as no one else does. It's a romantic ideal I carry into all my books for relationships between men and women, but the great thing is, it comes naturally for moms with their kids.

Books by Abby Gaines

HARLEQUIN SUPERROMANCE

Don't miss any of our special offers. Write to us at the following address for information on our newest releases.

Harlequin Reader Service
U.S.: 3010 Walden Ave., P.O. Box 1325, Buffalo, NY 14269
Canadian: P.O. Box 609, Fort Erie, Ont. L2A 5X3

CHAPTER ONE

THE LETTER ENDED the same way they all did. *Thank you for caring.*

"I'm too damn busy to care," Tyler snarled at his secretary, who'd just deposited today's stack of heartrending pleas for cash on the corner of his steel-and-glass desk.

"You always are," Olivia Payne agreed cheerfully. With her graying hair held back in a bun, she looked staid and professional—an appearance that was entirely deceptive. She nodded at the letter Tyler held in his hand. "Anything interesting?"

Tyler fanned out the four pages of closely written text dotted with exclamation points. "Some guy wants two hundred grand to save the red-spotted tree frog. If we don't act fast, we might never see the frog again."

He picked up another letter—a single-page e-mail asking for thirty thousand dollars to buy computers for a preschool—and weighed it against the frog letter, as if he could somehow gauge the relative worthiness of the two causes.

The Warrington Foundation, whose purpose was to give away some of the multimillion-dollar profits earned by Warrington Construction, had hired extra staff in the new year to do the preliminary evaluations. It was their job to send polite rejections to the men who wanted bigger breasts for their wives and the people seeking donations to surefire lottery schemes.

But that still left anywhere up to a hundred potentially genuine requests for the chairman—Tyler—to read each day. Many of them ended with what seemed to be that mantra: *Thank you for caring.*

Tyler folded the first page of the frog letter into a paper airplane.

All he cared about right now was convincing the powers that be in Washington, D.C., that he was the right person to head up their new think tank, established to determine how charities and government could work together to support families. They were looking for someone who understood the concerns of ordinary American families. And Tyler had ended up on the shortlist thanks to the foundation's good work with various children's charities.

Presumably, he was at the very bottom of that shortlist. Yet he wanted the job to an extent that surprised him and would have amazed his family, who would doubtless say he was more suited to a think tank on how to get more fun into people's lives.

Tyler flipped his hand-forged-silver Michel Perchin pen between his fingers as he contemplated his possibly irredeemable reputation. Every news report about his work at the foundation was countered by a juicy piece in the gossip pages about "playboy bachelor Tyler Warrington." He'd made a major lifestyle adjustment—dating the same woman every night the past two weeks—but he wasn't sure that act of heroism was enough. Correction: after the headline in this morning's *Atlanta Journal-Constitution,* he knew it wasn't.

He smoothed out the paper plane, slapped the two letters together, handed them to Olivia. "The frog's a no go. Invite the preschool to pitch at the next committee meeting."

What could be more *ordinary* and *American* than preschool?

Maybe his PR team could write an opinion piece about early-childhood education and submit it to the *Journal-Constitution* in Tyler's name.

Olivia tucked the letters into her folder. "I'll deal with these right after I go downstairs. Joe called to say there's a delivery for you. He sounded pretty excited."

"Just as well our security guy doesn't make the allocations." Unlike Tyler, Joe was a sucker for the attention-getting ploys to which some people resorted when they asked for money. "If it's balloons, cake or cigars, tell him to take them home to his kids." He raised his hands in self-defense against Olivia's daggered look. "Okay, okay, hold the cigars."

OLIVIA RETURNED carrying a faded green duffel bag in a fierce grip, the straps wrapped around one hand, her other arm underneath the bag. She cradled it with a delicacy that suggested its contents were at least as valuable as the Venetian-glass sculpture she'd spent hundreds on last week.

Tyler shoved his chair back from the desk, got to his feet. "What is it?"

Very gently, she slid the bag across the surface of the desk; Tyler saw the zipper was open. "Take a look," she invited, her voice curiously high.

He parted the top of the bag, peered in. And met the unblinking blue gaze of a baby.

Wrapped in a whitish blanket and wearing a soft yellow hat so that only a little round face showed… but definitely a baby.

"What the—" Tyler leaped backward, glared at his secretary. "Is this a joke?"

Olivia blew out a breath as she shook her head. "A young woman came in, told Joe she had a delivery for you. She excused herself to go to the bathroom and left the bag on Joe's desk. After a couple of minutes, the baby sneezed—gave Joe a heck of a fright. That's when he called me."

Tyler raked a hand through his hair. "For Pete's

sake, the woman's probably still in the bathroom. Or by now, back out with Joe and wondering where her kid's gone. Take it back down."

Olivia handed Tyler an envelope, his name written on it in blue ink. "This was in the bag."

It had already been opened—Olivia read all Tyler's correspondence. The paper crackled: thin, cheap, almost weightless. Yet it felt far heavier than those requests he'd been reading a few minutes ago. Tyler unfolded the page.

The handwriting was young, or maybe just uneducated, and the message brief.

Dear Mr. Warrington,
I know you are kind and generous and you help lots of people. Please can you adopt my baby? I just can't do this. Thank you very very very much for caring.

No signature.

So much for the she's-still-in-the-bathroom theory. Tyler read the letter again. *Damn.*

With a caution that would have amazed the college buddies he played football with every month, he advanced on the duffel. The infant was still there, still staring. It had worked one little hand loose and was clenching and unclenching a tiny fist against the blanket.

Hey, kid, if you're frustrated, how do you think I

feel? "What the hell am I supposed to do with you?" he said, the words rougher than he'd intended.

The baby blinked, and its mouth moved. If it cried now Tyler would be screwed. He patted the small hand as gently as he could, while he tried to think of words that might soothe. Snatches of nursery rhymes flitted through his head but were gone before he could catch them. "I meant heck," he said at last.

The kid still looked worried, so Tyler moved out of its line of vision. He looked out the window, over Peachtree Street, where courier bikes scraped between cars and vans with no margin for error, and the crosswalks thronged with businesspeople. No place for a baby.

"We have to find the mother," he told Olivia. "Ask Joe to send up the security-camera footage."

"I already did, but he doesn't think it'll help," she said, cheerful now she'd handed the problem to Tyler. "The woman wore a woolen hat pulled right down, and she had a scarf wrapped around her face. It's cold out, so Joe didn't think anything of it."

"Someone has to know who she is," Tyler persisted. "We'll give the tape to the police. And you'd better call social services—they can take the baby until the mom turns up."

"And they say you're just a pretty face," Olivia marveled. "I don't know why that young woman didn't go to social services in the first place." She chuckled. "I mean, do you know anyone less suited to looking after a baby than you?"

"You," Tyler returned sharply. Stupid to let her "pretty face" comment needle him. He might not be an expert on diapers and drool, but he knew he could do whatever he set his mind to. And that made him good for a whole lot more than simply doling out the money his brother Max made in the family's "real" business. Which he was about to prove by winning the job in Washington, D.C.

Olivia, who'd never married, never had kids, and as far as Tyler knew, was having too much fun to regret either omission, laughed at his insult.

She didn't know about Washington. She and Tyler's mom were close enough that there was no chance she wouldn't spill the beans. No one knew, not even Tyler, officially. The news that he was under consideration had come from his cousin Jake, who had reliable political connections. But the whole thing was so sensitive, so confidential, there was no way Tyler could do what he knew would work best—jump on a plane to D.C. and talk them into giving him the job.

All he could do was continue his strategy of raising his profile in the media—his political profile, not his social profile. He glared at the duffel from his safe distance.

"The press will be all over this," he told Olivia, "no matter how fast we palm the kid off to social services."

"It can't be as bad as today's story." She ruined the comforting effect by snickering.

Two women Tyler had dated in the past had gotten into a tipsy argument at a nightclub a couple of evenings ago, apparently over which of the two he'd liked best—he barely recalled either of them. In a misguided attempt to emphasize her point, one had slugged the other with her purse.

None of that would have made the newspaper if one of the women's pals hadn't posted the purse for sale on eBay. The purse had been of supreme disinterest to most of the world, but the bidding in Atlanta was fierce and the story had spread in the media as one of those quirky "I sold my grandmother on eBay" tales. Tyler could only hope it hadn't reached Washington.

He needed damage control, and he needed it now. Pacing in front of the window, he tried to think of a political angle he could play up with the baby that might counter the gossip. How about a photo opportunity of him handing the baby to social services, commenting about the challenges facing young mothers?

Then it hit him—or, rather, smacked him in the head with a force that left him dizzy.

There wasn't just one political angle to the baby story, there were *dozens*—the foster system, parenting, money, infant health, who knew what else?— that he could tap into. This was his chance to show the world how well he understood the concerns of families.

"On second thought, don't call social services," he told Olivia. "Nor the police." He grinned at the duffel, suddenly feeling a whole lot warmer toward its occupant. "We need to get the baby out of the bag."

"We?" she said, horrified.

"You," he amended.

She backed off. "Uh-uh, no way."

Tyler directed his most cajoling smile at her. "Please."

She rolled her eyes, but came back and reached into the bag. He steadied it while she lifted the baby out. Olivia held it in a grip that he judged possibly too tight, but the baby didn't protest, so Tyler bowed to its superior knowledge. He looked around his office, all hard surfaces, sharp corners, glass and metal. "How about we spread the blanket on the floor," he suggested, pleased with his own parental-improvisation skills.

He managed to get the blanket out from around the baby, who turned out to be encased from head to toe in yellow terry. "We'll use your office," he told Olivia.

"My floor has slate tiles." With the unnaturally pointed toe of her shoe—and with undisguised triumph—she nudged the plush rust-colored carpet that enhanced Tyler's luxurious work space. "Yours is much more suitable."

Too bad she was right. He spread out the blanket, smoothed it confidently—because looking after a kid wasn't rocket science—then nodded at Olivia, who knelt down to lay the baby on its back. She rubbed her own back as she got to her feet. "Now what?" she said.

Tyler looked down at the infant. Two short, pudgy arms waved at him, but there was still no crying. *Thoughtful of the mom to give me a well-behaved kid.* "You'd better organize a crib or whatever it is babies hang out in."

"You can't be thinking about keeping this child," Olivia said, shocked.

"Of course not. Just until we find the mom." At least a few days, he guessed, even if he put a private investigator onto it today. Maybe as much as a week or two. He would call his PR manager, tell her to arrange some media opportunities for him right away—just as soon as she found someone to get him up to speed about kid-parent issues.

"But—" Olivia shook her head, nonplussed "—you don't know the first thing about looking after a baby."

"That's what sitters are for. Call an agency, see if you can get someone immediately."

"I didn't even know you *liked* children." She was practically wringing her hands with worry, which Tyler considered an overreaction.

"I only have to like this one." He didn't even *have* to do that, but he was willing to try.

Olivia picked up a pad and pen off the desk. "Then I guess we need to think about food. Special baby formula." She jotted that down. "And diapers. They go through those pretty fast." She shuddered.

The baby hiccuped, its face contorted. Hell, was it about to puke? They did that all the time, didn't they?

"We should call a doctor," Tyler said. "Find out if the kid's okay before I make any plans." He pulled out his handkerchief in case of an emergency wipe-up situation. "Call that woman we gave money to last year. The pediatrician doing the kidney research."

"Great idea." Olivia's voice warmed. "She's a real peach."

Tyler frowned. "Are we talking about the same woman?"

"Dr. Bethany Hart."

"That's her." He would have described Bethany Hart as more frosty than peachy. And she was quite possibly the most ungrateful woman he'd ever met. The Warrington Foundation had granted her a generous sum for her research into childhood kidney disease which was part of a wider research project at Children's Healthcare of Atlanta, attached to Emory University. Instead of the thank-you letter most people wrote, she'd sent Tyler a curtly worded missive to the effect that if he was at all serious about helping young kidney patients he would give a lot more money.

Unlike everyone else, she'd accused him of not caring. Tyler had found her ingratitude refreshing.

Just a couple of weeks ago she'd written to him again. The money, intended to cover her salary, along with admin support and the use of lab facilities and equipment, was almost gone: she'd asked him to renew her funding. She'd enclosed a comprehensive—in his opinion, *boring*—report on her work to date, and had invited him, rather insistently, to visit a bunch of sick kids in the hospital.

"She may not be your biggest fan," Olivia said with rare diplomacy. She'd read the pediatrician's letters, too. "But she sure loves kids."

Tyler had noticed the way Dr. Hart's blue eyes lit up when she talked about the children she worked with. "Then she'll want to check out this baby."

He didn't plan to give her a choice. Bethany Hart might have complained about the amount of money she'd received, but no one else had offered her a dime. The foundation had given more than her presentation to the Philanthropic Strategy Committee had merited.

Tyler had swayed the PhilStrat Committee in her favor. Not because she'd wowed him with her presentation—despite her obviously high intelligence, she'd been inarticulate to the point where he'd been embarrassed for her. Definitely not because of that spark of attraction that had flared between them, despite her frostiness—he never let that kind of thing get in the way of business.

When she'd bumbled to the end of her appalling pitch, she'd shot Tyler a look of angry resignation that said she might have messed up, but it was his fault.

He shook her hand as she left, and couldn't help smiling at the furious quiver in her otherwise stiff fingers. Which enraged her further. She looked down her nose at him as she said, "You haven't heard the last of me."

He sighed. "I was afraid of that."

She reeked of do-gooder earnestness, coupled with the kind of instinctive, misguided courage that led people to pursue hopeless causes without, unfortunately, actually losing hope.

So Tyler had believed Bethany when she said he hadn't heard the last of her. During the PhilStrat Committee's deliberations, he'd cast his vote in her support largely to shut her up.

Now, as it turned out, that might have been a smart move. He needed her discreet cooperation over this baby and he expected her to give it, however reluctantly.

Because Bethany Hart owed him.

CHAPTER TWO

BETHANY WAS IN THE SHOWER sloughing off the fatigue of three straight shifts in the E.R. at Emory University Hospital when the phone rang in the studio apartment she rented near the campus.

It was Olivia Payne, Tyler Warrington's secretary, asking if Bethany could come to the Warrington Foundation offices right away. "Tyler would like to meet with you." Olivia paused. "At this stage I can't tell you why."

He wants to give me more money. Jubilation surged through Bethany; adrenaline transformed her exhaustion into energy. She punched the air with the hand that wasn't holding the phone, then had to clutch the towel she'd wrapped around herself before it slipped to the floor.

After she'd hung up, she celebrated with an impromptu dance around her living room singing, "I aaaaam a reeesearch geeenius" to the tune of Billy Joel's "Innocent Man." But the room was too small for her to burn off this much excitement: as she danced, she grabbed the phone again and dialed her parents.

"Mom, it's me. Bethany." She slowed down, suddenly breathless. Crazy that she still felt compelled to identify herself—it was fourteen years since her sister's death, there was no chance of confusion. Without waiting for a reply, she said, "Looks like the Warrington Foundation plans to extend my research grant."

Her mom squawked with delight, none of her usual listlessness evident. "Darling, that's wonderful. Just wonderful."

"I'm seeing Tyler Warrington this morning. The foundation can extend the grant for a second twelve months at its discretion, without me having to pitch again."

"That's the best news—let me tell your dad."

Bethany heard her mom calling out to her father, heard his whoop of excitement. Then a muffled question she didn't catch, and an "I'll ask her" from her mom.

"Uh, honey," her mother said into the phone, "is there any chance they'll give you more money than last year? You always say you could get so much more done if you could afford to pay your assistant for more hours."

The familiar defensiveness—the urgent need to impress upon her parents that there just wasn't enough money around to fund all the research into kidney disease—constricted Bethany's chest. She puffed out a series of short, silent, relaxing breaths. Her parents weren't worried about other projects, only about hers. She understood; she even sympathized. Brightly, she said, "Of course I'll ask for more, but I may not get it."

Mentally, she doubled the figure she would propose to Tyler Warrington. If she started high, even ridiculously high, chances were she'd end up with more than if she went in low.

"I know you'll do your best," her mother said warmly.

Bethany basked in that praise. No use telling herself she was too old to be grateful for the crumbs of parental approval that came her way; some things never changed.

The moment she'd finished the call, her phone rang again. It was Olivia. "I forgot to say, you'll need to bring your medical bag."

Bring her bag so Tyler could hand over a check? *Uh-oh.* A chill shivered through Bethany, the kind that either meant she was ill or something bad was about to happen. And in her own expert opinion, she wasn't ill.

Should she call Mom now and admit she might have been hasty with her talk of more money? Her finger hovered over the phone's redial button.

Then her natural optimism took over, binding itself to the remains of that energy surge. Okay, so

Tyler likely had a nephew or niece with a chest cold, and His Egoness figured he had dibs on Bethany's time now that he'd contributed to her research. But if he didn't plan to renew her funds, surely he wouldn't dare summon her help? And that report she'd sent a couple of weeks ago had made an excellent case. Whatever he wanted today, she could still talk to him about money.

Provided, of course, she could string together more than two coherent words. As always, the recollection of how she'd mangled her last pitch to the super-smooth Tyler mortified her. No matter how often she prayed for selective amnesia—either for her or Tyler—her memory stayed depressingly clear. His was doubtless just as sharp.

But with any luck, he was so hopelessly in love with his new girlfriend—according to the newspapers, he was embroiled in a hot-and-heavy romance with Miss Georgia—that he'd see everything, including Bethany, through rose-tinted lenses.

"All you have to do is stay calm," she told herself out loud as she fished through her wardrobe for something to wear. Last time, she'd borrowed a suit from a colleague, but Banana Republic navy chino hadn't stopped her messing up.

She tugged a burgundy-colored woolen skirt off its hanger. Maybe she'd have better luck with this—unmistakably homemade, it was a gift from a young patient's grateful grandmother. If anything could fire Bethany up to get more money from Tyler it would be a reminder of the kids she hoped to help. She pulled the skirt on, added a long-sleeved black T-shirt, then inspected herself in the mirror.

Hmm, maybe the skirt was a bit too peasant style, with those large felt flowers appliquéd around the hem, and—she twirled around—maybe said hem wasn't entirely straight—the old lady's eyesight had been failing—but Bethany's high-heeled pumps would dress it up.

Besides, she didn't have a lot of choice. Thanks to her huge student loans, her wardrobe consisted of scrubs, lab coats and a bunch of stuff she could hide beneath them.

Bethany waved the blow-dryer briefly at her shoulder-length reddish-brown hair, then, in deference to the importance of the funds she was about to request, not to the man who was to bestow them, she applied some mascara and a pinky-red lipstick.

"Calm," she reminded her flustered, wild-eyed reflection as she rolled her lips together to smooth the lipstick.

She couldn't afford to screw up again. Last time, Tyler hadn't bothered to hide first his boredom, then his amusement at her inarticulateness. Then, of course, he'd done that *stupid thing* that had left her feeling like the joke of the day.

Maybe she'd been oversensitive, she chided herself. There was probably a good explanation for his behavior. A nervous tic. Tourette's syndrome. Thirty-something years of silver spoon-slurping, privileged existence that had blinded him to the needs of—

Okay, now she was being uncharitable, the very thing she'd accused Tyler of in the letter she'd sent after her pitch. Besides, Miss Georgia was apparently committed to working tirelessly for world peace. Clearly Tyler's charitable instincts were in full working order.

Bethany would give him the benefit of the doubt and ask him politely—and coherently—for more money.

Olivia Payne gave Bethany a warm welcome, then phoned through to tell Tyler she had arrived.

When he appeared in the doorway of his secretary's office, Bethany was struck anew by his good looks. The camera loved him—she knew that from the newspaper photos—but real life suited him even better. She might not like the guy, but she'd have to be blind not to notice he had dark hair just too long for decency and when he smiled, as he was doing now, his eyes gleamed with a dare that plenty of women might be tempted to accept.

She doubted anyone could consistently achieve a smile like that without hours of practice in front of a mirror.

"Good morning, Dr. Hart." His voice was part of

the package, low and warm, as if she was the person he most wanted to see right now.

Poised, calm, smooth, she cautioned herself. She shook his hand firmly, noted the gold links that punctured the crisp white of his cuffs. In his immaculately tailored charcoal suit he looked more put together than a *GQ* cover, and for some unspecified, illogical reason, Bethany disapproved. "Good to see you again, Mr. Warrington—Tyler."

"How is your research going?" he asked courteously.

"Quite well, given the funding shortfall." Not subtle, but definitely articulate.

His lips twitched. "That shortfall would be my fault, I assume?"

"Nothing you can't rectify," she said encouragingly, and he chuckled outright. Was he laughing at her again? She plowed on. "As you'll have seen from my report, I'm on the verge of a breakthrough into therapies that interfere with antibody production. If the foundation would consider—" she thought of her parents, drew a shaky breath "—*tripling* its investment in my work, there's every chance—"

"I didn't ask you here to talk about your funding." His interruption confirmed her fears, sent her spirits into free fall. Bethany clenched her toes inside her shoes to counter the sagging of her knees. Less abruptly, Tyler continued, "But if you want to call Olivia next week and ask her to set up a time in my diary…"

Bethany's hopes shot back up again. Her first instinct was to grab the opportunity he offered. Then he favored her with that calculated smile that seduced socialites and beguiled beauty queens. And distracted Bethany? *Not this time.* She folded her arms and said deliberately, "And what will Olivia say when I call?"

Tyler blinked. Olivia made a strangled sound. Bethany waited.

Then he grinned, something much more genuine—as if to say, "You got me." "She may say there's no room in my diary," he admitted.

"Just like there was no room for you to visit the kidney patients I work with?"

"I have a lot of demands on my time." He spread his hands disarmingly. "You wouldn't believe the number of people who want a piece of me."

Most of them female. Even before Miss Georgia, the newspapers had reported his dating exploits so comprehensively, Bethany wondered how he found time to make it into the office. But evidently he did, because lately the press had been covering the foundation's charitable activities, and in that sphere, at least, it seemed Tyler was a saint. Albeit one untroubled by anything so pesky as a vow of celibacy.

"I want a piece of you, too," she said. Tyler raised

his eyebrows, and she stuttered, "I—I want you to guarantee me that appointment to talk about my funding. Please."

For a long moment Tyler stared at her. Then he said, "I like a woman who knows what she wants." Before she could decide if he was being provocative, he turned to Olivia. "Give Bethany some time next week. And when I tell you to fob her off, don't listen to me."

That frank admission of his lack of interest in her work floored Bethany...and, amazingly, made her want to laugh. Which she was not about to do: she took her work seriously, even if he didn't. She compressed her lips, picked up her bag. "Olivia asked me to bring this. I assume there's a patient you want me to look at?"

"In my office." He held the door open for her.

Tyler figured it was the oddness of Bethany's skirt that drew his attention to the neat round of her bottom as he followed her into his office. That, and the same kick of awareness that had surprised him at their last encounter.

He couldn't think why he found her so intriguing. Yes, that polished-cherry-wood hair waved nicely around her heart-shaped face. But her nose was too pointy, all the easier for her to look down it at him, and her mouth a trifle wide for that stubborn chin. She was pretty, but Tyler dated beauties.

He was still puzzling over his attraction to her

when she stopped; he almost bumped into her. She'd seen the baby.

"Oh, you gorgeous little thing." She sounded awed, breathless, as she dropped to her knees on the carpet. "Hello, precious," she crooned. The baby's face split in an enormous smile, and Bethany laughed out loud.

Humor widened her mouth to even more generous proportions and revealed a dimple in her chin. All trace of obstinacy vanished, and she was much more the peach Olivia had suggested. A cute-but-not-his-type peach. Women who went gaga over babies usually had him hightailing it out the door.

She looked up at Tyler, confusion wrinkling her brow. "Who's this?"

He shifted on his feet. Now that he had to explain, he realized just how weird this was. "Someone left it downstairs for me."

"*It?*" Her eyebrows drew together, and the effect in combination with that skirt was of a disapproving pixie.

"Uh…her?" Damn, he should have had Olivia check.

Bethany unsnapped the terry garment. She hooked the front of the baby's diaper with one finger and peered inside. "Him," she corrected as she refastened the snaps. "What do you mean, someone left him?"

Tyler handed her the note. Watched curiosity turn

to shock to alarm, all telegraphed across her face. She stared at him, mouth slightly open, apparently dumbfounded.

"This woman…" She groped for words. "This child's mother thinks *you* would make a good parent?"

As if her intimate knowledge of children's kidneys put her in a position to judge him. "I'm one of Atlanta's favorite sons—and its most generous."

Bethany sat back on her heels. "You hadn't even figured out he's a boy."

"I believe in equal-opportunity parenting. Gender is irrelevant."

She pffed. "You need to call social services."

"My lawyer says I don't." He was glad he'd clarified the legality of the situation in the forty-five minutes that he'd waited for Bethany. "The mother's letter effectively appoints me the baby's guardian. According to my attorney, that may not carry weight long term, and I'll need to meet with social services. But if they're satisfied he's well looked after and that efforts are being made to find the mother—which I'll hire a private investigator to do…"

Bethany leaned over to scoop up the baby, then scrambled to her feet. As she hoisted the infant to her shoulder in a casual, practiced movement, Tyler caught a glimpse of slim, winter-pale midriff where her T-shirt pulled away from her skirt.

"You mean, you plan to keep him?" she said.

"What about your incredibly busy schedule? Babies take time and attention."

"I'll organize a sitter."

"You can't tell me you care about this baby." She sounded suspicious and she was doing that looking-down-her-nose thing, one of his least favorite memories from the first time they'd met.

"I care about families, about children." What the heck, he might as well try out some of the lines he planned to use in media interviews. "Children are our future."

"Wonderful," she said brightly—to the baby. "Your new guardian is a graduate of the Whitney Houston School of Philosophy." She looked at Tyler and her eyes sparked, not with the tenderness she'd directed at the baby, but with something more... electric.

Tyler's senses stirred in response to that spark, and he struggled to keep his mouth from curving, his wits from deserting him to go frolic with his imagination in a place that involved him and Bethany and not much clothing. Definitely not that skirt. "Are you saying children *aren't* our future?" he asked with spurious confusion.

She shifted her hold on the baby, and the movement emphasized the high, full curve of her breasts. "You made it plain you're not interested in my kidney patients, so why should I believe you have any real concern for this child?"

But he hadn't invited her here to examine his motives. All he needed was for her to check the baby over and leave. Then he could get Operation Family Man under way. Still, he couldn't resist saying, "You're carrying a grudge because I didn't give you all the money you wanted, and it's clouding your judgment. You need to admit that was your own fault."

Bethany's face heated. So much for Tyler being either amnesiac or love-struck to the point of forgetting her humiliation. Yes, she'd brought it on herself…but he hadn't helped. She'd been sucked in by his charm—the charm she'd been too naive to realize was hardwired into him and freely dispensed to every female he came across—and in the misguided belief she'd already won him over, she'd wandered away from the scientific facts to support her case and detoured into anecdote.

Halfway through her pitch, she'd realized she'd lost Tyler's attention. He'd still been giving her that encouraging smile, but he'd glanced at his watch a half-dozen times, yawned more than once. She'd scrambled to get back onto the solid ground of medical fact, lost track, dropped her notes and been too nervous to take a break and sort them out. She'd garbled her way through, and just as she hit the crux of her case, Tyler—

"You winked at me!" she accused.

"I did not." He widened his eyes, as if to prove

there was no winking going on. At the same time, his brows lowered in a puzzled frown that hinted she was being irrational.

"When I pitched to your committee." The baby hiccuped and she rubbed his back in a circular motion. "You sat there not listening to a word I said and then you winked."

"*That's* why you're so touchy? Because I winked?" Tyler ignored the way Bethany stiffened at being called touchy. "I could see you felt awkward and I guessed it was because of that thing between us…"

"What thing?" she demanded.

"That…awareness, that—" he flung a hand wide to encompass the full spectrum of sexual attraction "—*edge*. It's here again, right now, even when you're mad at me."

Her face was blank. "I have absolutely no idea what you're talking about."

Tyler snorted. No way was this all on his side. There'd been a real and definite connection between them and it hadn't abated. He was used to women finding him attractive and, less often, to experiencing a mutual chemistry. If the situation wasn't appropriate, he could shrug it off and get on with the job. But he could see Bethany inhabited a less sophisticated planet than the women he dated. That big doctor brain of hers was probably a handicap when it came to something as simple as sexual attraction.

"You winked," she said again, a note of revelation creeping into the words.

Being an egghead was no excuse for not understanding the basics. "I told you," he said impatiently, "I did it because you—"

"While I was putting my heart into that pitch, you were *flirting?*"

CHAPTER THREE

"I WAS READING your signals," Tyler corrected her. "And I acknowledged them. I was being *polite.*"

Just when Bethany had thought she'd reached the pinnacle of embarrassment, he'd thrown this at her. Why didn't he just come out and say he thought she was an all-round loser, and sex-starved to boot?

"I was pitching for the most important thing in my life," she said in a tight, strained voice. If she hadn't been holding the baby, she would have yelled.

The baby whimpered. Through his hat, she nuzzled the top of his sweet little head with her chin, a caress intended to soothe herself as much as him.

No wonder Tyler hadn't taken her pitch seriously, if his rampant ego had decided she was making a pass at him.

"If you weren't giving me any signals—"

"I wasn't," she snapped.

"Then my…wink was out of order. I apologize."

Bethany saw the opening and dived for it. "You need to let me pitch again, right away."

He grinned. "Nice try."

The baby wriggled against her, and automatically she noted his good neck control—he had to be at least a couple of months old. "You can't have made an objective decision, if you thought I was flirting."

"Women flirt with me all the time. I don't take it seriously," he said, half laughing, half irritated. "Look, Bethany, I promise the reason you *only* got fifty thousand dollars was because that's the maximum the team thought your work deserved. I didn't underpay you because I thought you were flirting."

"And you're certain you weren't—" it sounded stupid, but she had to say it "—so distracted by your attraction to me that you failed to grasp all aspects of my presentation?" Because that happened to her all the time. *Not.*

"I swear I wasn't." His face was so grave she just knew he was laughing hysterically inside. "It wasn't even an attraction. It was an awareness, a spark. Not that you're not very attractive," he added hastily, as if she was about to take offense on a whole new scale. "But...you must know your presentation didn't do you any favors."

The fire left Bethany, and suddenly she was cold. "No," she agreed quietly. And now that she'd accused him of being in the thrall of an overwhelming attraction to her, how likely was it he'd give her more money when they met next week?

She'd blown it again.

"Can we start over?" he said, evidently deciding he'd neutralized her.

Start over. That's what she'd have to do with her research funding. Nausea churned in her stomach.

"I asked you in here to examine the baby, to check if he's healthy," Tyler said.

"Of course." She could at least do something for this child, get that right.

"There's a meeting room that adjoins this office." Tyler pointed to a door halfway along the far wall. "You can use the table in there." He looked at the baby, now dozing against her shoulder. "I'll carry your bag."

She followed him into a room that, like his office, had expansive views over midtown. Instead of a desk, it held a long table flanked by leather-upholstered chairs.

"How about you hold this little fellow while I set up?" Bethany said.

Tyler took the infant from her, held him at arm's length, like a puppy that had rolled in something nasty and needed a good hose-down.

"He won't bite," she said.

"It's more the barfing I'm worried about." He glanced down at the fine wool of his jacket, which fitted his shoulders snugly enough to reveal their breadth, while still allowing fluidity of movement.

"That's why I don't buy custom-made suits," she

sympathized. "I don't mind dropping a thousand dollars on a new suit, it's the twenty bucks for the dry cleaning that kills me."

He gave her a hard look, but he took the hint, held the baby closer. The little boy's head flopped against Tyler's chest, a tiny thumb went into his mouth. Then a fist curled around Tyler's lapel. Tyler looked less than thrilled.

Bethany tore open a plastic pack and pulled out a sterile mat. "I hope you've baby-proofed your house, because these critters get into everything." The baby was several months away from that stage, but why not give Tyler a scare?

"Luckily I had that done last year, on the off chance someone abandoned a baby on me."

She frowned so she wouldn't smile.

"But even if I hadn't," he continued, "this guy looks too young for me to worry about him digging out the magazines from under my bed."

Her head jerked up.

"Car magazines," he said blandly. "I only buy them for the pictures."

From her bag, Bethany took out the items she'd need for her examination. She rescued the baby from Tyler, laid him on the mat. Instantly wide-awake, he gurgled up at her. "Can you imagine how desperate his mom must have been," she mused aloud, "to abandon a cutie like this?"

"Why do you think she did it?" Tyler perked up.

"It's more common to abandon babies at birth if the pregnancy was a secret or if the mom had no support. At this age...possibly if he had a birth defect or a serious illness she couldn't handle..." She unsnapped the yellow sleeper and began to remove the garment. "But there's nothing obviously wrong with this guy." She appreciated the healthy pink tone of the baby's skin. Too often the youngsters she saw in the E.R. were either pale or flushed from illness. "I'm wondering if there'll be some clue to his name, maybe a wristband or ankle band under these clothes."

"Uh-huh." Tyler was looking at the baby, but the tapping of one black loafer on the carpet told her his thoughts were elsewhere.

A thought struck Bethany. "You don't know his name, do you?"

That brought his gaze back to her. "It wasn't in the note, so how could I?"

She waited before she replied, listening through her stethoscope to the baby's heart. He'd flinched when the cold metal touched his chest, but he didn't cry. Heart rate of one-fifty, perfectly normal.

"It occurs to me," she said carefully as she coiled her stethoscope, "that this might be your son."

He jerked backward. "Mine?"

"I mean—" she put a thermometer to the baby's ear, relieved she didn't have to meet Tyler's gaze as she elaborated "—your...love child."

She didn't expect the silence. It was unnerving, so much so that even after the thermometer beeped a normal reading, she kept looking at the display.

"Tell me that's a joke," he said.

She swallowed. "I have to ask. I'm a doctor, I have my patient's best interests in mind."

"You're not just a gossip with a juicy story to spread?" he asked silkily.

"Certainly not." She put the thermometer away.

"Because if a rumor like that got around, it could do me a lot of damage."

Bewildered, she said, "Tyler, according to the newspapers, you've dated half the women in Atlanta and the other half are eagerly awaiting their turn. Miss Georgia must know she's the latest in a long line."

"Professional damage," he elaborated. "And for your information, dating a lot of women doesn't mean I'm siring *love children*—" he embellished her euphemism with sarcasm "—all over town, then neglecting them until their mothers abandon them."

"Only one love child," she corrected reasonably. Then, when his face darkened, "If you say he's not yours, I believe you. But like you said, you're Atlanta's favorite son, you could get away with—"

"Forget it," he said with flat finality.

Bethany pressed her lips together and conducted the rest of her checks on the baby in silence. She put a finger in his mouth, ran it over his gums. Next, she pulled a brightly colored rattle from her bag, held it above and in front of the baby. His eyes focused on the toy, and when she moved it to her left and then her right, his gaze followed. When she put the rattle down on the table, the little boy turned his head to see it. His hand reached out, found only air, and he gave a squirm of frustration.

Bethany picked up the toy, held it to the tips of his fingers. He curled his fingers around it, held it for a moment, then dropped it. "Hmm, I'd say he's hit three months."

"How do you know that?"

She'd forgotten momentarily that she wasn't talking to Tyler after he'd accused her of being a gossip. Nonetheless, she magnanimously decided to share her conclusions with him. "He's able to follow an object with his eyes and grasp it, but he's not rolling over, though he's in good health, with plenty of fat, plus good muscle development. And there's no sign of teething."

There was a knock, then Olivia stuck her head around the door. "I have diapers. And something called baby wipes."

"Perfect timing." Bethany pulled the tapes on the diaper the baby wore. "Bring them in."

She tugged the wet diaper out from under the baby. She gave his private parts a quick check, then Olivia handed her a fresh diaper and a wipe. The secretary left the room double quick.

"On all the obvious measures he's fine, a healthy

little guy," Bethany said as she fastened the clean diaper. She glanced at Tyler. "I still think it's best if I call social services and have them pick him up." She began to dress the baby again.

Tyler shook his head. "I can't throw him into the welfare system when his mom asked me to take him. Who knows what might happen to him."

"*I* know." She gathered the baby in her arms. "Social services will send someone to get him. They might be satisfied with my medical assessment, or they might take him to another doctor. While they try to find his mom, they'll place him with a foster parent *who knows how to look after a baby,*" she said with heavy emphasis. "Someone who'll *care about him.*"

He looked at her for a long moment, then his gaze flicked down to the baby in her arms. "Thanks very much for your professional advice, Dr. Hart. Be sure and send Olivia your bill."

Just like that he was dismissing her. He even had the nerve to offer her that meaningless smile, the one he'd given when he'd dismissed her pitch.

He would do the same at their meeting next week. It wouldn't make any difference if she was coherent, babbling or speaking Swahili.

Bethany's future flashed before her eyes, and it wasn't a pretty sight. She'd have to pull out of the research team at Emory; she'd been a late addition to the team, accepted on the basis of her funding from the foundation. Every cent was allocated, they couldn't carry freeloaders. She would have to start traipsing around the charitable foundations, submitting applications, presenting her case. And every time, she'd be up against dozens of other worthy projects.

This could mean the end of the goal she'd worked toward since she was thirteen years old.

She could find a way to deal with the recriminations from her parents—she just wouldn't answer her phone for a year—but knowing she'd failed to do the one thing that would make any sense of Melanie's death…that would haunt her.

Now Tyler stood before her, frowning with faint confusion, as if he couldn't understand why she was still in his office, still holding "his" baby. He didn't give a damn about the children she hoped to save. Did he care about anyone, other than himself?

Bethany's mouth set in a determined line. "I'm not leaving until I'm certain you've made acceptable arrangements for this baby."

"For Pete's sake." His hands came together in a throttling motion that she hoped was involuntary. "I told you, I'll find a sitter. I'll have Olivia call you later and let you know how I get on."

"Does that work the same as, 'Call Olivia and have her slot you into my diary'?"

A smile tugged at Tyler's mouth. Surprise, surprise, he wasn't taking her seriously again.

"Do you know how to choose a sitter?" she demanded. He probably planned to ask one of his girlfriends. Goodness knew what sights the poor baby might be subjected to. "You need someone qualified. And I mean capable of more than sashaying down a catwalk."

He laughed out loud. "Modeling is a very demanding profession," he chided. "I've been told many times."

"I'm trying to say—"

"I *am* saying, this is none of your business," he interrupted. "I assure you, though I don't have to, and I really don't know why I'm bothering, that I'll hire a qualified, professional sitter, the best that money can buy."

Everything came back to money.

He had it, she needed it.

Which seemed so monumentally unfair, Bethany wanted to cry.

"We're done here." Tyler took a step toward the door. "I'll be happy to update you about the baby at our meeting next week. If you'll hand him over to me…"

"No," Bethany said. Because an idea was glimmering in the recesses of her mind, and she just needed a minute to tease it into the open.

"You don't want an update?" He added hopefully, "Or you don't want to meet next week?" It obviously didn't occur to him she wasn't about to hand over the baby.

It was coming closer, her idea, coalescing into a plan. A plan to get money out of him, without her having to beg, or rob him at gunpoint, both of which had occurred to her in the course of this encounter.

"I want," she said casually, confidently and—best of all—coherently, "you to hire me as your babysitter."

The allure of Bethany's feisty brand of cute was wearing off fast, Tyler decided. And the way she was holding on to the baby as if he was a bargaining chip was decidedly alarming. "No way."

"I've worked with social services in the emergency room," she said. "They know me, they trust me. When I tell them you're not a fit guardian for this baby, they'll be around here faster than you can proposition a supermodel."

"I doubt that's possible," Tyler said coolly. "But, humor me here, why exactly would you want to tell social services that?"

"Because it's true." Her tone said, *Duh,* and he could see she believed it. "I'm not going to let you risk this child's well-being because you want, for whatever reason, to keep him—" She stopped. "I bet you see this baby as some kind of chick magnet."

"*I'm* a chick magnet. And I don't need you telling lies to social services." Just the thought of her carrying out that threat made Tyler go cold. He imagined the resulting furor when the news hit the headlines. He might as well go out and have *Don't choose me to run a family think tank* tattooed on his forehead right now.

"If this is about the handbag incident," he said, "I swear I was nowhere near that nightclub, and I haven't seen either of those women in a long time."

"What handbag incident?" She shifted the baby to her other shoulder.

Great, why didn't he make things worse? "Just kidding. Look, how about I let you choose a sitter— one who meets whatever standard you want to set." He reached for the baby. "Here, he looks heavy, why don't you pass him over."

She squinted at him and held the infant tighter. "The standard is, it has to be me."

"You're overqualified," he said. "And you have lives to save. Your research, remember?"

"The research I've run out of money for," she pointed out. "I've been pulling shifts in the E.R. for weeks now, so I can use some of the foundation's grant to extend my assistant's hours. But as of this week, she's working for someone else until I get more money."

The money. Again. "I find it difficult to believe you have a burning ambition either to work for me or to be a babysitter."

"I admit I have an ulterior motive—access to

you." She turned her cheek to avoid a sudden grab by the baby. "I'll use up the vacation time I'm owed looking after this little guy until his mother is found, and I'll spend every minute I can educating you about my research."

The days and weeks stretched before Tyler in a *Groundhog Day* nightmare of lectures about kidneys and caring.

"Did you think of demanding a renewal of your funding in exchange for your butting out of my business?" Not that he would have paid her off, but it would in theory have been simpler than this Machiavellian scheme.

"That would be blackmail," she said, shocked. "All I want is a fair hearing." The baby blew bubbles, and she wiped gently at his mouth with her finger. "I'll work for you—" the hardness of her voice, at odds with that tender gesture, startled Tyler "—and I'll make you listen."

She couldn't *make* him do anything. But he couldn't afford to have her bad-mouthing him to social services. And he did need a qualified sitter. Plus, her knowledge, not just of how to look after this baby, but of wider child-related issues, might come in handy.

Tyler made a decision—*his* decision, for *his* reasons. "You can have the job." Her eyes lit up, so he said hastily, "But if you think that's going to make me listen to you…all I can say is, hold your breath."

She blinked. "I believe the expression is *don't hold your breath*."

"Ordinarily," he agreed. "But in this case I'm hoping you'll suffocate yourself."

"And then this poor baby will have no one who cares." She patted the little boy's back. "Let me tell you how much I charge for my services." Bethany named a sum that had Tyler's eyebrows shooting for the ceiling.

"I had no idea babysitting was such a lucrative profession."

"One of a thousand things you have no idea about," she said loftily. "Now, when can I move in?"

"Move in?" Tyler felt as if his brain was ricocheting around his head, trying to keep up with her twisted mind. What was she planning next?

"You're aware that babies wake in the night?" she asked. "That they need feeding and changing 24/7?"

Tyler had been vaguely aware of the unreasonable nature of infants, but he hadn't yet translated that to having to violate his privacy by having someone move in. He'd never even had a live-in girlfriend. "You're not moving in."

"Okay, if you think you can handle the nighttime stuff…" She shrugged. "I guess with your dating history you're used to not getting much sleep. But those middle-of-the-night diapers are the worst. Just make sure you buy a couple of gallons of very strong bleach and three pairs of rubber gloves. Oh, and have you had a rabies shot?"

Was she suggesting he could get *rabies* from the baby? He stared at her, aghast. She looked back at him and there was nothing more in her blue eyes than concern for his well-being. Which made him suspicious. But he wasn't willing to take the risk.

"Fine," he said, "you can move in."

She didn't blink. Only a sharp breath betrayed that she hadn't been certain he would agree. Immediately, he wished he hadn't. "But don't get too comfortable. I don't imagine I'll have custody of him for more than a few weeks, max, before either his mom is found or social services take over."

"That's all the time I'll need," Bethany said.

"I'll have Olivia get me some earplugs," he said. "When you're nagging me about your research, I won't be listening."

"While she's out buying those, she can buy or rent some baby equipment and supplies," Bethany said. "I'll write you a list—do you have a pen?"

Tyler handed over his silver pen with a sense of impending doom.

Bethany scribbled a list of what looked like at least two dozen items, and handed it to him.

"If you like, I can take the baby to your place right now and—" She stopped. "We can't keep calling him 'the baby'—how about you choose a name for him?"

"Junior?" he suggested.

"A proper name. One that suits him."

Tyler rubbed his chin. "Okay, a name for someone with not much hair, a potbelly, incontinent... My grandfather's name was Bernard."

Bethany laughed reluctantly. "Bestowing a Warrington-family name on him might create an impression you'd rather avoid."

Good point. Tyler looked the baby over. "Ben's a nice name for a boy."

"Ben," she repeated. "It suits him." She dropped a kiss on the infant's head, as if to christen him. "Okay, Ben, let's get you home." To Tyler, she said, "I don't have a car. Are you going to drive me, or call me a cab? Better order one with a baby seat."

"How did you get here today?"

"By bus," she said impatiently.

"Everyone has a car," he said.

"Underfunded researchers don't."

Pressure clamped around Tyler's head like a vise. He massaged his aching temples.

Bethany had promised to give him hell, and she didn't even have the decency to wait until she'd moved in.

CHAPTER FOUR

BETHANY PULLED her knitting out of its bag, propped herself against two large, squashy pillows and checked out the view. Of Tyler's bedroom. From Tyler's bed.

This was so undignified, being forced to wait for her employer on his *bed*. No doubt he'd be less than impressed to find her here.

"It's his own devious, underhanded fault," she muttered as she untangled a knot in her wool.

She'd been full of self-congratulatory delight at having inveigled her way into Tyler's multimillion-dollar home in Virginia Highlands so she could brainwash him into giving her money. Her sense of triumph had lasted through three nights of interrupted sleep, fifteen bottles of formula and thirty thousand dirty diapers.

At least, that's how many it felt like. It was now Thursday evening, and Bethany hadn't seen Tyler since the meeting they'd had with social services on Monday afternoon, at which it had been agreed that Tyler would have temporary custody of Ben. Correction: she hadn't seen him in the flesh. Beside her on the bed was today's newspaper, featuring a photo of Tyler and Miss Georgia at the opening of an art exhibition in Buckhead on Tuesday.

She tossed the newspaper across the deep crimson bedcover. Who would have thought crimson could look so masculine? It must be the combination of the white walls, the dark polished floorboards, the Persian rug woven in rich reds and blues.

Her cell phone rang, breaking the silence and startling her. Bethany fumbled her knitting, reached for the phone's off button. She'd spent the past few days dodging calls from her mother and stalling the head of the emergency department at Emory with vague promises that she'd be available for work "soon."

The one person she wanted to talk to was Tyler. But she hadn't even said two words to him about her research.

Because the man was never here.

So now, when Ben was napping and Bethany should have been sleeping—the dark circles beneath her eyes were growing dark circles of their own—she was instead relying on the irregular clack of her knitting needles to keep her awake. If she wasn't careful, Tyler would make one of his lightning raids on the house while she dozed.

She didn't know how he managed to figure out exactly when she'd be out taking Ben for a walk, or catching forty winks, or at the store stocking up on diapers. But at some stage every day she'd arrive home, or come downstairs into the kitchen, and there'd be…no actual evidence of his presence, just an indefinable sense of order shaken up. And, occasionally, the scent of citrus aftershave, freshly but not too liberally applied.

Tyler wouldn't elude her today, she promised herself as she hunted for a dropped stitch with little hope of rescuing it. No matter how much Bethany knitted, she never improved, probably because knitting was a means of relieving tension rather than a passion.

Since she'd arrived at Tyler's home, she'd knitted most of a sweater.

Today, she would relieve her tension by delivering Tyler a brief but salient rundown on childhood kidney disease. Waiting on his bed meant he couldn't sneak past her; she wouldn't let him out of the house until she'd said her piece.

Bethany yawned and leaned back into the pillows, letting her eyelids droop just for a moment. Her bed in Tyler's guest room was very comfortable, but this one was in a different league. It was like floating on a cloud….

THE NEAR-SILENT SWISH of a well-made drawer sliding stealthily closed woke Bethany. She jerked upright.

And saw Tyler standing frozen next to the dresser, holding a plastic shopping bag, watching her watching him.

Bethany roused her wits. "Who are you, and how dare you barge into this house?"

She had the satisfaction of confusing him, but only briefly. Those full lips curved in irritated appreciation of her comment.

"Sorry I haven't been around, I've been busy." He crossed the room, a picture of relaxed grace, and dropped the shopping bag onto the end of the bed. He stood, clad in Armani armor, looking down at her as if she were a territory he had to conquer before dinner.

"I've been busy, too," Bethany said. Unlike him, she bore the ravages of her day, evidenced in the baby-sick that blotted the shoulder of her sweater, in her lack of makeup, in the hair she hadn't had time to wash this morning.

"You mean, busy doing something other than snoozing on my bed?" He took a step closer. "Or are you here because you want…something?"

"I *want* to talk to you." She scowled. "You were hoping to sneak in and out without waking me, weren't you?"

"You looked so sweet," he said blandly, "it seemed a crime to disturb you. Where's Ben?" He glanced around with casual interest, as if she might have stowed the baby under a pillow. For all he knew, that was exactly what she did each day.

"He's sleeping."

Tyler sat on the other side of the bed from Bethany, and farther down so he was facing her. Still too close for her liking. She'd have liked to stand up, but one foot was still asleep, and she'd probably topple over if she tried. She settled for edging away from him.

"That kid's amazing," he said. "Every time I come home, he's fast asleep. I feel as if I've hardly seen him." He must have noticed the anger kindle in her eyes, for he continued hastily, "So, how are you?" His gaze flicked over her from top to toe. "You look tired."

Didn't every woman love to hear that?

"I," she said deliberately, "am exhausted. The reason Ben is asleep whenever *you're* around—" she pointed her knitting needles at him for emphasis "—is because he's awake every other minute of the day. And night."

"Careful, Zorro." Tyler reached out and deflected the needles, which were almost stabbing him in the chest. "It's not my fault if I don't hear Ben at night."

"The only way you wouldn't hear him is if you're wearing those earplugs Olivia bought you."

He shook his head. "Uh-uh."

Bethany narrowed her eyes. "Maybe you can't hear him because you're sleeping somewhere else."

He appraised her through thick lashes. "I've been right here every night. In this bed."

She didn't need to think about that.

"Alone," he added mournfully.

With that newspaper article visible from the corner of her eye, she couldn't help saying, "Things not going well with Miss Georgia?"

"That would be your business…how?"

"It's the whole city's business, if you read the newspaper. Besides, if she dumped you," Bethany said hopefully, "and you're looking for an excuse to see her again, you can set me up to brief her about my research. She gets a lot of media coverage, she might be a useful spokesperson."

"Nice idea, but I think she has her hands full with world peace. And in the unlikely event of a woman dumping me, I won't need your help in patching things up." He leaned forward and grabbed the plastic shopping bag, which bore the logo of a local independent bookstore. He pulled out several books, stacked them on the nightstand on his side of the bed. Among them, Bethany recognized one that many of her patients' parents recommended: *What to Expect the First Year.* He crowned the pile with *Real Dads Change Diapers.*

He caught her watching him. "Obviously I'm philosophically opposed to this last one."

"I noticed," she said. "Still, it looks as if you're willing to be educated. So you'll be interested to learn that if researchers could figure out how to control antibody-producing cells, kidney patients might be able to accommodate transplanted organs from incompatible donors."

"Who do you think Ben's dad is?" Tyler asked.

Bethany counted to five and managed an ungracious "How would I know? Has the private investigator come up with something?"

"Nothing yet. I was just wondering… What if his dad is looking for him?"

Bethany blinked. Tyler had noticed she did that whenever he disconcerted her…which wasn't as often as he'd like. Too often it worked the other way around.

"Good question, I've been thinking more about his mother," she admitted.

"That's because you're a woman," he said smugly. "It's hard for you to acknowledge that Ben's dad has just as much claim on him." It was a line he'd found when he'd skimmed *Real Dads Change Diapers,* a somewhat political tome, in the bookstore. He'd also skimmed the index of *What to Expect the First Year* and found no reference to rabies, which gave him another score to settle with Bethany.

She frowned. "In my experience, fathers love their kids just as much as moms do, though they're not always as good at showing it. But every kid needs a dad he can rely on. Maybe not so obviously at Ben's age, but in a few years' time he'll need someone to show him what being a man is all about."

Tyler was sorely tempted to pull out a pen and make notes. Bethany was more useful than any number of books when it came to getting up to speed on baby issues.

Bethany continued. "I'm not a guy—" stating the obvious, he thought, scoping out the fullness of her breasts in her thin, ribbed sweater "—but I'd bet being a father is the most rewarding, fulfilling, hope-giving experience a man can know. It'd beat those other coming-of-age experiences—first car, first girlfriend, graduation—hands down."

Enthusiasm lit Bethany's face, emphasizing its pixieish quality. Very cute. Then she added, "If you talk to some of the fathers of children in the kidney ward at Children's Healthcare of Atlanta—"

Okay, now she'd gone past quotable and was riding her hobbyhorse into earnestness.

"Fascinating though this is," Tyler interrupted her, "I'm due at dinner in half an hour. You're welcome to stay, but I need to get changed."

"Miss Georgia again?" she said coolly, ignoring his invitation.

He folded his arms. "You seem overly interested in Miss Georgia."

Bethany flushed. "I'm interested in the fact you're never here with Ben."

"Right," he said dryly. They both knew she wanted him here so she could spout kidney facts. "The fact is, I pay *you* to care for him." Damn, he could sense another of her lectures coming. He said quickly, sympathetically, "You know, you wouldn't be the first woman to be jealous of Miss Georgia."

Her outraged gasp had him stifling a smile. "I'm about as jealous of Miss Georgia as I am of that table leg." She waved at the nightstand.

"That's a very shapely table leg," he conceded, "but you shouldn't put yourself down." He eyed her sweater again, noticed that it had worn perilously thin in places. "You have a great figure."

She drew herself up, and her indignation had the interesting effect of swelling her bosom. "My figure has absolutely nothing to do with—"

"There's every chance you'll find a boyfriend one day," he continued.

"I have a boyfriend," she snapped.

That was unexpected. Even more out of left field was Tyler's sudden urge to tear a telephone directory in half with his bare hands—he'd never indulged in primal-male competitive behavior. Finding Bethany curled on his bed asleep, one arm flung behind her head, her lips parted, must have struck a chord with some unconscious fantasy, and it had obviously unbalanced him. He forced himself to say lightly, "Is he deaf?"

"Of course he's not deaf!"

"I just wondered how he puts up with you." He dodged vengeful knitting needles. "What does he think about you living with me?"

"He's not *exactly* a boyfriend," she admitted. Tyler's testosterone surge ebbed slightly. "Kevin is just…someone I see sometimes."

"Ah." Tyler put all the knowledge of a man who knew every nuance of dating into the syllable. "Someone convenient. I've had plenty of those."

Bethany raised an eyebrow. "Convenient boyfriends?"

He grinned. "Plenty of convenient girlfriends."

She sniffed. "Emphasis on the plenty."

"Emphasis on the convenient," he corrected. "Did it occur to you that you might get further convincing me about your funding if you were nice to me?"

"You have more than enough people being nice to you," she said. "I plan to stand out from the crowd."

No matter that even sitting on the bed she was discernibly shorter than him, she was giving him that superior look down her nose. He said, "I don't have any trouble noticing you."

No trouble at all.

His gaze locked with hers across the bed, and there was a connection that Tyler figured even Bethany couldn't deny. It made no sense that he should find her so attractive—she dressed like a color-blind bag lady, she persisted in judging him according to her own overemotional standards and she was a pain in the backside.

But since when had sex and sense had anything

n common, beyond the fact that they were both
 one-syllable words starting with S?

He leaned closer to her, which prompted her,
gratifyingly, to lick her lips. His gaze zeroed in on
that full mouth.

"Tyler," she warned, "I am *not* sending out
signals. Not now, not ever."

He shook his head. "You are so deluded. One day
you're going to wake up to this attraction, and when
you do, I'll be here."

"Never," she insisted.

"You're making this hard on yourself," he chided
her. "The longer you hold out, the more there'll be
egg all over your pretty face when you have to admit
it."

Bethany put a hand to her face involuntarily, then
scowled when he laughed.

"Tell you what," he said. "I'm going to make this
easier on you."

"You're going to walk out that door and have
dinner with your *girlfriend?*"

"Uh-uh," he chided her. "Miss Georgia is fun, but
she's not my girlfriend. Now, Peaches, I'm going to
figure out a signal you can give me so you don't
actually have to say out loud that you want me." He
added kindly, "I understand that might just about
choke you."

He took his time pretending to think, all the while
enjoying the sight of her on his bed. Obviously

sensing he planned a hands-on demonstration, she
backed up against the headboard. "Don't touch me."
Her voice held irritation, panic…doubt.

"Just this once," he said, "so you'll know what I
mean."

In one graceful movement, Tyler shifted so close
to Bethany that she could see the gold flecks in his
blue eyes. Just as plainly as she could read the
amused condescension in them. He stretched a
finger toward her, and Bethany forced herself not
to flinch. *Let him play his stupid game.*

"This is what you need to do," he said softly. His
finger found the tender skin just below her left ear,
traced the line of her jaw. He tilted her chin so she
was looking directly into his eyes and smiled down
at her. Appreciatively. Seductively. And Bethany,
dammit, was only human. She smiled back. If more
world leaders were women, she thought, the USA
would have a secret weapon right here in Tyler Warrington.

"That's all you have to do, Peaches, to tell me
you want me."

Reason found her again, and Bethany jerked
away from his touch. "Never going to happen." To
her horror, she sounded breathless. And her jaw,
where his finger had traced, felt tight, tingly.

Tyler laughed. "Never say never." His mission of
throwing her off her stride apparently accomplished,
he got off the bed and said briskly, "By the way, if

don't see you when I get in tonight, I need you to bring Ben to my office tomorrow afternoon. Four o'clock."

Now he was done toying with her, he was dismissing her.

"Tyler," she said firmly, "I need to talk to you about my research. Now."

"Go ahead," he invited, surprising her. Then he unbuckled his belt. His hand hovered over the button of his pants. "You don't mind if I get changed while we talk, do you?"

If she'd been braver, or at least less prone to blushing, she would have told him to go right ahead. But with her face in flames, Bethany scrambled off the bed and almost ran from the room.

AT THREE-THIRTY on Friday, Olivia was typing the latest batch of rejection letters Tyler had asked her to send out, when the door to her office opened. She looked up.

And thought, *Call Security.*

A hobo stood framed in her doorway. A giant hobo, more than six feet tall, enormous shoulders made broader by a grubby overcoat. His hair, an unkempt salt-and-pepper mix of brown and gray, grazed his collar, and Olivia judged the matching stubble on his chin to be at least three days' growth.

She reached for the phone.

"I'm Silas Grant," the hobo announced.

Two things stayed Olivia's hand. First, his name seemed familiar. Second, the words were uttered in a voice that was slow to the point of sleepiness, gravelly...and unquestionably educated.

As she puzzled over that riddle, he walked toward her with a silent, purposeful tread at odds with his sleepy voice. That lithe, almost graceful gait would have worried her if she'd been walking down a darkened street, but here she couldn't believe he posed any threat. Other than to her discriminating taste in fashion. His brown corduroy trousers were pale and worn at the knees, and over them he wore a heavy shirt in brown and green plaid, buttoned to the neck, but untucked. But while they may have been more suited to gardening, the clothes did appear clean. Unlike the overcoat.

"I'm here to see Tyler Warrington," he said.

Now that he was up close, Olivia saw he had gray eyes, but they weren't at all cold. They held the deep, dormant heat of ashes, beneath which lurked the potential, if stirred by just a hint of breeze, for fire.

"Do you have an appointment, Mr. Grant?" She knew he didn't—neither she nor Tyler believed in Friday-afternoon appointments. Tyler invariably had a hot date to prepare for, and, often enough, so did Olivia. Today she planned to be gone by four; she'd promised Gigi Cato she would come by to approve the floral arrangements for this evening's soiree. It was inconvenient—she'd have to drive

ome from Gigi's to change, then turn around and
o straight back to the Catos' again—but what were
riends for?

Silas Grant frowned. "How could I have an ap-
ointment," he asked gently, "when Tyler Warring-
on can't see a conservation crisis when it's right in
ront of him?"

Conservation crisis? Olivia remembered where
he'd read those words.

"You're the man with the red-spotted tree frog,"
he said, pleased with herself. She couldn't quite
emember if the spots were red or yellow.

"Hyla punctatus," he said sternly.

It took Olivia a moment to realize he wasn't
ttering some dreadful curse over her, but rather
vas giving her the Latin—or was it Greek?—name
f the frog.

"It's on the verge of extinction," he said. "And
yler Warrington just signed its death warrant."

He spoke slowly, even for a Georgian. The pace
ent an unlikely authority to his words, went some
vay toward countering his oddball appearance. But
ot far enough.

"I'm Olivia Payne, Mr. Warrington's secretary.
'm afraid he's unavailable," she told him with the
lismissive, well-bred Atlanta-belle tone that had
erved her through her years as a debutante, then as
single woman. Olivia was an expert at giving men
heir marching orders. Over the years, she'd broken

off no fewer than six engagements. Possibly seven
if you counted Teddy Benson, who'd popped the
question three years ago. She'd seen the light faster
than normal, and broken it off even before the en-
gagement announcement hit the newspapers.

"Thank you so much for stopping by," she added
pleasantly to Silas. Because one should always be
polite in one's dismissal.

He planted both hands on her desk, which might
have intimidated her if he'd done it any faster than
a hedgehog crossing the road. The movement put
his eyes level with hers, close enough to break
through the professional distance she'd set with her
voice.

She dropped her gaze, and observed that his
hands were clean, his fingernails cut so neatly they
might be manicured. She recalled that the tree-frog
funding application had come from an address in
Buckhead—could this man really live in the most
expensive area of Atlanta?

"I won't take no for an answer," he said, and there
was a hint of steel behind the soft drawl.

While his announcement might be tiresome—at
this rate she'd be late to Gigi's house—it was
nothing Olivia couldn't handle.

"Mr. Grant, as you were told in the letter you
received, the foundation does not enter into correspondence about its endowment decisions." The
same clean-break policy worked well with fiancés.

he'd found. "I understand you're disappointed, but can assure you, Mr. Warrington will not see you."

He straightened, but only so he could reach one ong arm to pull up a chair. "I'll wait," he said, and ank into it, legs stretched out in front of him.

This had happened before, so she said, "As you vish," and returned to her typing.

Most people started to fidget within two minutes. After five minutes, they'd bluster some more. But when they saw she wouldn't be moved, they'd leave. The longest anyone had stayed was fifteen minutes. Something about silence unnerved them.

Today, it was Olivia who was unnerved. Silas didn't fidget, not once, for fifteen minutes. He sat with his arms folded, quite still.

She kept her gaze fixed on her screen and wished he phone would ring with a summons to collect something from another part of the building, so she'd have a reason to move. But for once, no one called.

"Who else have you refused money to lately?" Silas's abrupt question startled her, so that she mistyped a word and looked at him before she remembered not to.

"It's not my money to give," she said politely. She added, "Nor is it Mr. Warrington's."

"What are your views on conservation and the environment?" he asked.

He really did have an attractive voice, one that almost made her want to say those things mattered to her. But, in this respect at least, she was always honest. Better to admit an unnatural lack of sentiment than to pretend to care.

"I don't have any." She was concerned, of course, that the planet shouldn't be flooded or burned up as a result of global warming. But that wasn't going to happen in her lifetime, so she didn't lose any sleep over it.

"*Hyla punctatus* is a Georgia native, not found anywhere else in America."

"I'm aware of that. From your funding application."

He ran a considering gaze over Olivia. She half wished she'd had her roots done this week. She wasn't out to impress him, she scolded herself. And if she was, her hair, worn loose today in its sculpted bob, her artfully applied makeup and the emerald-green cashmere polo-neck that made her neck look longer and slimmer would surely withstand his scrutiny.

"You know what this world lacks?" he said.

She pressed a hand to her mouth and gave a ladylike yawn.

"People who care." Sharpness tinged his words.

Of course she knew that! She said lightly, "If you can't beat them, join them."

Fire sparked into life in his eyes, and his jaw jutted beneath the mouth that she now noticed was firm and well shaped behind all those whiskers.

Olivia had the same keen appreciation for good-looking men that she did for silk lingerie and French champagne. Each of her seven fiancés had been gorgeous by anyone's standards. So she could only look at Silas Grant and rue the waste of such a fine specimen.

She wondered why his bizarre appearance didn't exempt him from her appreciation. Discomfited by the thought that perhaps, now that she'd turned fifty-five, she might be desperate enough to let her standards slip, Olivia looked away.

"It's exactly your kind of apathy that's sending this world to hell in a handbasket," he growled.

She'd obviously pressed one of Silas's buttons, because he began to decry, albeit in an undramatic way, the parlous state of the world, the shallowness of materialism and the loss of life's simple pleasures.

Olivia, who collected designer handbags, liked to dine on Wagyu beef and had two real fur coats in her wardrobe that she resented being unable to wear, struggled to sympathize.

Yet still, Silas Grant mesmerized her, whether with that unexpectedly cultured voice or with his sheer size. When she found herself wondering what he would look like with a shave and a tuxedo, she realized this had gone far enough.

"What will it take to convince you to leave?" she said abruptly, heatedly. She'd never reacted like this before, not to any of the cranky rejectees who'd turned up here.

"Your promise that you'll ask Warrington to meet me." Either Silas had the good sense to say no more, or he'd run out of steam.

Olivia was so relieved to hear the end of that gentle diatribe that she agreed. "I'll let you know Mr. Warrington's response."

"Thank you." The two syllables stood stark, and for one moment, Silas sounded alone, as alone as Olivia.

CHAPTER FIVE

BETHANY PAUSED on the threshold of Olivia's office. Tyler's secretary was locked in a death glare with a bum in a dirty coat. Should she fetch help? She tightened her grip on Ben's car seat in case she had to run and said, "Olivia?"

The bum didn't acknowledge her arrival. He said to Olivia, "I'll be back," with about as much menace as a low-on-batteries Terminator. He swung around, loped past Bethany with his coat flapping.

Before Bethany could ask Olivia what that was about, Tyler opened the door of his office. "Olivia, have you seen my silver pen? I can't think where I—" He stopped, distracted by the disheveled appearance of the departing visitor, now out of earshot but still visible. "Who's that?"

Olivia cleared her throat. "Silas Grant, the guy who's saving the red-spotted tree frog. He wanted to see you."

"Was he bothering you?" Tyler took a step forward as if he might head down the corridor and grab hold of the man.

Olivia shook her head. "He's all right. Just… odd. I told him I'd find out if you're willing to meet with him."

Tyler cast another look at the guy, then turned to Bethany. He scanned her outfit—black leggings and a taupe crochet sweater, a by-product of the stress-relief technique that had preceded knitting, worn over a black slip. A taupe cardigan completed her layered look.

Bethany liked to think of it as Bohemian.

"Why is it that most do-gooders dress so badly?" he demanded. "It's like a badge of honor with some of you." He glanced down at his own clothing, which Bethany observed was unusually casual, yet as crisp and new looking as if he had a Calvin Klein store tucked in his office. "Nope," Tyler said complacently. "I don't see any reason why you can't look good *and* do good."

Bethany gaped. "You call yourself a do-gooder?"

He rubbed his chin. "Let me see…my job involves giving millions of dollars away to people in need, I'm an acknowledged expert on philanthropy, and now I'm fostering an abandoned baby." He nodded at Ben in his car seat but made no move to take him. "You're right, I'm evil."

"You spend money," she said, "but you don't care."

He groaned. "If you mean I don't respond emotionally to every problem, you're right. But if you mean providing practical assistance that makes a difference…"

"I mean," she said, "giving something of yourself, caring in a way that changes you as well as the other person."

He looked mystified. "Why would I want to change, when everyone loves me the way I am?"

Bethany was about to deliver a few choice words on that topic, when she saw laughter lurking beneath the innocent inquiry in his eyes. Tempted though she was to laugh—something she felt surprisingly often around Tyler—she chose not to indulge him. "That pen you're looking for," she said, referring to the question that had brought him out of his lair. "Would that be the one I borrowed the other day to write out a list of baby equipment?"

"So you did," he said.

"I took it," she admitted. "By accident."

He held out a hand. "May I have it back?"

"I haven't seen it in a couple of days." She frowned. "I know I used it to sign a check at the supermarket. I'm not sure if I put it back in my purse…"

"Could you think a little harder?" Tyler said. "It's my favorite."

Oops. Bethany grimaced. "I think I left it in the store."

"You're kidding, right?" His shock sounded out of all proportion to the loss of a pen.

"Keep your hair on," she said. "I'll buy you another one."

He folded his arms. "You're going to buy me another twelve-hundred-dollar Michel Perchin pen?"

She clattered Ben's car seat onto Olivia's desk before she dropped it. Olivia leaned back in her chair, looking askance.

"You didn't say twelve *hundred* dollars, did you?" Bethany pleaded. "You said twelve dollars."

Tyler glared at her.

She felt sick.

"That money's coming straight off your next research grant," he said. "Or it would, if I had any intention of giving you more cash."

In an instant, her fighting spirit was resurrected.

She planted her hands on her hips. "Twelve hundred dollars is an obscene amount to pay for a pen. You should be ashamed of yourself."

"*You* have an attitude problem." Tyler's effortless urbanity had vanished, and he spoke with the fulminating tension of a man goaded beyond endurance. "You've lost my handmade pen, which for all you know could be of great sentimental value, and somehow you've made this all about *my* flaws."

"*Could be* of sentimental value," she mocked. "But it's not, is it, because for that, you'd have to have a heart."

Into the seething pause, Olivia said, "What shall I tell Silas Grant? Will you see him?"

Bethany saw Tyler grapple to regain his control as he turned to his secretary. "I'm a family guy, not a frog guy," he said to Olivia with a passable replica of his normal ease, though Bethany's snort had his fists clenching at his sides. "I'm not interested."

Olivia looked relieved. "I'll let him know." She pulled a file out of her drawer. "In fact, I'll call and leave a message on his voice mail before he gets home."

Tyler frowned. "If you're worried about dealing with him, I'll do it."

His offer surprised Bethany. As far as she knew, Tyler didn't do anything for other people.

Olivia's face flushed. "It's no problem."

"Don't say I didn't *care* enough to offer," he said, with a pointed glance at Bethany. So that's what his sudden consideration was about. Then he said to her, "You'll be pleased to know I'll be *caring* for Ben personally tonight. I'm taking him out with me."

"Taking him where?" Bethany picked up Ben's car seat again. Somewhere that didn't involve Tyler's usual suit and tie, obviously. He wore designer-faded jeans, a long-sleeved fine-knit polo shirt, casual shoes. He looked like…like… Bethany struggled to define the annoyingly alluring blend of preppy and rugged. She failed.

"Babies don't go out at night," she told him. "You'll have to find another drinking buddy."

"My drinking buddies are all female, and believe me, there's no shortage of them." He grasped the car seat, one hand at each end, and tried to tug it from her. She held on. She wasn't about to pass Ben over until she was certain he wouldn't end up at some nightclub—she'd belatedly caught up with the eBay purse scandal, and it had reinforced her view that Tyler wasn't a suitable guardian.

"I'm taking him to a meeting of Divorced Dads International," he said.

Surprise loosened her clutch on the car seat, and he seized it. Bethany pretended she'd let him have it, and folded her arms. "That would be because you're divorced, or because you're a dad?"

His new look suddenly made sense. *He looks like a dad.*

A million-dollar dad, sure, but Tyler definitely looked like a guy who might have been woken by a baby at five this morning, who might have heated formula, who might even have changed a diaper.

Who knew appearances could be so deceptive?

"I'm the guest speaker at their quarterly meeting," he said.

"What the heck can you talk about?"

His gaze slid away from hers. "Motivational stuff. I figure I'm not qualified to offer actual advice." He added, "I know that doesn't stop some people."

She sent him a withering look. "What's in it for you?"

"Excuse me?" He put Ben's car seat down on Olivia's desk, which drew a resigned groan from his secretary.

"Like you said, you prefer to sign checks. What makes you want to motivate a bunch of dads?"

"The press will be there, it's good publicity for the foundation. The more people know about our work, the more partners like government and other charities will want to get involved in joint ventures with us." He spread his hands. "Which means bigger checks for all those people I love to help."

The challenge in his eyes dared her to object to his noble purpose. She longed to—something about this didn't add up. But his argument was technically sound. With something approximating good grace, she handed Tyler the bag containing Ben's diapers, bottle and other essentials. "Here's all his stuff. He'll need a diaper change before you go."

He frowned. "Can't you do it?"

"I would," she said sweetly, "but it'll help you empathize with the divorced dads."

"I don't do empathy," he said. "I do checks."

She smiled sunnily and headed for the door.

"Olivia," Tyler cajoled behind her.

"If you ask me to change that diaper," his secretary said, "you'll be looking for a new assistant. There are only two certain things in this world, Tyler—you're selfish, and I'm even more selfish."

Maybe it was the shock of hearing the truth about

the adult who'd taken responsibility for him, but Ben started to cry. Olivia began typing as if her life depended on it.

Tyler cursed. "Bethany!"

She'd just made it out the door. Though she told herself not to, she stuck her head back around.

"He's crying."

She gave him a thumbs-up. "Well done—you're a natural at this parenting stuff."

"Can't you do something?" And when she would have pulled the door closed and left, he added, "Please?"

Darn it, he was projecting the kind of male helplessness that called to a woman's maternal instincts, then subverted those instincts, thanks to the addition of a sexy smile, into something far less wholesome.

Drawn by a force too strong to resist, Bethany eased back into the office. "I'm doing this for Ben. Not for you."

"Of course." She could tell herself that if she liked, Tyler thought, but he was the one she hadn't been able to turn down.

"If this was about you, I'd be out of here so fast you wouldn't see me."

"Dust," he agreed.

Her blue eyes turned calculating. "And you understand that I have never, ever given you any kind of signal? You agree that I am not attracted to you in any way?"

Tyler was aware of Olivia's bristling speculation. What was the bet his mother would hear about this conversation within the hour?

Ben's cry turned to the kind of howling wail that would have someone at the far end of the building dialing 911.

"I agree," he lied. He sent Olivia an intimidating look. She winked in reply.

"Sweet baby," Bethany cooed to Ben as she unclipped his harness. She lifted him out of the seat, and for one second the sobbing stopped, but then it was back full force. She grimaced as Ben got too close to her ear.

She had pretty ears, Tyler noticed, with her red-brown hair tucked behind them.

Bethany swayed with Ben in her arms, her attention so focused on the baby that Tyler felt as if she no longer saw him or Olivia. Softly, sweetly, she sang, "Rock a bye baby, on the treetop, when the wind blows the cradle will rock."

"With lyrics like that, it's no wonder I don't remember any of those old rhymes," he said. "Who would put a baby up a tree?" Ben's cries had quieted somewhat, but Tyler figured any guy might shut up and listen with Bethany crooning at him, no matter how psychotic the words.

"When the bough breaks—" Bethany frowned at Tyler as she sang on, lowering her voice to a murmur as the baby's sobs turned to wet hiccups

"—the cradle will fall, and down will come baby, cradle and all."

"You'll give him nightmares," Tyler protested.

"He doesn't understand the words," Bethany said in the same low voice she'd used for the song.

"You don't know that for sure. This is probably why you're having so much trouble with his sleeping."

"If you think you can do better…" Eyes sparking, she offered the baby to Tyler. He got the message loud and clear: if he didn't shut up, she'd walk right out of his office.

He shut up. Bethany held all the aces when it came to Ben, though, fortunately, she didn't seem to realize that.

Suddenly, taking Ben to the divorced-dads meeting didn't seem like such a great idea. What if he started yelling again? But without a kid in tow, Tyler would look too much like his old playboy self, despite the clean-cut, low-key outfit he'd adopted for the occasion.

He propped himself against a filing cabinet, made no effort to take Ben from her arms. "No way can I do better than you," he soothed her. "How would you like to come along to this meeting and show the single fathers how a pro does it?"

"No, thanks, this is my night off." With Ben now settled, she headed into Tyler's carpeted office. Tyler picked up the change bag she'd left on Olivia's desk and followed her.

Bethany spread a changing mat on the floor and whipped off Ben's wet diaper.

As Tyler watched, Ben's soft unfocused gaze found him, then sharpened into a kind of bemused recognition. It struck Tyler just how vulnerable this little boy was, bare bottomed in a roomful of strangers, with the office door open so even Olivia could see the whole process.

"Give the kid some privacy," he told Olivia, who was observing with a kind of fascinated repulsion.

Olivia rolled her eyes. "I saw your cute baby bottom more times than I can remember when you were this age. Doesn't seem to have done you any harm."

"Great." Tyler moved to block her view of Ben. "My secretary has not only seen my butt, she talks about it."

"Don't they all?" Bethany asked in surprise, and it took him a second to realize she was joking. He glared at her, and heard Olivia snicker.

"How about I give you a whole day off on Sunday, instead of tonight?" he said. To remind her how irresistible he was to women, he added, "Miss Georgia's always saying she loves kids, I'll invite her over on Sunday for some hands-on experience."

Bethany knew she should refuse to help him out, should make him fend for himself with Ben tonight. And she didn't feel a need to humor Miss Georgia's desire to play mommy.

But something had shifted in the dynamic

between Tyler and Ben just now. Something had clicked.

One minute she'd been changing the diaper, with Tyler looking and yet not looking, with his usual disinterest.

Then everything had changed.

She'd seen it in his sudden straightening, in the flaring of compassion in his eyes, in his admonishment to Olivia and his not-so-subtle shielding of the baby.

Bethany didn't know why it had happened, but she knew what it meant. As of right now, Tyler saw Ben as a person, with dignity in his own right.

She wasn't naive enough to believe Tyler had suddenly developed a fully evolved conscience in place of his throw-money-at-the-problem attitude. And certainly Ben's need for privacy was not one of the more pressing issues.

But maybe that moment of recognition had been a first step—a baby step, if you will—on the journey to becoming a less selfish human being.

And once Tyler Warrington learned to care, who knew how much help he'd give her for her research?

THE RATIO OF MEN to women in the ballroom at the Excelsior Hotel was pretty well what she'd expected. After all, this was a convention for single dads. Among the fathers chatting in clusters, taking their seats in ordered rows or handing babies and preschoolers over to the woman running the day-care area in the back left corner of the room, Bethany counted just two female hotel workers, the daycare woman, plus herself.

Everyone else had a Y chromosome. A couple of hundred divorced dads, a handful of male reporters—Divorced Dads International had a reputation as a vocal and sometimes aggressive supporter of fathers' rights—and Tyler.

Tyler insisted on putting Ben in the day care so he could "meet some other kids," once again showinghis skewed prioritization of Ben's needs. Bethany suspected Tyler wanted to fit in with the other dads.

The meeting was called to order. The organization's chairman introduced Tyler as the man they'd all seen in the news this week as the remporary guardian of baby Ben. He used terms that couldn't have been more glowing if Tyler had delivered Ben himself while surrounded by raging fire in the middle of an earthquake, rather than just opening a duffel bag and finding the little boy lying there. Tyler wore a self-deprecating, and very appealing, smile that said he was just your regular hero, no need to make a fuss, folks.

He eased into his speech with a couple of jokes about diapers and sleepless nights. So what if he knew nothing about either? He had the kind of charisma that made people—even tough, tattooed men, as some of these guys were—pay attention, laughing when they should, murmuring in sympathy or agreement in key moments.

As he moved into what Bethany guessed was the main part of his speech—as unfazed as his audience by the occasional squeal of laughter or cry of frustration emanating from the day care area—Tyler acknowledged he didn't have a lot of experience with babies.

"But," he said, "I'm starting to figure that being a father is the most rewarding, fulfilling, hope-giving experience a man can know. It beats those other coming-of-age experiences—first car, first girlfriend, graduation—hands down."

Now that was impressive.

And familiar.

The rat was repeating exactly what she'd said last night.

"Heck," he said, "I'd go so far as to say it's better than sex."

Okay, that was original. Obviously he didn't mean it, but it got a big laugh from the audience.

"In my experience, fathers love their kids just as much as moms do," Tyler continued. "They're just not as good at showing it. But every kid needs a dad to be a role model. Maybe not so obviously at Ben's age, but in a few years' time he's going to need someone to show him what being a man is all about."

The audience cheered, a couple of cameras flashed white lights at the stage. Bethany seethed. Once again, the master manipulator had played her. That softening she'd seen back at the office had doubtless been a ploy to persuade her to come along tonight, just so Tyler wouldn't have to get his hands dirty actually looking after the baby.

"I may not be in Ben's life then," Tyler said soberly. "But I'll do my best to make sure he's got someone—some guy—to look up to."

Empty words.

Tyler issued a couple of insightful suggestions that hadn't come from Bethany, so she assumed they were straight out of *Real Dads Change Diapers.* Then—surely by now he was skating at the extreme limits of his capacity to talk about parenting—he began to wrap things up.

"In the few days that I've had responsibility for a baby, I've realized just what hard work parenting is," he said.

Bethany snorted. A man in the back row whose muscled forearms and low-riding pants suggested he might be a construction worker turned to frown at her.

"You guys have my respect," Tyler said. "Give yourselves a round of applause." There was a stutter of self-congratulatory clapping, which at Tyler's urging grew more solid, then thundered through the ballroom. When it died away, Tyler leaned forward at the lectern, fixed his gaze on the audience with an intimacy that suggested he was making eye contact with every man in the room.

He lowered his voice, but in the silence his masculine presence commanded, his words carried to the farthest corners. "Guys, I don't know much about looking after a baby, but if there's one piece of advice I can offer from my limited experience, let it be this…"

He paused, and the suspense just about killed Bethany, so she could guess what it was doing to people who actually believed this garbage. "Please, guys, no matter how busy you get with your precious kids…please, I know it's hard…but take some time for yourselves."

The room erupted into applause, punctuated by whoops and hollers. The tough-looking construction worker in front of Bethany blew his nose into a none-too-clean handkerchief.

The man who took more time for himself than anyone Bethany had ever met stepped down from the stage. His progress toward the back of the room, where she knew he'd arranged to chat to a couple of the reporters while the meeting continued, was slowed by men wanting to clap him on the shoulder, shake his hand or discuss their child-rearing issues. Tyler accepted the first two with buddylike equanimity and managed to deflect the last with a charming admission of ignorance that somehow came across as authoritative.

Bethany stepped forward. "I had no idea you knew so much about being a father," she said coldly.

On a high from the applause and the adrenaline rush of having spent twenty minutes talking on something he knew nothing about, Tyler grinned. "Nor did I, Peaches. It's amazing how it all just came to me."

He took advantage of Bethany's speechless outrage and moved on to greet the reporters who were his only reason for being here. One of them was a stringer for the *Washington Post*. Tyler had no doubt the think-tank crowd would soon be reading about tonight's success.

He managed to hold up his end of the interview by talking common sense—no, he didn't think men should resort to illegal methods to see their children, and yes, he thought mediation between estranged parents was a great idea—and by throwing in a few more of Bethany's pearls of wisdom.

He could tell from her pursed lips that his parenting muse wasn't happy…but too bad, what could she do?

The interview moved on to the search for Ben's mother.

"Social services is trying to locate her, and we're boosting those efforts with the help of a private investigator I hired," Tyler said.

"What consequences will the mother face for abandoning her child?" asked the *Post* reporter.

Tyler would bet the divorced dads would have some suggestions. "We don't know yet how old she is…what her circumstances are. Until we do, none of us can judge her," he said. "The priority will be to make sure Ben ends up in a loving, supportive environment. It's too soon to say whether that will be with one or both of his parents."

Both reporters had brought photographers, and both wanted to take a picture of him with Ben.

Interrupting his own reply to a question about joint-custody agreements, Tyler turned to Bethany. "Could you fetch Ben from the day care?"

Her infinitesimal pause should have warned him.

"No," she said. A battle light glinted in her eyes, and something in her tone had both the reporters turning to her.

Uh-oh. No way did Tyler want them copping her views about him as a parent. "The number-one problem facing a lot of dads who share custody," he said to the reporters, "is finding a good babysitter. Sometimes you end up scraping the bottom of the barrel." He twitched his head in Bethany's direction, then winked to show his audience he was teasing.

But he knew how sensitive Bethany was—she had no sense of humor when it came to him winking—and, true to form, she got mad. So mad that she stalked off, red-faced, almost frothing at the mouth. Even if she'd stayed, he figured she would have been incoherent with anger.

Of course, that meant he had to get Ben himself. He excused himself from the reporters with a promise he'd be back in a minute, then headed for the day care.

"You were great, Mr. Warrington," the woman in charge said.

"Thanks." He gave her his warm, playful Super-dad smile, and her hand moved involuntarily to cover her heart. "I'd like to take Ben out for a photo."

"Sure, I'll just—"

"Excuse me." Bethany spoke from beside Tyler, startling him.

So she'd caved, huh? He might have known her do-gooder instincts wouldn't let her butt out where Ben was concerned. She didn't look quite as mad as before, but she held herself stiffly, as if her calmness was the product of rigid self-control. Tyler rewarded her with a full-on dazzling smile.

But she wasn't looking at him. She said to the day care woman, "You see that little girl over there?" She pointed to an angelic-looking girl wielding a pink fairy wand to deal punishing blows to two smaller boys. *The innocent-looking girls are the worst,* Tyler thought, remembering how Bethany had blackmailed him. She deserved whatever grief he gave her.

"I'm a pediatrician and I noticed she's showing signs of an allergic reaction," Bethany continued.

The day-care woman's forehead crinkled. "You're a doctor? Not a babysitter?"

"A doctor *and* a babysitter," Bethany said. "Mr. Warrington insists on nothing but the best care for Ben." Understanding dawned on the woman's face, and Bethany went on, "The girl's allergy doesn't look too serious, but you might want to notify her father."

The day-care woman looked horrified. "Of course I will. Thank you so much for letting me know." As she leafed through her list of names, looking for details of the girl's father, she said distractedly to Tyler, "Can you get Ben yourself, Mr. Warrington, I need to deal with this."

She found the information she was looking for, and scanned the crowded room.

"You go and find the dad," Bethany encouraged her. "I'll keep an eye on the kids for a minute."

The woman gave Bethany a look of such gratitude that for an instant, Tyler could see how rewarding it must be to have a job like Bethany's. If you liked that kind of thing.

He left her chatting to a couple of toddlers and made his way over to the infant section, where half a dozen babies snuggled in their car seats.

Half a dozen *identical* babies.

In half a dozen car seats as near as dammit identical.

Hell. Which one was Ben? Panic gripped Tyler and he forced himself to slow his thoughts. Ben was wearing a white romper. That eliminated the baby in the red sailor suit and the one in the yellow dress—which was probably a girl, though you couldn't be sure these days.

Four babies wore white rompers, obviously some kind of must-have infant fashion. Perspiration beaded on Tyler's brow. The baby second from the left had much more hair than Ben, he was certain. Darker, too. The one next to it looked too fat. That left two—one at either end—to choose from.

Tyler looked from one to the other. Now he could see they weren't identical at all, but he still had no idea which one was Ben.

Bethany spoke at his elbow. "Need some help?"

Relief flooded him. Then he saw the glitter in her eyes.

"I'll show you which baby is Ben," she said coolly, "but it'll cost you."

Blackmail, her weapon of choice.

"How much?" He couldn't afford to blow an interview with the *Washington Post* and if the reporter, or anyone in the audience here, suspected Tyler didn't have a clue which baby he was responsible for, his family-man image would be shot to pieces.

He figured her price would be something to do with those kidney kids. Not the research money, for some weird reason she considered that unethical, though she didn't hesitate to make other demands.

She drew a deep breath, and Tyler braced himself

for whatever new way she'd devised of making his life difficult.

"Two hours of your time, every day, to be spent with Ben."

She surprised a laugh out of him. "What's the catch?"

"No catch." Her blue eyes were serious.

"Two hours a day doing whatever I want with Ben?" he said skeptically.

"Two *waking* hours," she amended, "for both of you."

Tyler couldn't believe his luck. He would probably need to spend that much time with Ben anyway, with all the media appearances his PR manager had lined up over the next couple of weeks. For once, Bethany's naiveté was working in his favor. She'd be sick to know how much better a deal she could have scored if she'd been tougher, if she'd realized how important this interview was. He didn't let his inward smile show on his face, just stuck out a hand. "Deal."

Satisfaction glinted in Bethany's eyes. Ignoring his hand, without another word, she bent to pick up one of the infant car seats, passed it to Tyler.

She'd chosen the fat baby that hadn't even made his shortlist. Dubiously, he inspected the pudgy white bundle. "Are you sure this is Ben? I didn't think he was so, uh, round."

"Of course I'm sure," she said scornfully.

Tyler's departure from the baby area was hindered by the arrival of the day-care lady and an anxious-looking man in a suit.

"This is Lucy's father," the woman said to Bethany.

Bethany's brow creased in perplexity. Then it cleared. "I'm so sorry to have worried you," she said to the guy. "From a distance I thought your daughter looked a little flushed and swollen, but I can see now there's nothing wrong with her. My mistake." The reassuring smile she gave the girl's father might not have dazzled on the scale of Tyler's, but it was sweet enough that the guy—who Tyler now saw was good-looking, in a weedy kind of way—perked up.

Her *mistake?* Tyler pinned Bethany with a glare, willing her to look at him. The connection between them was as telepathic as it was sexual. It took only a second for her to glance his way. The bland innocence of her countenance didn't fool him for one second. Then she couldn't help herself, and a pleased-as-punch smile broke out.

The manipulative little witch.

Though, he had to admit, that had been pretty quick thinking for a babysitter scraped from the bottom of the barrel. It bespoke the same almost poetic cleverness he liked to think he possessed himself. His mouth twitched, and he clamped it back into line.

"Don't apologize." Lucy's father put a hand on

Bethany's arm. "I appreciate you taking so much care." *Care, that word again,* Tyler thought sourly. The guy darted a lightning-quick glance at Bethany's left hand, pushed his trendy rimless glasses higher up his nose and said, "Maybe I could buy you dinner soon. Just to say thank you."

Someone should warn Bethany that divorced dads had more than gratitude on their minds when they asked a pretty woman to dinner. Tyler coughed significantly. All three of them—Bethany, Lucy's dad, the day-care woman—turned to stare at him.

"I'd love to," Bethany said. "But my employer is very unreasonable and I don't get a lot of time off."

Which didn't stop her giving the jerk her cell-phone number along with an invitation to call her.

He could be an ax murderer, for Pete's sake.

"Do you realize you just put Ben's safety at risk, inviting a stranger into your life?" he demanded as they headed back to the journalists.

Her nose went up in the air. "I am so not talking to you."

"You can't go out with that guy," he persisted.

She stopped suddenly, but her force field of self-righteousness prevented him from bumping into her. "What's your problem, Tyler?" she demanded. "Are you jealous that despite this supposed attraction that's rampant between us, I gave my number to another man?"

He narrowed his eyes. "I'm as jealous of Mr. Specs as you are of Miss Georgia."

"Okay, you're not jealous," she agreed. "You've got the right baby, thanks to me, and all you had to do was agree to spend a lousy two hours a day with him. I'd say things are going pretty well for you."

She flounced away.

CHAPTER SIX

BETHANY WATCHED from a distance as the photographers did their work and the reporters threw in a couple more questions that seemed designed to make Tyler look good. She couldn't decide if she was furious with him—the cretin, not even recognizing Ben—or elated that she'd pinned him down to that daily two hours.

It might not seem like much, but Bethany was certain that she was on the right track.

Tyler might have faked that moment of connection with Ben back in his office this afternoon, but once he was spending more time with the child, there was no way he wouldn't fall for him. Then he'd be more open-minded about her research and a whole host of other issues where he could do some good.

She was going to *make* him care.

As they drove home in Tyler's BMW M6, Bethany's cell phone rang, breaking the loaded, wary silence that so far not even Ben had dared breach.

Overwrought by the tensions of the day, Bethany

nswered the phone without checking her display.
nd immediately wished she hadn't.

"Where have you been?" her mom said. "I've
een calling. The hospital said you're on vacation."

Bethany closed her eyes. Her parents had to know
ooner or later. "I'm taking a short break from my
esearch to look after Tyler Warrington's baby." From
ne corner of her eye, she saw his head jerk around.
Although it's not actually his baby," she amended.

"The little boy who's been in the papers?" her
nother said, flabbergasted.

"That's right," Bethany enthused. "He's such a
utie, you'd love him." They both knew that wasn't
ue. Mom was all out of love.

"But what about your work?" Her mom's voice
irned high and thin, and Bethany's conscience
ricked. "You said you were getting more money."

"I—I wasn't quite right, as it turned out. But,
Mom, Tyler Warrington, the guy I'm working for,
the man with the money."

Next to her, the money pot's eyebrows knitted in
isapproval. Bethany shifted in her seat so she
ouldn't see him.

"This job puts me close enough to Tyler to
onvince him to fund my work for another year."
Anxious silence down the phone. Bethany pictured
er mother twisting the cord in her fingers, trying
ot to blurt out her disappointment. "Another *two*
ears," she said desperately. She ignored Tyler's

snort. "Believe me, by the time he's had me livi
in his house a few more weeks—"

"You're *living* with him?"

"It's a live-in job, Mom. Nothing's going on."

The sound from Tyler might have bee
emphatic agreement.

"Sweetheart, you know we love you." Her mom
voice dropped to a coaxing note.

Did they? In their own way, perhaps. But nev
as much as they'd loved Melanie.

Mom said, "But I'm worried you're losing sig
of what you're working for."

Her work was all Bethany ever thought about, :
the unfairness of that comment stung. She ended t
call as fast as she could, then let out a long, slo
breath.

"Good thing I was under no illusions about ho
you feel about me," Tyler said. "Discovering you on
wanted my money could have been quite a shock."

She stuck out her tongue.

"You've been spending too much time with juv
niles," he said.

"You haven't been spending enough time wi
them." She folded her arms. "But that's about
change."

She held on to that single bright spark.

TYLER WOULD HAVE SPENT his promised two hou
with Ben on Saturday, but he'd already arranged h

monthly football game with his pals before he'd made that commitment to Bethany. He couldn't let the team down on such short notice. He told Bethany so, and explained that although the game didn't take long, they always went for a few beers afterward, then ended up at one of the guys' houses to watch a game on TV. Obviously, he couldn't mess with tradition.

She made a big show of counting to ten, hands behind her back, gazing at the ceiling, then grudgingly accepted his explanation with the rider that he had to start with Ben tomorrow.

On Sunday, his almost-genuine intention to spend time with Ben was derailed when Tyler remembered that today was the two-weekly lunch at his mother's house.

He canceled the planned visit from Miss Georgia and left for Mom's. Unfortunately, he wasn't able to take Ben with him because Bethany had taken the baby out for a walk, even though it was her day off. Tyler had to admire her work ethic.

He left her a note to say where he was, and in a fit of generosity that he'd probably regret, added a P.S. promising to spend extra time with Ben on Monday.

It was a sunny day, though cold, so lunch was set up in the conservatory. As always, Tyler was the last to arrive, right behind Olivia, who was an honorary member of the family. Max, his brother, would have been first there, followed by their cousin Jake.

Jake's mother had died some years ago and he was estranged from his father. Susan Warrington, Jake's aunt and godmother, treated her late husband's nephew as a surrogate son.

"I can't believe you didn't bring the baby with you," Susan complained as they started in on the appetizer of smoked-salmon roulade.

"If you smelled him you'd know why." Tyler broke open a hot, freshly baked bread roll and savored the aroma.

His mom rapped the back of his hand with her fork. "That's mean, and so are you for not bringing him."

"Are you sure you didn't put him in the trunk and forget about him?" Max said.

It was a referral to an incident from their childhood. A friend of their parents had given Max and Tyler, aged six and four, respectively, an enormous chocolate teddy bear each. Tyler had eaten his in about an hour. Max, possessed of much greater self-control—which he still was, now that Tyler thought about it—planned to eat his bear over the course of a month.

By day three, Tyler's bear was a distant memory—he didn't fully believe he'd ever had one, let alone eaten it all himself—so he began pestering Max for a share of his. Max had a strong sense of what was fair and right—again, he still did—and refused.

After a week, Tyler convinced himself that not only was Max the greediest kid alive, he must also have taken Tyler's bear and eaten it. From there, it was

short step to finding a way to right this terrible
wrong.

When Max was having his piano lesson, Tyler
took the remaining three-quarters of chocolate teddy,
and hid it in the trunk of their mother's car. Amazingly, it took Max two days to notice the theft. By
which time Tyler had forgotten where he'd put it.

Now, twenty-seven years later, Tyler figured his
guilty conscience had blotted out the whole
incident. No one had believed he couldn't
remember, and he'd had the sore backside to prove
it. They found Max's chocolate, or what was left of
it, the next time Mom opened the trunk—on a
scorching July day about a month later. They'd
never gotten the trunk completely clean. And Max
had never let Tyler forget the incident.

But these days it was a subject of humor, not
acrimony, so when Max made that comment about
leaving Ben in the trunk, Tyler laughed along with
him. "I have a babysitter who'd never let me get
away with that."

He wondered if Bethany was home yet, what she
was doing.

"I can't imagine you looking after a kid," Max
said.

Tyler spread butter on his roll. "He's kind of cute."

"Yeah, but—ouch!" Max lifted the tablecloth
and glared under the table. "Mom, that mutt of
yours bit me."

"Don't be silly, darling," Susan said. "Mitzy is th sweetest-natured dog in the world."

"She sure is," Tyler agreed, happy to let hi mother's unreasonable devotion to her agin Cavalier King Charles spaniel deflect his brother' curiosity. He grinned in response to Max's scowl.

His respite didn't last long. Jake was gazing pas him out the window of the conservatory with an ab stracted expression, twirling his wineglass betwee his thumb and forefinger.

"It's been a while," his cousin said thoughtfully "since an enraged female has descended on thi place with the intention of amputating a sensitiv part of your anatomy, Tyler."

Yet another youthful memory that kept the famil amused.

"Those were my wild-oats days," Tyler said. "I'v grown up."

Jake gave him a pained look, then focused bac out the window. "Funny how those things can com back to haunt a guy."

All eyes followed Jake's. Tyler had to turn in hi seat.

"What the—?" He inhaled a crusty flake of brea roll and began choking.

Bethany was walking—no, stomping—up th driveway, Ben strapped into his front-pack. Tyle had an awful feeling she'd taken a bus here from hi place, which doubtless involved two transfers and a long walk in between. He imagined it wasn't the sort of journey that left one in a happy frame of mind. He couldn't actually see a knife, but even from this distance, he could read in Bethany's black look the intention to emasculate him.

"Hell." He coughed, managed to dislodge the rogue bread crust, swallowed. Cutlery rattled as he shoved his chair back from the table.

"She's pretty, but she's not your usual type," his mother said, interested.

"She's the babysitter." Tyler threw his napkin onto the table. "I'll go see what she wants."

Jake snickered. "Apart from the obvious."

Tyler hurried out into the hallway so he could head her off at the pass.

When he opened the heavy front door, Bethany's teeth snapped together and she began unclipping the front-pack. Seemed she was too mad to speak.

"Let me help," he said, and was rewarded with a filthy look from flashing blue eyes. He was fairly sure Bethany wouldn't actually throw the baby at him, but just in case, he kept a tight grip on Ben while she wriggled her arms free of the harness. That achieved, she dropped the diaper bag on Tyler's foot. Manfully, he didn't flinch.

"Take your baby and look after him," she said through gritted teeth.

"Would you like to come in?" He knew she

wouldn't, but he was intent on scoring points fo hospitality.

"Do I *look* like I've had a lobotomy?" sh demanded. "If I step through that door, you'l have me feeding Ben, changing his diaper, puttin him to bed…"

"You mean, all the things I pay you to do?"

She rammed fisted hands onto her hips. "Yo promised me two hours a day."

"And you'll get them. Soon. Look, I'm sorr about today, but I promised my family I'd be here and Ben wasn't around when I left." As he explaine himself, which he *never* did to, say, women h dated, Tyler's sense of personal grievance grew She'd blackmailed him into this two-hours-a-da thing, and hadn't made any allowances for hin needing to carve out that time. "I can't just drop ev erything to suit you—do you have any idea how busy I am?"

"Too busy to have taken a good enough look a Ben's face to remember what he looks like."

Damn.

"Too busy to visit a bunch of sick kids who migh die if researchers don't figure out how to help them."

Double damn.

"Too busy to—"

"You've made your point," he snapped, before sh convinced even him he was lower than…whateve the lowest bug was in the bug hierarchy.

"*You* made a promise. And I'm yet to hear a decent excuse for breaking it. Don't give me busy." She shoved a sticky-out piece of hair behind one ear. "*I'm* so busy with Ben, I haven't had a proper meal in a week. You're a—a—"

"He's a brute," Tyler's mother said from behind him.

Just what he needed.

Bethany blinked, adjusted her focus. "Yes, he is."

"It's my fault," his mom said.

Bethany blinked again.

"I gave birth to him," Susan apologized. "I inflicted him on the world, then I brought him up to have no regard for anyone other than himself."

"Thanks, Mom," Tyler said.

"Why would you do that?" Bethany asked, so mystified that Susan laughed.

"We all make mistakes. In my defense, he does have very good manners." She clasped Bethany's hands. "My dear, I'm Susan Warrington, mother to this wretched creature."

Belatedly, Tyler remembered his famous manners. "Mom, this is Dr. Bethany Hart."

"I've heard all about you from Olivia," Susan said, and Tyler knew that had to be bad. "The research you're doing into kidney disease is so important, it quite captivates me."

Just like that, Bethany melted. She made an indistinct sound that left her lips parted, so Tyler could see the pink tip of her tongue, and she swayed slightly toward his mother.

"My dear, you're clearly in need of a decent meal," Susan said. Tyler rolled his eyes. "We just happen to be sitting down to a salmon roulade, followed by citrus-roasted goose, then peach cobbler with homemade ice cream."

Bethany's stomach growled, and she clamped her hands over it. "I can't come in," she said reluctantly, "because *he*—" she jerked her head at Tyler "—won't do a thing for Ben if I'm here."

"I'll insist that he does," Susan said. "Besides, who could refuse this gorgeous baby anything?" She leaned down to goochy-goo at Ben, which immediately sent her to the top of Bethany's approval list—no easy feat, Tyler knew.

"He'll con you into doing it instead," Bethany said morosely.

Susan tugged on Bethany's hands. "Absolutely not. You're right, my son should face up to his responsibilities. Did you knit that sweater?"

Tyler was certain no reputable store would stock anything as odd as the open-knit blue sweater with the asymmetrical hem that Bethany had teamed with a long skirt and boots.

Bethany put a self-conscious hand over a particularly large hole in the weave. "I'm not very good."

"The wool is lovely and the color is gorgeous on

you," Susan said diplomatically. She pulled Bethany over the threshold. "Come in, and I'll show you the shawl I'm knitting. But first I'll just shut Mitzy—that's my dear little dog—away, not that she would *ever* hurt Ben. And you must tell me more about your work." She spoke so rapidly, darting from subject to subject, that Tyler could see Bethany caving in under the gentle, inexorable force.

"We'll set an extra place for lunch," his mother said, "and I promise Tyler will be solely responsible for the baby while you eat."

Tyler scowled at his mom's treachery, but she just laughed over her shoulder as she led Bethany to the conservatory.

Tyler carried Ben, still in the front-pack. With a jerk of his head, he requested Jake to hold on to the pack so he could release Ben from his confinement. It took half a minute of wrestling the little wriggler, but at last he got the baby out. Tyler was holding Ben from behind as Jake tugged the front-pack away. His cousin started to laugh.

"What's so funny?" So what if Tyler wasn't a natural when it came to holding a baby?

Max took one look at Ben and guffawed. Tyler turned the little boy around so he could share the joke.

Ben had an oval sticker plastered to his navy blue romper. One of those stickers they hand out at conferences.

Hello, my name is Ben.

Tyler slammed Bethany with his glare.

"I wanted to avoid any confusion," she said snootily as she accepted the chair Susan proffered.

Before Tyler could wreak revenge, Bethany was sitting down, eating the smoked-salmon dish with a knife and fork and with a leisurely bliss that suggested she wasn't even thinking about the baby.

Tyler, on the other hand, held Ben in one hand and a fork in the other, and struggled constantly to ensure the two didn't meet. Ben's wandering hands—this kid had a great future as a horny teenager—made it almost impossible for Tyler's fork to connect with his meal.

Max couldn't stop chuckling every time he caught sight of that name sticker, Jake was flirting with Bethany, and Susan was going all out to ensure Bethany's comfort. The only person who had any evident sympathy for Tyler was Olivia, who winced every time she looked at him, but nonetheless steered a wide berth around Ben.

Bethany's instinct was to shovel her food in as fast as she could, before Tyler handed Ben back. But the atmosphere in Susan Warrington's house was so genteel, her hostess so gracious, that she couldn't bring herself to abandon good manners. She found herself delicately forking food, laying her knife aside, transferring salmon to her mouth with a sense of relaxation that felt otherworldly.

"Give us the scoop, Bethany," Max said. "Is Tyler the world's worst dad?"

Max wasn't as handsome as Tyler, but he had a commanding presence and a hard charm that probably attracted a lot of women.

Even though Bethany knew Tyler would win a Least Likely Father contest hands down, she replied with a noncommittal "He's adjusting."

She caught the flash of surprise in Tyler's eyes before Ben stuffed four fingers up his temporary dad's nose, and the surprise turned into a yelp of pain.

"He's certainly the best-looking daddy a boy could have," his mother said fondly. When Max groaned, she patted her older son's hand across the table, "So would you be, dear, it's just you don't have a baby."

Max sent her an impatient look. "Neither does Tyler. This is just his latest fad."

"Hey," Tyler protested. "This kid's mother left him with me."

"The Warrington Foundation strikes again," Max said dryly. "Leaving us to make millions of dollars, while you change diapers."

By "us," he meant Warrington Construction, Bethany presumed. Max's joke fell flat. Tyler got a resentful look in his eye, but he obviously wasn't about to admit he'd never changed a diaper, which limited the responses he could make to his brother's comment.

Just when the silence threatened to get awkward,

he recovered his equanimity and said with a self-righteousness that made Bethany giggle, "It's sad how you rate the ability to make money so much higher than the ability to look after an abandoned child."

"Now, boys, you know I don't like to hear you arguing about business." Susan smiled at Bethany. "The foundation is my baby."

"Oh," Bethany said politely.

"Ten years ago, it didn't exist. My husband and I used to get a lot of personal letters asking for money, so I decided to set up a charity to help people."

"It was a hobby, like her knitting," Max said, which Bethany read as an older-brotherly attempt to put Tyler in his place.

"In those days we were giving away small amounts to hundreds of people," Susan said. "After my husband died, Tyler moved out of Warrington Construction and took over the charity. He created the Warrington Foundation." She reached over and ruffled Tyler's hair before he could duck. "It was perfect for you, darling—all that schmoozing you're so good at."

Tyler's smile was tight.

Jake, who had an easy, relaxed manner that Bethany imagined would encourage women to lower their guard way too fast, spoke up. "Auntie Sue didn't explain, Bethany, how Tyler transformed the whole concept of a family charity. The Warrington Foundation has one of the best returns on funds given away, by any measure—it's a business in its own right."

"Do you have any involvement in the foundation?" Bethany asked Max.

He shook his head. "I'm the chairman of Warrington Construction. Jake's the vice president for major projects. The foundation fits around Tyler's social commitments." He raised his glass to his brother in a toast.

"Which reminds me," Susan said, "I'm hosting the Save the Children afternoon tea next Tuesday. Do you think you could come along, Tyler? The old ladies give so much more money when you do the asking."

"Mom, I have work to do," Tyler said. Bethany read exasperation beneath his casual tone. "And you know those women give me their daughters' phone numbers, then complain to you if I don't call them."

"It's for a good cause," Susan said reproachfully, but Tyler shook his head.

"I might have some time on Tuesday," Max said. He sounded disinterested, but Bethany saw the alertness in his eyes, which were the same blue as Tyler's.

His mother shook her head. "It's okay, darling, I'll manage."

Max's jaw firmed, almost imperceptibly. How strange that he should be annoyed he wasn't needed for a charity afternoon tea.

"But I do need someone to look after Mitzy when I'm away next weekend," Susan said.

Horror was uniform across the three men's faces.

"Forget it," Max said flatly.

Jake muttered something about a date who was allergic to dogs.

"Ugh, this baby stinks," Tyler said.

"COULDN'T YOU HAVE SAVED this until Bethany's back on duty?" Tyler asked Ben as, one-handed, he spread the changing mat on his mom's guest bed.

The baby smiled and made a razzing sound.

Tyler pulled the tabs on the diaper and a choking smell filled his nostrils. "Go easy on me, kid," he muttered.

Half a box of wipes and three diapers later, he had the baby clean and changed. He was exhausted.

When he got back to the lunch table, the appetizer had been cleared away, though Tyler hadn't finished his, and Max was carving the roasted goose.

"Can I put the baby down somewhere?" Tyler asked Bethany.

"There's a blanket in his bag. You can lie him on the floor with a rattle to play with, if you want to ignore him for a few minutes."

Once Ben was installed on the floor, Tyler wolfed down his goose in case he didn't get to finish it. But Ben dozed off on his blanket, and Tyler ended up with plenty of time to observe Bethany with his family. For someone who made no effort to be nice when he was around, she was sweet-natured, even cute. Neither Tyler nor Jake had ever been attracted to sweet women, so that sour feeling Tyler was experiencing had to be surprise at the amount of attention his cousin was paying his babysitter.

IT WAS FOUR O'CLOCK by the time lunch broke up. Susan escorted her guests out to the antebellum home's pillared front porch.

She cooed at Ben, kissed Bethany on the cheek and caught Tyler in a tight squeeze. "Anytime you have an errand and you need to leave Ben somewhere, bring him to me," she told Bethany.

"Thank you," Bethany said. Tyler's mom's willingness to get involved with Ben was a welcome contrast to her son's reluctance.

At the same time, Tyler said, "I pay Bethany to look after him."

His mother swatted him.

"Mom, who's that guy loitering outside your gate?" Max asked.

Susan stepped forward, as if moving a few inches might make all the difference in her ability to see what was happening a hundred yards away. "I'm not sure."

Olivia said something inarticulate and started down the steps.

Tyler shaded his eyes against the late-afternoon sun. "It's the wacko frog guy."

CHAPTER SEVEN

OLIVIA STUMBLED on the bottom step.

Tyler brushed past her. "I'll get rid of him."

"No." Olivia caught his arm. "Let me do it."

Tyler's brows drew together. "He's already harassed you once."

"I—I feel sorry for him." Silas Grant was looking up the driveway, right at her. She gave him a merry wave, so as not to alarm Susan. He didn't wave back. "He's harmless, I'll be fine," she assured Tyler.

Tyler looked confused, and she knew why. Like him, she didn't generally do anything that wasn't in her own immediate interest—the two of them worked so well together because they understood each other. She wasn't about to admit to him that Silas did interest her. After he'd left her office the other day, she'd read his funding application right through, and been quite intrigued.

Olivia hopped into her sporty little Mazda RX-7, wondering if she had time to apply a fresh coat of her Chanel Crimsonite lipstick before she reached the gates. She didn't take the chance because she was worried that, if she didn't keep an eye on him, Silas might barge into Susan's property.

But it was Olivia he was looking at. Her stomach tightened. A quick run of her tongue over her lips confirmed her lipstick had indeed been wiped away by that delicious lunch. But she'd had her hair styled yesterday, and she was wearing one of her nicest outfits, a soft pink dress with a matching belt and a large gold buckle that showed off her still-trim waist.

Silas, on the other hand, looked every bit as disreputable as he had the last time. That overcoat hadn't got any cleaner, and she was certain those were the same pants and shirt. Just maybe, she thought, he'd washed his hair—it looked springier, shinier. But if he had, he'd forgotten to comb it.

She pulled over to the curb, got out of her car, beeped the remote lock.

"Hello, Olivia." His deep, well-modulated voice sparked a sense of inevitability and excitement that set her heart thudding. Too silly at her age. And at his—she'd learned he was sixty years old, five years older than she was.

"You shouldn't be here." She tried to sound cross but didn't quite pull it off. The men she'd met recently had all been so underwhelming, even the handsome— and definitely interested—cardiologist Gigi had introduced her to at Friday's soiree. In contrast, a powerful undercurrent of excitement pulled her toward Silas.

"As I said on your answering machine, I did ask, but Mr. Warrington won't see you."

As if to reinforce her words, Tyler's BMW M6 swept out of the gates behind her, and turned in the opposite direction.

"How did you know I was here?" she asked Silas.

He frowned and said slowly, "I didn't. I came looking for Tyler Warrington."

Of course he had. Embarrassment heated Olivia's cheeks.

Silas gave her a measuring look. "But since he's gone and you're still here, I suppose I could talk to you instead."

You'd never guess from his slow talk that this man had one of the state's finest scientific minds. The excitement in the air must all be on Olivia's side. She told herself the cardiologist's overt appreciation was looking more appealing every second.

Silas looked around, took a hesitant step in the direction of Susan's house.

"Not here," Olivia said. "There's a café around the corner."

She glanced at her car, and regretfully dismissed the idea of driving to the café, no matter that walking would do a distressing amount of damage to the hand-lathed leather sole of her Italian pumps. If Silas got in the Mazda, not only would his coat likely permanently stain her custom white leather trim, but if someone saw him…

In her fanciful imaginings about him, she'd decided he was a trust-fund kid from impeccable stock, who'd dropped out back in the seventies— but you couldn't explain all that in the half second it would take for anyone Olivia knew to look at Silas and decide she'd lost her mind.

"Let's walk," she said. He was probably too tall to fit comfortably in her car anyway. This way, if she saw someone she knew, she could put enough distance between them to make their proximity look accidental.

AT THE PEPPERMILL CAFÉ, Olivia led the way to a table tucked right in the back. She ordered a double espresso; Silas asked for a filter coffee.

At first, they waited for their drinks in silence. When the scrutiny of those gray eyes set beneath bushy eyebrows became too unnerving, Olivia spoke.

"Mr. Grant, or should I say—" she paused delicately "—*Professor* Grant, I understand you're very passionate about those frogs. But you need to realize everyone who applies to the foundation is passionate about something." She thought about Bethany and her research—a lovely girl, but far too serious.

Silas didn't acknowledge her use of his title. He reached into his shirt pocket and pulled out a pair of spectacles, which he slid onto his nose. When he leaned forward, Olivia had the uncomfortable sensation those glasses were magnifying the lines around her eyes and mouth. She smoothed the edges of her lips with her index finger.

"What are you passionate about?" he asked, his voice betraying no more than academic curiosity.

"Er, excuse me?"

"There must be something that keeps you awake at night."

Good grief! The thing that had kept her awake at night over the weekend had been the memory of Silas's voice. Olivia glanced around, but no one at the nearby tables appeared to have heard that leading question.

"Something you want to fight for," he prompted.

She drew a blank.

Their coffees arrived. Olivia added half a sachet of sugar to hers. Silas topped up his cup liberally with cream. Then he launched into a meandering monologue about the red-spotted tree frog. If he was right, the amphibian's situation was certainly dire. But by the time he'd finished, Olivia cared no more about the frog than when he'd started.

She wished she did. Wished something in her life fired her up to the extent that nothing else mattered. Imagine being willing to be seen in public dressed like a bum. Imagine not minding that people thought you were crazy.

Olivia wanted to feel passionate about something more than shoes and dresses and custom white leather trim.

But it was hard to care so deeply for anything—or anyone—when no one had ever loved you like that.

"There's nothing." She flung the words at him to put an end to her own thoughts.

"Humph." Silas's eyes bored into hers, disbelieving.

Something prickled in the air between them, and Olivia felt as if she'd just had one of those facial treatments that use electrical pulses to tighten the skin. She rubbed her cheeks with her palms. She shouldn't let this mad scientist provoke her into dissatisfaction with her life. Whatever instinct had prompted her interest in him, she no longer wanted to pursue it. No matter how many letters Silas Grant got to put after his name.

She brought the conversation back to the reason they were here. "Silas—" she liked his name, it was strong and honest "—the foundation's rejection wasn't personal."

He smiled, a sudden movement of the mouth that lit his eyes, then vanished before she could add it to her impressions of him.

"Not for Warrington, no," he agreed. "But sometimes, things matter for reasons that are intensely personal, don't you find?"

For the umpteenth time in her life, Olivia felt as if she'd been measured on some depthometer and been found lamentably shallow.

"I can't say I do," she said haughtily, seeking

refuge in the knowledge that she was a scion of Atlanta society, who over the years had given her time to numerous worthy causes. Not a gala ball, not a charity fund-raiser, had taken in place in this city without some involvement on her part.

Silas assessed her. "You're an interesting woman." He nodded, as if to reinforce his assessment, picked up his cup and drained the contents. "Guess I'd better go." He stood, stuck out a hand.

Having already ascertained it was every bit as clean as it had been the first time they'd met, Olivia didn't hesitate to shake it. His fingers were as strong as the rest of him looked, and his hand dwarfed hers.

"I'd appreciate if you can do what you can for me with Warrington." Briefly, he tightened his clasp.

"I already told you," she said, frustrated, all tendency to simper evaporating. "There's nothing more I can do."

"Goodbye, Olivia," he said.

She told herself she was relieved when he and his coat flapped out of there. Leaving her to pay the check.

THAT NIGHT, Ben woke at 2:00 a.m. wanting his bottle. As Bethany bent over the crib to pick him up, Tyler stopped inside the nursery doorway.

"Nice panties," he said with the air of a connoisseur.

Bethany scooped Ben up with one hand, and with the other she tugged down the back of the butt-skimming Medical College of Georgia T-shirt she slept in, covering up her skimpy pink-and-white lace panties.

He ran a hand through sleep-tousled hair. "What's wrong with Ben?"

"He's hungry, I usually give him a bottle around this time."

Tyler's interest in her underwear was apparently of the "out of sight, out of mind" variety. Which made it vastly unfair that he should turn up wearing only a pair of blue silk boxer shorts. Bethany had to work hard to keep her gaze on his face, well clear of his bare torso, which the briefest of glances had told her was solid, muscular and very sexy. Didn't he know it was winter, for Pete's sake? She ignored the fact that Tyler's house was so warm she herself hadn't bothered to pull on a robe.

"I thought he must be in mortal pain, he was yelling so loudly." Tyler moved closer to look down at Ben, as if to check he was really okay.

Bethany stepped backward. "It's the same noise he makes every night." She pulled the bottle out of the electric warmer. "He'll drink this pretty fast, then he'll drop right back to sleep."

Tyler watched as she settled herself and the baby in the armchair he'd moved into the nursery at her request. Ben latched on to the bottle the way Tyler latched on to a beer after a game of football. As the baby chugged the white stuff, his eyes traveled from Tyler to Bethany.

He smiled around the teat of the bottle, and there was a strangely adult tentativeness to it. Then his eyes fastened on Tyler's face, and one hand flapped in a half wave. Feeling stupid, Tyler waggled a couple of fingers back…and felt an unexpected tug somewhere inside him.

Ben's smile widened, so that milk dribbled out of his mouth.

"You're distracting him," Bethany griped. But as she wiped the baby's chin with a piece of flannel that Tyler had learned was called a receiving blanket, her eyes were warm with something unfamiliar—he was startled to realize it was approval. She said, "You did an okay job with Ben at your mom's today."

He put a hand on his heart. "No, please, you're gushing."

Bethany laughed and, maybe because it was the middle of the night and she was tired, or maybe because Tyler had only just walked in and so hadn't had time to say anything to annoy her yet, she seemed more relaxed than usual.

He soon tired of watching Ben, but it was no hardship to watch Bethany, intent on her task, her mouth soft and curved in a half smile. A lock of russet hair had fallen over one cheek, pointing toward the tip of her nose. Her T-shirt was stretched wide at the neck and as Tyler watched, it slowly slipped to bare one smooth shoulder.

That glimpse of silken smoothness was somehow even more enticing than that peek at her panties.

She tugged the bottle out from between Ben's gums, and hefted him to the shoulder still protected by her T-shirt. Right away, the baby emitted an enormous belch. "Good boy," she crowed.

"My mother would have smacked my behind if I'd done that," Tyler said.

She laughed as she settled Ben in her arms to drink some more. "Not at this age, she wouldn't have."

When she laughed, the dimple in her chin showed up. Tyler wanted to kiss it. How bizarre that his first specific thought on how he would act on the attraction between them should be so tame. And that his desire to kiss that dimple should be so strong. Maybe Tyler was only capable of G-rated fantasies with Ben around. It was an alarming thought, which he banished by reminding himself that the dimple was just a starting point. From there, he'd move to other, more exciting places. Mmm, yes, that was better.

As if he'd floated the idea into the ether, Bethany leaned down and kissed the baby's forehead.

A resentful noise escaped Tyler.

Her puzzled gaze met his. "Did you just... growl?"

"What if I did?"

"*Why* did you growl?"

"Maybe I didn't." But she wasn't about to accept that, so he said, "Maybe I thought you're spoiling Ben with all this attention."

Which probably was the lamest thing he could have said. Laughter gurgled out of her, confirming it.

"You're jealous because I kissed him." Mischief warmed her eyes, and she taunted, "Jealous of a little-bitty baby."

He scowled. "No way. Now, if you were breast-feeding him maybe…"

She wrinkled her nose, pixie style. "Ugh, that's sick."

"Not from where I'm sitting."

Bethany realized his gaze had dropped down, and the way she was leaning forward, he could see right down the gaping neck of her T-shirt.

She spread a hand over the expanse of bare skin, and Tyler's smile widened. "Grow up," she said.

A few minutes later Ben was drawing only air from the bottle, so she sat him up and patted his back until he belched again. She glanced at Tyler. "Do you want to do his diaper?"

He scowled his answer to that, and she sighed with theatrical disappointment. She made swift work of the wet diaper and soon had Ben snugly taped up again and back into his pajamas patterned with space rockets improbably piloted by teddy bears.

Bethany eased him down, tucked the blankets

around him. Ben lay with his eyes open, but he blinked with a frequency that suggested he would soon be asleep.

"Guess he had a long day," Tyler said. "Meeting all those new people."

She nodded. "He liked your mom."

He shot her a glance. "You mean, *you* liked her."

"That too," she agreed. "She was really charming."

"Mom's a sucker for a cute smile."

About to reply, she realized he'd said her smile was cute. And, of course, no matter how hard she fought it, no matter that he'd made what was doubtless an autopilot flirty comment, she couldn't help smiling right then. And smiling automatically lowered her guard and allowed her to check out his torso again. *No fair.*

Tyler's eyes followed the curving of her lips with enough interest to suggest that he did actually think her smile had something going for it. Then his gaze dropped lower, into territory that was clearly beyond anywhere Mrs. Warrington might find cute, and strictly within the expertise of Atlanta's favorite playboy.

Aware of the responsive tightening throughout her body, Bethany folded her arms across her chest. "Your brother is kind of bossy."

"He plays to his strengths."

"And Jake is fun."

He frowned. "He's a workaholic."

"I had the impression he plays hard, too. He invited me to a ball game."

Tyler scowled. "I need you to look after Ben that day."

"I haven't told you when it is yet," she said, annoyed.

"Doesn't matter."

She gave a hiss of irritation, and Tyler smiled.

"What I don't understand," she said thoughtfully, "is how come when your dad died, Max and Jake ended up at Warrington Construction, and you ended up at the foundation?"

It was a reasonable question. One Tyler wasn't fond of answering. "My compassion and do-good instincts made me a shoo-in for the job."

She snorted.

He wondered what she'd say if she knew the truth. That no matter how highly the rest of Atlanta regarded him, when it came to anything important, his own family had no faith in his abilities.

"How long ago did your father die?"

"It'll be four years next month." He glanced at Ben, whose eyes were still open. "Dad was flying his chopper, he came down in bad weather."

"I'm sorry," she said.

He nodded. "He was such a larger-than-life character, his death left a big hole in our lives. Mom's only been herself again the last year."

"You and your brother must miss him, too." She plunked herself into the armchair, tugged her T-shirt down. She looked as if she was settling in for a chat Tyler didn't want to have. He should just walk out, but to do so while Ben was still awake felt as if he'd be leaving a job half done.

Tyler eyed her bare legs—might as well get some enjoyment out of this. "Max and I haven't been on great terms since Dad died. I used to work in the construction business, but the first thing Max did after Dad died and the board appointed him chairman and president of Warrington Construction was fire me."

She gaped.

"Not so much fire me," he admitted, "as insist I take up the job at the foundation."

"But…why?"

He leaned against the changing table. "Dad and I got on pretty well, he knew my capabilities, he had me in the company as VP of marketing." He shrugged. "Turned out all everyone else, including Max, thought I was good for, was charming customers and making stockholders feel secure. Max decided those skills didn't justify my inflated salary."

Bethany looked troubled, and Tyler guessed his history had tapped into that deep vein of compassion that ran through her.

He braced himself for a whole lot of questions he didn't want to answer. And was saved when Ben belched again. There was a wet quality to it, and when Tyler looked at the crib, he saw the boy had been sick over his sheets.

"Poor baby." Bethany lifted him up. "Can you hold him while I change his bed?"

Tyler took Ben; he smelled of sick, but it wasn't offensive. As Tyler watched Bethany strip the crib and put new linen on, he reflected on how helpless the little boy would be if Tyler and Bethany walked out of here right now…if no one fed him…if his mom had abandoned him in the street, rather than bringing him to Tyler's office…

He shook off the unpleasant thoughts. Ben was safe, he had Bethany lavishing love on him, and Tyler providing for his material needs.

"Maybe I should start a trust fund for him," he pondered aloud.

Bethany looked up from the sheets she was tucking in with precise hospital corners and chuckled.

"You find his lack of financial security amusing?" Tyler said loftily.

"That's so typical of you. Ben starts to look as if he might need something, and you think of money."

"Money's good," Tyler said.

"I know why you woke up when Ben did tonight." Her smugness would have been irritating if it hadn't been so cute.

"It was the nightmares I had from changing that stinking diaper at Mom's place today."

She tsked. "It's because when you were forced to look after Ben today, you bonded with him."

He recoiled. "No, I didn't."

"You feel something for him."

"Only disgust at his stinkiness." Tyler didn't know why, but he felt he had to convince her of that.

She sent Tyler that disapproving look he knew so well. But for some reason, most likely because of her preposterous theory about him bonding with Ben—how could he bond with someone who couldn't talk, couldn't understand and probably didn't have a clue who Tyler was?—the look was mellower than usual.

"He'll need clean pajamas, too," she said. While Tyler held Ben, she removed his clothing. When the cool air hit him, the baby instinctively snuggled against Tyler, who equally instinctively cupped the back of Ben's head with his hand.

She rummaged through the dresser drawer, pulled out a pale blue terry sleeper, turned around. "Here we—"

Bethany stopped, mesmerized.

"What?" Tyler said defensively.

"You and Ben," she said. "You're cuddling him."

He rolled his eyes. "I'm keeping him warm. I am *not* bonding."

"I wish I had my camera," she said. "I'd make a killing in the greeting-card business."

His dark eyebrows drew together. "Excuse me?"

"You know. Gorgeous near-naked guy holding gorgeous, near-naked baby. On second thought, it' an advertiser's dream. We could sell aftershave."

"I have no idea what you're talking about. Except she suspected from the quirk of his lips h *had* gleaned that she thought he was gorgeous.

"It's the sort of thing that turns women on," sh explained, and added hastily, "Emotionally."

"Emotional turn-on, huh?" His tone said, *Righ* His gaze held hers.

"Only very late at night," she said, and suddenl it seemed neither of them was talking *emotional.*

Without warning, he leaned forward and plante a quick, hard kiss on her mouth. Its very brevit made it demanding, hot. She wanted more, wante to protest she hadn't had time to register the exac firmness of his lips.

She stepped backward, mustered coolness "Don't do that again."

"Why not?" His eyes narrowed. "You liked it."

Was *liking* it what made her mouth burn, mad her feel as if she hadn't eaten in weeks, made he want to reach out and—

She did reach out, but only to take Ben from Tyler. "You told me you wouldn't act on your one sided—" her voice shook, making a liar of he "—attraction to me unless I gave you a signal." She took refuge in self-righteousness. "Did I give you any kind of signal?"

"Not consciously," he admitted. "But you were talking about turn-ons."

"I was talking about emotions." She laid Ben on the changing table, slipped him into his clean pajamas. Without looking at Tyler she said, "For someone who's supposedly good with women, you can be pretty dense."

Tyler's chuckle carried all the confidence of a man who knew everything about women's responses to him. "Whatever you say."

She slipped Ben back under his covers. His eyes closed immediately.

"Looks like my work here is done," Tyler said. He took a step toward Bethany, his eyes on her mouth.

"I told you…" Bethany warned.

She was ready to jerk away from an attempted kiss—she didn't expect him to reach around and pat her bottom. His touch made her leap forward, so she bumped into him.

"See, Peaches, you can't keep away from me." Tyler tapped her nose with his finger, then sauntered from the room, his bare shoulders golden in the dimmed light.

Bethany sat down heavily in the armchair, touched an experimental finger to her lips. It couldn't be true. No way could one kiss, followed by one pat on her bottom, have pulled together all the pieces of a puzzle she hadn't even known existed.

Tyler had been right all along. She wanted him.

BY WEDNESDAY, Tyler was sleep deprived and sex starved. Every night since Sunday, he'd been woken by Ben crying for his middle-of-the-night meal.

Every night, he tried hard to ignore the wailing. But even after it stopped, even when he was certain Bethany must be with Ben by now, something compelled him to go and check.

Of course, she was there every time, always dressed in some horrible item of nightwear bearing the logo of an academic institution or pictures of fast food. There was that panty-baring MCG T-shirt, a longer and thus less appealing—to Tyler—Emory University Hospital sweatshirt, a pair of shortie pajamas with rather phallic hot dogs on them. They all led Tyler to one conclusion. Bethany had great legs.

Only for looking at, not for touching. Because no matter how conscious Tyler was of that attraction, her extreme cussedness meant she continued to deny it was mutual. She'd told him not to kiss her again, and he'd decided to respect that, mainly with the intention of driving her crazy with longing for him.

But he was the one who couldn't forget that brief sweet sensation of her lips beneath his. He was the one whose imagination had bought a season ticket to a quite extraordinary variety show. He was certain Bethany was having the same thoughts—he saw it in her skittishness every time he showed up in the middle of the night. She went out of her way to avoid bumping into him, and since he'd planted that kiss on her, she'd barely met his eyes. He just had to get her to admit the obvious.

Then they could all get some sleep. And some other things, too.

ON THURSDAY MORNING, Tyler called Bethany from work.

"The investigator just came by. He thinks he's found Ben's mother."

Tyler explained that an old lady had informed the investigator that her young neighbor had looked pregnant but had denied it repeatedly. "She's a whole lot thinner now," the old woman reported, "and there's no sign of a baby."

Bethany thought about the footage she'd seen so many times of Ben's mother leaving him at the Warington Foundation. Although the mother's face was almost entirely concealed by her black woolen hat and a long knitted purple scarf, Bethany had decided she was young, mainly on the basis of her loping walk.

Why had she given Ben away? Did she want him back?

I don't want to give him back.

The possessiveness that gripped Bethany shocked her. Ben wasn't hers, wasn't Tyler's.

"Is social services going to check her out?"

"I haven't talked to them yet. I thought," Tyler

said, unusually hesitant, "maybe you and I shoul
visit her first."

"But social services—"

"She's not necessarily his mother," he said. "An
if she is, and if she's just a kid who's been in a dif
ficult situation, we may be able to help smoot
things with the authorities."

Bethany approved of his compassion. That jus
left one hitch. "You want us to go together?"

"Of course together," he said, irritated.

Apart from those inevitable—and oddly intimate—
midnight sojourns in the nursery, Bethany had bee
trying to stay out of his way. He'd been putting in hi
two hours a day with Ben, and on each occasion sh
handed Ben over, then left him to it. Because now tha
she'd realized she...liked him, every contact fanne
the attraction.

How could she *like* someone as selfish as Tyler
If she was ever to fall for a guy—*this is sexual at
traction, I'm not falling*—it would be someone wh
would put her first. Who would, when the tim
came, put their children first.

"If she's a kid, she might need reassuring she'
not in trouble," Tyler said. "And she might prefer t
talk to a woman."

"We'll go together," Bethany agreed.

She tried to imagine handing Ben back to hi
mom. Maybe it wouldn't be that straightforward

depending on the circumstances. Maybe Ben would stay a little longer—

What was she thinking? Tyler didn't want to keep Ben, he wasn't father material. Bethany had only been here ten days, but she had the sudden feeling it was high time she got back to her real work. High time she got away from Tyler's increasingly captivating presence.

As she loaded Ben's dirty clothes into the washing machine, Bethany decided she was thankful they'd found Ben's mom. She was looking forward to resuming her research.

What research? She realized with a shock she hadn't pushed Tyler about the money at all these past few days. That she didn't have any work to go back to unless the foundation paid up, and she was doing a miserable job of making that happen.

She'd let his kiss deflect her, take her mind off what really mattered. *I need to persuade Tyler to give me the money, then I need to get out of here.*

CHAPTER EIGHT

TYLER AND BETHANY'S visit to a surprised, scared
sixteen-year-old in Augusta proved a false alarm.
The girl had been pregnant, and her parents had
forbidden her to reveal the pregnancy to anyone.
They'd convinced her to hand the baby over to some
childless cousins, who'd filed a formal application
to adopt the baby.

Tyler was silent most of the long drive home.
Bethany had no clue how he felt about still being
Ben's guardian. She, herself, felt only relief.

The kind of relief experienced by someone who
jumps off a sinking ship and hauls herself into a
lifeboat, only to find the lifeboat is leaking. She and
Tyler were back to square one.

Only it was a whole lot hotter in here now.

OLIVIA'S MAZDA RX-7 was far too conspicuous for
the errand she had in mind, so she'd borrowed her
friend Margie Biedermeyer's maid's Toyota.

Olivia couldn't quite believe she was disguising
herself so she could cruise the streets of Buckhead

Atlanta's most elegant neighborhood—where she'd lived all her life—and check out Silas's home.

She had chosen this time of day, four-thirty, because it was just starting to get dark, which left her enough light to get a good look, but minimized the chances of Silas looking out a window and recognizing her.

Her hands tightened on the steering wheel at the thought of him seeing her skulking. But how else could she find out more about him?

"You're acting like a lunatic," she told her reflection in the rearview mirror. She'd had two dates with Gigi's cardiologist, a charming, *normal* man, and yet here she was, pursuing a crank. Maybe her lunacy had nothing to do with Silas, who on every measure other than his good looks wasn't her type. Maybe it was menopause's parting shot.

She flicked her turn signal, headed left onto Armada, Silas's street. Like much of Buckhead, the homes were large, prepossessing. Some of them had been divided into apartments, and she envisaged Silas living in one of those. Alone.

She didn't know for sure he wasn't married, but he didn't wear a ring, and no woman would let her husband go out looking the way Silas did. No woman in Buckhead, at least.

When she got to the two hundreds, she slowed down. Silas had given 280 Armada as his address on his funding application. She left her headlights

off to aid her anonymity…274, 276, 278… Olivia
eased her foot off the gas, let the automatic trans-
mission move the car forward at a snail's pace.
Number 280 had a high brick wall across the front,
which meant she wouldn't see much until she was
right outside the gates.

There was only one letter box set into the wall—
no indication that the house was apartments. The
gates were beautiful black wrought iron, elaborately
patterned. Most unusual. Olivia came to a stop
across the road from the house.

And stared.

She buzzed down her window to get a better look.

Silas's home was stunning. A huge, gracious Federal-style brick house, three stories, shutters at the
windows. The wide, paved driveway had a fountain
in the center, and bisected rolling green lawns on its
path from the gate up to the grand front steps that ran
the length of the house, then back around to the gate.

It was Olivia's dream home.

As she sat there, lost in wondrous contempla-
tion, the gates swung open. Even with her window
down, Olivia couldn't hear any intrusive mechani-
cal operation. They moved silently, as if by magic.

Too late, she realized *why* they were opening.

A car whose approach had been obscured by the
brick wall appeared in the driveway. A black
Maserati, sleek and gorgeous, its powerful Italian
engine purring like a well-fed tiger.

The driver paused at the gates, checking for traffic in the street. Even in the half-light Olivia recognized the tall, broad figure behind the steering wheel.

Silas drives a Maserati.

She was so glad she'd come.

He moved forward and the car's headlamps swept the road, bathing Olivia in their glow before she could duck down.

She froze.

Silas stared right at her.

ON SATURDAY MORNING, Tyler took Ben on a protest march in support of cheaper day care for low-income families.

"You've got to be kidding," Bethany said when he told her where they were going.

"You said I could spend my two hours with him any way I like." He jiggled Ben, who was getting fractious, against his hip. "You can come too, if you like."

"I'm going back to bed. I was up three times last night."

"Let the record reflect that you put your beauty sleep ahead of the crisis in day care," he said.

"Let it," she said, and went upstairs.

Naturally, it turned out Tyler wasn't just attending the march. When Bethany switched on the TV news during Ben's dinner that night, she saw him at the front of the protest—one of the leaders. He carried Ben in the front-pack, and held a placard that proclaimed, Poor Kids Need Day Care Too.

"If that was all you were worried about, you'd have been happy to walk at the back of the line," she lectured Tyler as he grabbed a beer from the fridge.

"I would have been delighted to, but that wouldn't have done the foundation any good," he said virtuously. "It's no picnic being constantly in the public eye, you know."

"That's why you're taking Miss Georgia to the red-carpet premiere of that new show tonight." She put her TV dinner in the microwave and set the timer. "I'm surprised she has time to date you when she's so busy working for world peace."

His eyes gleamed at the edge in her voice, which sounded, she had to admit, like jealousy.

He sighed. "She needed cheering up. Poor girl, I fear she's losing heart over the peace thing."

Right after he left, Bethany's mother phoned to ask if she'd secured the new funding yet.

"I'm working on it." Bethany decided it was an aspiration rather than a lie.

BETHANY WAS SURPRISED to hear Tyler let himself in before midnight. Had he and Miss Georgia had a fight?

Normally, she would have been asleep at this hour, but Ben had picked up a cold. This was the second time he'd woken already.

Tyler appeared in the nursery doorway. "Everything okay?" He propped himself against the doorjamb, relaxed and self-assured in dark pants and a gray shirt. He didn't look as if he'd had a bust-up with his girlfriend.

"Your protest march gave Ben a cold." Bethany wiped away a trail of mucus from Ben's nose.

"Hell, I'm sorry." He came into the room, and she saw real remorse in his eyes. "Will he be okay?"

"Tyler, it's a cold, not the bubonic plague."

"You may not appreciate this," he said, "but guy colds are much more serious than girl colds."

"I'd heard." She smiled—it was much easier to talk to him when he was fully clothed.

"Just so long as you're aware." He looked down at her, took in her shortie pajamas decorated with rainbow-pastel soft-freeze cones. "Did I ever tell you that you have great legs?"

"No, but you look at them often enough, I figured it was either that or you're trying to creep me out."

"Both," he said.

There was a moment's silence. Then Bethany said, too loudly, "Ben's asleep, I'm going back to bed."

BEN WOKE at one o'clock, fretting, unwilling to be pacified.

Tyler watched Bethany walk the baby up and down the small nursery. He started to walk along-side her, matching his steps to hers. Eight steps down, turn, eight steps back. It soon grew tedious. "I prefer circuit training."

"Then why don't you carry the weight?" She passed Ben, still wide-awake and peevish, to him.

They resumed their pacing. The room wasn't that wide, so they were forced to walk close together. Maybe this exercise was more strenuous that he'd thought, because heat prickled all over Tyler.

"I forgot to ask how the show was tonight," Bethany said.

Tyler grimaced. "It was one of those interminable family dramas—a whiny bunch of people who didn't like each other much."

"A pretty ordinary family, then."

"You've been talking to your mother again," he said.

She stopped midpace. "How did you know?"

"Maybe I'm not as self-absorbed as you think," he said smugly. "I noticed last time you spoke to her you kept scratching your neck afterward. You've been doing that tonight."

Since at that very moment Bethany's hand was curled at her nape, she wasn't in a position to deny it.

"I'm not allergic to my mother," she muttered.

"No, but you're tense." He clasped Ben with one hand so he could jog her elbow. "Keep walking."

She did as she was told. After a moment he said, "Where do your folks live?"

"In Madison."

He'd never been there, but he knew the town was around an hour from Atlanta. "Any siblings you're allergic to?"

She sucked in her cheeks and said reluctantly, "I had an older sister, Melanie. She died when she was fourteen."

Tyler waited.

Bethany screwed up her face, revealing her struggle not to say more. Eventually, the pause became so pregnant it threatened quintuplets.

"Of acute kidney failure," she blurted.

What the—

Bethany kept moving, staring straight ahead at the teddy-bear height chart on the wall. Tyler wondered why the baby planner he'd enlisted to stock the nursery had decided he needed a height chart for a baby he would have only a few weeks.

He halted Bethany with a hand on her arm. "How old were you when she died?"

"Thirteen. We were born fifteen months apart."

"That's tough," he said. "I'm sorry." He resumed walking, and Bethany followed. "Any other kids in the family?"

"My younger brother, Ryan—he was just a year old when Melanie died."

Tyler exhaled against Ben's head, and the little boy batted Tyler's chest. "So that's why you chose kidney disease as your specialty?"

"I guess."

He searched her face. "Is it why you became a doctor?"

Bethany shifted. "Maybe…indirectly."

Tyler was still trying to process what he'd learned. There had to be more to it. "I think it's strange you didn't say anything before, about your sister."

"It was a long time ago."

He reached over and tucked a strand of hair behind her ear. "Strange."

"IS HE OKAY?" Tyler asked at 2:00 a.m. Once again, with an uncanny sense of timekeeping, Ben had woken almost on the hour. "He's…snorty."

"He's blocked up. I need to get these saline drops into him." Bethany squeezed the contents of a dropper into Ben's nose, much to his outrage. She soothed the screaming baby with her usual lack of perturbation; as always, Tyler was impressed by the way she got on with the job without complaint. "He'll be fine, we'll just have to wait this thing out." She peered at Tyler. "Or, rather, I will. You look tired, you don't need to get up to him every time."

"Oh, yeah," he said. "If I sleep through, I'll have you accusing me of selfishness."

She actually looked guilty. "I won't," she promised. "You've been great tonight."

That unqualified praise hung in the air between them.

"Why don't you go to bed." She sounded as if she really, really didn't want Tyler there.

Which had to mean he was getting to her.

Deliberately, he eyed her legs. "I don't mind staying."

So that's what he did. He stayed, and let his mind wander to how Bethany's legs would look and feel wrapped around him.

THREE O'CLOCK WAS TIME for Ben's feed. Bethany hoped like heck Tyler hadn't heard him crying, but he got to the nursery at the same time as she did.

"After you." He sketched a bow in the doorway.

Ben was both ravenous and ill, his face was redder than a tomato. Bethany hastened to heat his bottle.

Tyler picked Ben up. "His diaper is full." A pause. "Shall I change it?"

"I must have fallen asleep for a second," Bethany said. "I just dreamed that you offered to change—" Tyler's darkening expression made her cut her little joke short. "Yes, please."

He grumbled something about ingratitude as he untabbed Ben's diaper, threw it in the trash can.

"Uh, Tyler, you might want to have the new diaper ready before you—"

Too late. Ben shot a steady stream of pee into the air. Tyler leaped backward, but not before the full force of the spray hit his bare chest.

"Damn." Several other curse words followed as he grabbed a couple of baby wipes and began rubbing his chest with such distaste that Bethany burst out laughing. She fastened the clean diaper on Ben and put him back in his crib, which he protested loudly.

"Need any help?" she asked Tyler, still chuckling.

"No, no, my life's goal is to keep you amused and I seem to be doing fine."

She plucked the wipes from his hand and picked up a clean receiving blanket. "Let's dry you off."

The second the blanket made contact with his chest, she realized this was a bad idea. The soft flannel fabric afforded her hands no protection against the heat of his torso. Involuntarily she uncurled her fingers from around the cloth, then spread them wide in a futile attempt to span the firmness of all that muscle and sinew. Her wiping motions slowed, slowed. Stopped.

Tyler covered her hands with his own, securing them against his chest. Bethany felt the thud of his heart, felt his gaze on her, willing her to look up. She kept her eyes locked on their joined hands.

Then Ben squawked, and Tyler released her. They both turned their attention to the baby. Bethany gathered him in her arms; Tyler patted the back of Ben's head, his fingers brushing across Bethany's. Static electricity snapped between them, and she jumped back, fixed him with an accusing look.

He smirked. "Told you there was a spark."

Bethany rubbed her fingers against her thigh. "That was science, not sex."

AT 4:00 A.M., Bethany could hardly stand up straight, she was so tired. Yet one part of her—the sad, pathetic part that held out for any glimpse of Tyler seminaked in the middle of the night—was wide-awake. Each time he appeared in the nursery, she noticed something new about him. The shadow on his jaw, the whiteness of his teeth as he smothered a yawn, the cording of his biceps as he ran a hand around the back of his neck to ease his exhaustion.

Was it her imagination, or was he standing closer to her each time they leaned over Ben's crib together? Like now, as she stroked Ben's head to help him get back to sleep, she felt as if Tyler was only an inch behind her. To test the theory, she leaned back, and instantly encountered the hard warmth of his chest. When she would have pulled away, his hands descended on her shoulders, keeping her there. His chin dropped onto her head. "Tired?"

"Uh, yeah." Best to let him think that was why she was leaning on him.

"Me too." He turned her around to face him, and his eyes were unfamiliarly compassionate. "But this has got to be tougher on you than on me. You're doing all the work."

"Not all," she demurred. She added mischievously, "Ninety percent, tops."

He laughed. "I don't know where you get the energy to joke at this time of night."

"You think I'm joking?"

He laughed again, and it chased away Bethany's fatigue. Her whole body went on alert, every corpuscle pulsing with energy. His fingers burned into her shoulders, ten points of radiant heat. Even though he'd had as little sleep as she had, Tyler looked so strong, so vital, so red-blooded, that Bethany could stand it no longer.

She'd said this moment would never come, that she would never give him a signal. But she'd been wrong. Just plain wrong. *Nothing to be ashamed of in that.*

She lifted her hand, reached to a point just below Tyler's left ear, ran a finger from there along his jaw to his chin.

She waited.

Tyler gazed down at her, intense, unreadable.

And yawned.

He ran a hand over his eyes, cutting her off from that intensity. "Guess I'll hit the sack."

He was turning her down! Bethany braced herself against the wave of mortification, somehow managed not to let it topple her.

"Good idea," she muttered. Blindly, she turned back to the crib. "I think Ben's asleep now."

She waited, frozen in her humiliation, until she heard Tyler's bedroom door click shut; then she made her way back to her own room.

WAS IT POSSIBLE to feel more tired, Tyler wondered as he sank into bed. His head swam, red and black spots hovered before his eyes like demented ladybugs. He hadn't slept a wink tonight—he'd been unable to drift off between stints in the nursery, partly because he was worried about Ben, mainly because he was hyperaware of Bethany.

How did she manage to look so good when she must be every bit as exhausted as he was?

She smelled good, too. Tyler had given up the fight to keep his distance and moved closer to her, just so he could absorb that fragrant blend of lemon and mint and something floral that he'd come to associate with her. Then there was the feel of her, her shoulders satiny smooth beneath his fingers.

And somehow she retained the energy to backchat him at every stage of the night. He liked the way her eyes sparkled with humor when she tried to stomp on his ego—she'd doubtless be disappointed to know it wasn't as fragile as she thought.

Then there were those touches. He didn't know what it was about that woman, but every time she touched him, he felt as if he'd been set alight. It had taken all his willpower just now not to react to the featherlight touch of her hand against his jaw.

Her hand...his jaw...

Tyler sat bolt upright. Dammit, Bethany had given him the signal.

He leaped out of bed, fatigue forgotten, only one thought in his mind.

Get to Bethany. Now.

He barged into her room without knocking, cursed when he stubbed his toe on what felt like a book. It was pitch-dark; he heard scrambling movements as she sat up in bed. "Tyler? Is it Ben?" She sounded alert, worried.

He reached the bed, fumbled for the lamp on the nightstand, snapped it on. She blinked at him, her face flushed, tilted toward him so that a minimal movement would join his mouth to hers.

"You gave me the signal," he said.

She dropped her gaze. "What signal?"

"I was tired, it took me a couple of minutes to click. I'm sorry."

"Oh…that." A forced laugh. Her fingers plucked at the duvet. "I'd forgotten already."

"I'm here to take you up on your offer."

Panic widened her eyes. He might have known she'd get cold feet. She'd had such difficulty getting this far, when from day one Tyler had seen it as their obvious destination.

"It wasn't an offer." She pulled the bedclothes higher, up to her neck. "I changed my mind."

He tugged the duvet so sharply that the unexpectedness made her let go. "Oh no you don't." He sat down on the edge of the bed, stopped her moving away from him by simply putting a hand at either side of her. "I've been waiting forever for this."

Bethany snickered nervously. "I've been here not quite two weeks. That's hardly forever."

"It feels like ten years."

"That's because I nag you."

"It's because I want to do this," Tyler corrected her. He leaned in, kissed her, wanted desperately to devour her. But that would likely scare her off, so instead he took it easy. Which had the unexpected and very pleasant benefit of allowing him to fully savor the sweetness of her lips in a way he didn't remember doing since he was a teenager. He murmured against her mouth, "You don't get to change your mind now."

All the same, he pulled back a little.

"I suppose it would be rude," she agreed, her eyes fixed on his lips.

Yes! He kissed her again, harder, felt the response of her mouth to his. Her lips parted and he went in. This was what he'd been waiting for; it felt even better than he'd imagined…and he only realized now just how much imagining he'd done.

She made a mew of pleasure as her tongue met his. He pushed her back against the pillows and lay down so he was half on top of her, pressing into her delicious curves, soft against his hardness. Her arms went around his neck.

Bethany abandoned herself to the delight of

Tyler's kiss. His hands stole beneath her pajama top, caressed the skin of her waist, sending her arching against him. His thighs were hot against hers, combustible.

If she didn't stop right now, she wouldn't be able to stop at all. She didn't want to stop. Then she remembered, and suddenly, stopping was easy. She shoved hard against Tyler's chest.

"Hey." He pulled away, surprised. "What's wrong?"

"You went out tonight. With Miss Georgia." She pressed her palms to her cheeks, but her hands were as hot as her face and didn't cool her.

"And?" he said impatiently.

"Did you think you'd go straight from her bed to mine?" Bethany swiped the back of her hand across her mouth, to erase the imprint of his two-timing lips.

His eyes narrowed. "I don't treat women like that. I told you, Sabrina's not my girlfriend."

So, Miss Georgia had a name.

"Do you really think I'd kiss you like that if I was dating her?" he demanded.

Who would have thought playboy Tyler Warrington had a streak of decency? He looked so offended, Bethany decided it would be impolitic to answer. "So you're certain she wouldn't be upset about…what we just did?"

He laughed, incredulous. "You're worried about her feelings?"

Bethany shifted up the bed, so she was semi-upright. "I don't steal other women's men." Not that she'd ever been in a situation where that was even a remote possibility. But it seemed like a sensible rule.

Tyler wanted to laugh at the seriousness with which Bethany was treating a kiss. A great kiss, a hot kiss…but just a kiss.

Trouble was, Bethany didn't take anything lightly.

"So," she said, "you're not dating her, and you're kissing me like that…"

She wanted to know if she and Tyler were dating.

Did he have to decide that right now? Before he'd even finished kissing her?

Typical of Bethany to complicate matters.

One part of him wanted to say yes, then take her to bed to seal the deal.

But maybe having a baby in his life was making him more cautious, because what stopped him from acting on that impulse was the thought of tomorrow and the day after.

If he was honest with himself, he'd admit that his attraction to Bethany was just a little out of control.

He thought about her all the time. About kissing her. And other things. Disturbingly, not all of those things were physical. He wasn't used to being pre-occupied with a woman, and it didn't seem a smart place to be.

Especially not with Bethany, when they were living under the same roof. Things could get tricky.

He measured her lips with his gaze, resigned himself to the fact he probably wouldn't taste them again anytime soon. He shuffled down the bed a bit. "I'd rather not overanalyze what just happened," he said. "We kissed, it was nice." *Understatement.* "Let's not suck all the fun out of it."

Her eyes narrowed. "You think talking takes the fun out of a relationship?"

Definitely. "You think we have a relationship?" he countered.

She opened her mouth, then closed it again. "We have an attraction," she said tentatively.

"Agreed." He watched her face in the lamplight, the progress of her thoughts across her face.

"But in your mind that doesn't lead to a relationship, not even if we kiss and…stuff?"

Tyler shifted at the thought of *stuff.* "A relationship is based on more than attraction." He felt the way he had when he'd talked to the divorced dads about parenting—out of his depth.

"That's true," Bethany said. "And the fact is, I'm here to ask you for money, nothing more than that."

Couldn't she forget the damn money?

"Getting close to you emotionally could screw things up." She bit her lip. "And chances are, you and I don't have anything in common, apart from that attraction. A relationship would be an unnecessary risk."

"You could be right." Had he misread her question about relationships? Was she saying she was up for no-strings sex? Tyler's entire body went on alert. He moved so he could see inside her pajama top, the first few buttons of which were undone. He got a glimpse of an enticing, pale swell of breast.

"I mean," she said, "you're rich and famous."

He dragged his gaze up from her cleavage just long enough to shoot her a wary look.

"And I'm intelligent, hardworking and caring. So, Tyler—" she paused and the silence made him look up again "—I don't think this is going to work, do you?"

She held his eyes as, with deliberate movements, she refastened all the buttons on her pajama top.

CHAPTER NINE

ON MONDAY MORNING, Olivia set an unsolicited cup of coffee on Tyler's desk. Since he usually had to ask her to bring coffee at least three times, her consideration inspired suspicion rather than gratitude. He sat back, waited.

"I've met someone I like," she said.

Tyler stuck his fingers in his ears. "I don't want to know."

"It's complicated."

"It always is," Tyler said bitterly. He couldn't believe Bethany had ended up giving him the brush-off on Saturday night. No matter that common sense told him it was the right thing to do. "You're always meeting men you like," he reminded Olivia. "You're worse than I am. With women," he clarified.

"I like this guy more than the others," Olivia said.

Tyler looked at his secretary. She was very attractive, slim, always well groomed, her graying hair carefully highlighted. Olivia was a class act. "I'm sure he'll like you back."

"I doubt I'm his type. I think he's looking for someone…deeper."

"Ouch," Tyler said. Because neither he nor Olivia was good at deep. He had the same problem with Bethany, who was— He pulled himself up. "Don't you have girlfriends you can have this conversation with?" he said. "Like my mom?"

"I don't want your dating advice," she snapped. "I need a favor."

"I'm not going to ask him if he likes you."

She laughed, but without enthusiasm. "It's Silas Grant."

It took a moment. Then: "The frog weirdo!"

Olivia didn't object to having her romantic crush referred to as a weirdo. Tyler figured that was for obvious reasons.

"Olivia, have I been putting too much pressure on you?"

She plunked herself down in a chair with none of her usual elegance. "As if I'd let you. I know it's crazy, Tyler, but I like the guy. Now, are you going to do me this favor, or do I have to call your mom and have her order you to help me?"

"You've told Mom you like Frog Guy?" he said, incredulous.

"Of course I haven't." She shuddered. "Please don't make me."

He sighed. "What's the favor?"

"Let Silas pitch to the PhilStrat Committee."

She'd never tried to influence how the foundation spent its money before. They both knew she was overstepping the mark. But Tyler couldn't get angry. Sometimes, you met someone who made you want to act out of character. He was strong enough to resist that temptation, but Olivia obviously wasn't.

"You think that'll impress him?" he asked.

"It's the only thing I've got." The words fell out of her, startling both of them.

"Take it easy, Olivia," Tyler said.

She grimaced. "I can't believe I'm telling you this. It seems like only yesterday you were—"

Tyler held up a hand. "This had better not be about my bare baby bottom again."

She clamped her lips together. But only for a moment. "Did you know Susan asked me to be your godmother when you were born?"

"No," he said, surprised.

"I refused, told her it wasn't my thing."

He nodded. Olivia had doubtless been too busy partying.

She crossed her legs, flexed one black patent-leather shoe. "It wasn't true. I just didn't think I'd be a very good godmother."

"Of course you would," he said automatically. He couldn't see that godmothering was too difficult a task.

Olivia took his assurance more seriously than he

intended. Her smile might have been skeptical, but her eyes lit up. "You really think I could have done it?"

"I wish you had," he said, and realized he meant it. "Instead, I had Lyddie Hudson telling Mom that, 'dear Tyler would look so adorable wearing a suit and tie to church, you really must have him fitted.'"

Olivia shuddered. "You were only six—I never saw a kid look so uncomfortable. I couldn't convince Susan to get rid of that suit until after you put a hole in the pants, climbing a tree."

Tyler narrowed his eyes. "You dared me to climb that tree."

"Did I?" she said innocently.

He grinned. "I definitely wish you'd been my godmother."

"If I'd known how fond of you I would eventually become, I might have accepted," she said, surprising him again. He had a lot of affection for Olivia, and he'd assumed she felt the same, but it wasn't something they talked about. "Truth be told," she added, "I didn't like you much at first."

"Even with my cute little…?" He waved in the direction of his behind.

"Even with that," she said dryly. "Your mother was so besotted with you, it was painful. She loved Max, of course, but I've never seen anyone as potty about a baby as she was about you." She laughed. "Susan couldn't think or talk about anything else after you were born."

"Sounds horrible." One thing about Bethany, no matter how devoted she was to Ben, she had plenty of time and energy to tell Tyler where he was going wrong. He chuckled at the thought.

"I was jealous," Olivia admitted. "I've known your mom longer than I've known anyone else—she's the person I'm closest to in the world."

Tyler shifted in his seat. "I guess we've all matured since then."

Her smile was wry. "Right now, I feel about twelve years old. I don't know what to make of this thing with Silas. I'm so confused."

"Sounds like it." He couldn't imagine what the attraction was.

"When you're twelve years old," Olivia said, "you're so *hopeful*. Dreadfully naive, but there it is."

Tyler sighed, spread his hands on the desk. "Fine, tell your boyfriend he can pitch to the committee. As long as he gets a haircut."

Olivia beamed, and for a second she did look like a girl, a hopeful, happy kid.

"Maybe you should trust your instincts," he said abruptly.

She stood, considering him. "Maybe *you* should trust *yours*."

What the hell was that supposed to mean? He wasn't the one who felt like a twelve-year-old. "This conversation is not about me."

She tutted, but she was still smiling. "That makes a nice change."

Troubled, Tyler watched her walk out of the office. Olivia had fallen for Silas hard and far too fast, which she had a habit of doing, as he knew from her multitude of past engagements.

But he'd never seen her put herself out for someone before. He'd never heard her talk about her fears, her hopes.

The world was turning upside down, and Tyler didn't like it.

WHEN OLIVIA CALLED Silas with the good news that he could pitch to the PhilStrat Committee, he didn't say anything about her presence outside his house last Friday.

So maybe he hadn't seen her. Had he been wearing those glasses?

She made herself believe he hadn't, because otherwise she'd be too embarrassed to proceed with her plan. It would be so blatantly obvious that she'd checked out his material wealth before she took this step.

"There's not a lot of time before the pitch meeting," she said casually, "so I thought I might…help you."

"Hmm," he said, neither encouraging nor discouraging.

"I know how the committee makes its assessment, so I can make sure you cover all the bases," she said. "And I'm a whiz with PowerPoint."

She was learning not to rush him through the silences he seemed to enjoy.

"That's very kind of you," he said at last.

Was it Olivia's imagination, or did a thread of amusement run through the words?

She was glad she couldn't see him. She clutched the phone tighter. "Would you like to come to my place on Wednesday night so we can plan your campaign?"

He thought about it. "Yes," he said, "I believe would."

TYLER HAD BEEN out of sorts the past couple of days. Ever since that kiss.

Since Bethany felt the same, though in her opinion she was doing a better job of hiding it, they didn't talk much. And they definitely didn't touch. They passed Ben from one to the other without the slightest contact.

As she fed the baby his dinner late Tuesday afternoon—Ben had graduated to rice cereal or pureed vegetables served in his high chair for his evening meal—Bethany admitted that, as far as the baby was concerned, Tyler was shaping up better than expected. He gave his two hours every day without argument. He took Ben out with him, often to a media interview. Bethany never heard him speaking to Ben in a way that was anything but kind, if disinterested. And he changed diapers, if not with enthusiasm then with tolerance.

"I think he likes you," she told Ben.

Tyler had shown less tolerance toward the pamphlets about kidney disease that she'd taken to leaving around as part of her new stealth campaign. She found a bunch of them in the wastepaper basket in his den. And the Your Kidney and You poster she'd pinned to the back of the bathroom door was unceremoniously torn down within hours. She never found it.

The head of Bethany's research team had called her yesterday to see if she would be rejoining them anytime soon. But while he was hopeful the team's budget might be expanded in the second half of the year, right now there was no money to pay her beyond what she could get out of the Warrington Foundation.

Which was big fat nothing. Nagging Tyler hadn't worked. Not nagging hadn't worked. And her strategy of getting him to fall in love with Ben and throw cash at her research was…well, that wouldn't succeed overnight.

The doorbell rang, interrupting the dismal inventory of her progress.

"Just a minute, sweetie," she told Ben.

On the porch stood the most gorgeous specimen of womanhood Bethany had ever seen. A blond, bronzed bombshell. Tall, slim, but with curves. Enticing curves, by anyone's standards.

"You must be Miss Georgia."

The smile was wide, warm, wonderful. "Sabrina Merritt," she said. A magical name for a magical creature. "Also known as Miss Georgia. And you're Bethany. May I come in?" She held up a small Tupperware container, as if it was some kind of admission token.

Doubt—and guilt—assailed Bethany. Could Tyler really not be dating this woman? And what if Miss Georgia was in love with him? What if she'd guessed about that kiss and wanted to confront the woman who was after her man? Maybe Bethany should just confess now that she'd forgotten the beauty queen's existence when she'd issued that reckless invitation to Tyler to kiss her. Let the woman club her to death with the Tupperware, and be done with it.

From the kitchen, Ben squealed, then hiccuped.

"Come this way," she told Sabrina. The presence of a baby would surely distract even the most jealous of lovers. Six feet of stilettoed beauty queen sashayed behind Bethany to the kitchen.

Miss Georgia caught sight of Ben in his high chair. "Isn't he adorable."

He'd made hay in Bethany's absence, dipping his hands into the bowl of rice cereal she should have removed from his tray, and was now squeezing the gooey mixture between his fingers.

Sabrina brought her face close to Ben's and made

clucking noises. Bethany had read that even babies recognize beauty; Ben took one look at Miss Georgia and paused in his play. His wide eyes roamed her perfect face, then a chubby hand reached for that spun-gold hair.

"Careful," Bethany warned her, just as Ben tugged hard.

"Ouch!" But nothing disturbed Miss Georgia's apparently flawless temper, and she was still smiling as she disentangled Ben's hand from her hair. "You little cutie, you're going to be irresistible to the ladies."

Ben chortled and waved with excitement at having the attention of this vision of loveliness. Bethany supposed making a fuss over babies was high on the list of a beauty queen's essential job skills, so she didn't take the usual pride she might have in Sabrina's praise of Ben.

Some contrary impulse stopped her mentioning that the woman had a large glob of rice cereal stuck in her hair. She picked up a spoon and began trying to coax the remains of Ben's dinner into his mouth.

"I told Tyler I'd call around this afternoon. He said he'd be home early—" Sabrina shook her head indulgently at Tyler's tardiness "—but maybe you and I can make girl talk until he gets here." As if there was nothing Bethany would rather do than be made to feel like a total frump.

The other woman slid onto a stool at the granite island, every movement as smooth as a performance of *Swan Lake*. She set the Tupperware container in front of her with a precise movement. The clump of rice cereal swung as she moved, attracting a few more strands of hair.

Bethany should say something. But right now that lump of cereal was the only thing that made Miss Georgia human enough to talk to. She'd mention it soon, she assured herself as she put the kettle on to boil. She offered her guest a drink. Sabrina chose herbal tea.

"Tyler tells me you're doing a great job of looking after Ben."

"He's a wonderful baby, anyone would want to help him," Bethany said.

"How did you end up getting involved?"

At Sabrina's urging, Bethany told her about her kidney research. The other woman was interested and compassionate but not, Bethany guessed, turned on by the cause. It seemed unlikely she could enlist Sabrina's help in persuading Tyler to spend more money.

She was surprised to find herself enjoying their conversation. The "girl talk" stayed at a level Bethany could follow—moisturizer, sunscreen, lipstick—rather than soaring into the realms of Botox, collagen, or, worse, men.

"Oh, I forgot—" Sabrina slapped her cheek in a charmingly ditzy way "—I made some food for Ben." One long, lilac fingernail tapped the Tupperware container. "Tyler told me you prepare Ben's food yourself, rather than buying cans."

Tyler talked about baby food with Sabrina? And he'd actually noticed Bethany pureeing carrots? "Uh…thanks, that's really thoughtful of you."

"It's coq au vin," Sabrina said. "I pureed it thoroughly so it's total mush, and there's no salt in it. I know salt's bad for babies."

Bethany peered at the container. "Um, did you say coq au vin?"

Sabrina chortled. "I'm Cordon Bleu trained, so I can't help cooking fancy meals. But there's no alcohol in it. I mean, there's a tiny bit of wine, but the alcohol evaporates during cooking."

As far as Bethany knew without consulting a textbook, Sabrina was right. There shouldn't be a problem giving a baby food that had de-alcoholized wine in it. But something about the thought of feeding a baby coq au vin seemed just plain wrong.

"He's only having rice and vegetables at this stage," she said. "Chicken won't be on the menu for another month or so. I'll put this in the freezer."

Before she could do so, Ben banged his spoon on the tray of his high chair and gurgled with such purpose that she and Sabrina turned to see the source of the fuss. Tyler had arrived.

He greeted Bethany, ruffled Ben's nonexistent hair, then moved on to their guest.

"Sabrina." After a swift glance at Bethany, he

dropped a kiss on Miss Georgia's beautiful mouth. "I forgot you were coming over."

"Do you have other plans?" She didn't seem miffed at the thought of being forgotten, and Bethany liked her for it.

"No. Yes." He stared at the cereal in Sabrina's hair. A few more tendrils had been drawn into the sticky mess, and it looked larger. Without commenting on it, he looked back at Sabrina, and Bethany saw concern in his face. Concern about something more than the state of Sabrina's hair. "Jake said he might call in for a drink."

Sabrina bit her lip, but not hard enough to mar her lipstick's perfect finish. "I'll stay a little while," she said, "then get out of your hair before he arrives."

That phrase, *get out of your hair,* had Bethany painfully aware she should say something about the rice cereal. Because when Sabrina looked in a mirror, she wouldn't have to be the sharpest file in the manicure kit to realize the mess had originated with Ben and that Bethany had seen it and not told. "Uh, Sabrina…"

The peal of the doorbell had Sabrina stiffening.

Jake let himself in, called out a hello as he made his way to the kitchen. "Hey, buddy, I know I said six o'clock, but—" He stopped at the sight of Sabrina, whose fingers had curled around the Tupperware container and were clenching it as if it was a talisman to ward off evil.

"Hello, Jake," she said coolly.

"Sabrina." His eyes swept her. "You have puke in your hair."

Bethany cringed. "It's not puke," she said, "it's rice cereal." As if that somehow made it better. Well, it did. Given the choice of having her hair clogged with rice cereal or puke, anyone would choose cereal.

Bethany couldn't figure out why the easygoing Jake had been so rude.

Sabrina colored, rummaged in her tiny, elegant Chanel purse, pulled out a mirror. After a quick inspection she stowed the mirror again, her expression neutral.

"I'd better get home and fix this mess." She pushed herself off her stool. Lightly, she said to Bethany, "It's funny, once you've been onstage in a swimsuit and a diamanté crown, no one ever tells you if you have lipstick on your teeth, or a smudge on your face, or—or puke in your hair." Her voice wobbled, but she brought it under control quickly.

Bethany felt lower than an earthworm, and Tyler was squirming too. Sabrina turned to Jake and said, "So, thanks, Jake. I guess this means right now you're my best friend in the world."

He flung her a look of such loathing that Bethany flinched on her behalf.

But Sabrina seemed to find that oddly cheering, and her smile warmed up as she said goodbye to Tyler.

"Thanks for bringing the puree." In a last-ditch effort to redeem herself, Bethany said urgently to Jake, "Sabrina made a meal for Ben. She cooked chicken." She wasn't about to specify coq au vin, she had a suspicion Jake would have a field day with that. As it was, he rolled his eyes rather than commending Sabrina for her thoughtfulness.

Sabrina acknowledged Bethany's feeble, belated effort to intervene in an obviously damaged relationship with a smile. But there was a distance in it that hadn't been there before. Bethany still felt like a heel.

When the beauty queen had left, Tyler grabbed a couple of beers from the fridge, handed one to Jake.

"Would you like a glass of wine?" he asked Bethany.

She had him pour her a glass of merlot.

Jake clinked the neck of his bottle against Tyler's. With Sabrina gone, he seemed his usual relaxed self. "I have news for you, buddy. I had a call from a pal in Washington, D.C."

Tyler glanced at Bethany, and said, "Let's go to the den."

TYLER SAT DOWN on the button-backed leather sofa that had seen him through years of TV ball games, dozens of Chinese takeouts and an immoderate amount of making out. "You have news on the think-tank job?"

"First, my usual disclaimer, none of this is written

in stone," Jake warned. But he was well connected—his father, Tyler's uncle, had been governor of Georgia—and his information was seldom wrong.

"Understood," Tyler said.

Jake took a swig of his beer, eyeing Tyler over the rim of his bottle. "Those guys in D.C. should be the last to believe what they read in the press, but that article in the *Post* about you at the single-dads conference made a big impression. As of this week, you're the front-runner."

Nervous excitement dried Tyler's mouth. He gulped down beer. "I'm up against some big names," he said, trying not to get excited. "People who've had years of working with families and kids."

"I hear there's some pressure to choose a candidate from the South," Jake said.

"There's plenty of competition down here, too. Carson, Lavelle…"

"You're the golden boy."

"That doesn't mean anything to those guys. Hell, it didn't mean anything to my own family."

Jake folded his arms, didn't disagree.

"If I get this job it'll be on my own strengths." Tyler didn't know if he could pass the test.

"Looking after the baby was a smart tactic." Jake was clever enough to figure out where Tyler's interest in parenting stemmed from, and cynical enough not to object.

Tyler didn't have to pretend with him. Still, he found himself saying, "Ben's a nice little guy."

"A bonus."

Which was true. Even if Ben had been the baby from hell, Tyler would have gone ahead with his plan.

"If you can swing another media coup on the scale of the *Washington Post*," Jake said, "you might just have yourself a job." He frowned. "I hope my family doesn't handicap your chances."

Jake's father had exited the governor's office in disgrace, and Tyler knew the shame still rankled with his cousin. "If they wanted to hold your father against me, they'd have ruled me out a long time ago."

"I guess." Jake stretched his arms behind his head. "How are you getting along with the cute kidney doctor?"

Tyler shrugged. Then suspicion hit. "Why do you call her cute?"

Jake laughed. "She have a boyfriend?"

"Yes," Tyler said, remembering the "convenient" guy he'd never actually seen. Plus the divorced dad who'd asked for her phone number. Had he called yet?

Jake looked skeptical. "You wouldn't have a problem if I ask her on a date, would you?"

"I heard you already did."

Jake grinned, unembarrassed.

Tyler couldn't explain the sudden coldness that

settled into his spine. "If she's out with you, I'll have to look after the baby. So, yes, I would have a problem."

Jake gave him a knowing look.

"I'm not interested in her," Tyler protested. He thought about that kiss, the memory of which still sneaked up on him at least a dozen times a day. "Not beyond the 'she's a pretty woman, I'm a red-blooded man' level. You know I don't go for the wholesome do-gooder type." He folded his arms and found himself staring his cousin down in a way that was vaguely reminiscent of years ago, when he and Jake both had crushes on Sabrina.

Back then, Jake had won, and it hadn't bothered Tyler. But Jake damn well wouldn't get to date Bethany. The strong surge of possessiveness caught Tyler by surprise, and he had to struggle to stay polite.

Maybe sensing that struggle, Jake didn't stay long.

"Remember what I said," he told Tyler as he climbed into his Alfa Romeo. "Find yourself another opportunity like the *Post* one, and do it fast."

After his cousin drove away, Tyler tried to enjoy the thrill of knowing he might soon win that job in D.C. But he kept thinking about Jake dating Bethany.

It wouldn't hurt to figure out exactly what Bethany thought of his cousin.

CHAPTER TEN

"DO YOU COOK?" Tyler asked Bethany when he walked back into the kitchen.

She looked up from the newspaper she was skimming as she stood at the counter. "I do a nice pureed carrot."

He tapped the tile floor with his foot. "I'll make us dinner."

"Aren't you going out?" she said, surprised.

"I don't go out every night."

She raised her eyebrows.

"I stayed home one night last year," he said, and she laughed. "Most boring damn night of my life."

"And that's what you're offering me?"

Tyler could think of any number of ways to spice up an evening in with Bethany. In fact, the breadth of his imagination startled him. "I've got to be better company than Ben."

"If you say so," she said dubiously. "But you don't have to cook. I usually eat one of the microwave meals out of your freezer."

Her hand reached over to Ben, still in his high

chair. She stroked his head, and Tyler wished it was him she had her hands on.

"I'll cook," he said.

BETHANY PUT BEN to bed before they ate, and when she came downstairs, Tyler had set the table in the formal dining room with cutlery, condiments…and candles.

She reminded herself he was hardwired for seduction and that this meant nothing. He'd made it clear he wasn't after a relationship, and she wasn't after sex. Or a relationship, she added hastily.

The table was huge, so they sat at one end, opposite each other. Tyler had cooked steaks with artery-clogging but delicious garlic butter, home-fried potatoes and—a nod to the health lobby—green beans. Bethany's steak was perfectly medium-rare, tender and juicy.

With the candle flickering between them, the atmosphere was way too romantic.

Bethany broke the mood. "My brother called, he wants to stay over on Friday, is that okay?"

Tyler shrugged, distracted. "I'll be out at a concert, do whatever you like." He put down his fork. "Did Jake tell you when that ball game is yet?"

"I thought I wasn't allowed to go."

"I can't stop you dating," he acknowledged. He didn't sound happy about it, which given he wasn't interested in her himself smacked of pettiness.

"Good, because I had a call from Scott, the father of that girl who didn't have an allergy."

He hissed his annoyance, and because her ego needed pampering, she added, "Maybe I'll go out with him next week, then Jake the week after, now that I have your permission."

He eyed her with disfavor. "Jake's not your type."

Bethany sighed as her ego took another tumble. "You mean, he wouldn't want an ordinary woman like me?"

"Don't put words in my mouth."

That drew her attention to his lips and the memory of that kiss.

"Jake's not a one-woman guy," he said. "You'll get hurt."

Nice of him to care. "What's with Jake's hostility toward Sabrina?" Bethany asked.

"They go back a long way," Tyler said vaguely. His gaze sharpened. "Why didn't you tell her she had that gunk in her hair?"

Bethany felt her face redden. "Why didn't you?"

He fixed her with a curious stare, and drummed his fingers on the table.

She held out as long as she could, then said, ashamed, "It made her seem more...human."

"Sabrina's lovely."

"I know that now. But, believe me, when you look like I do and you meet a woman like her, it's intimidating. She wasn't so frightening when her hair was a mess."

"You're not frightened of anyone," he said. "Besides, you're pretty, you have no reason to feel insecure."

As compliments went, it wasn't a top-ten, all-time great one.

"So why didn't *you* tell her about the rice cereal?" Deliberately provocative—not to mention pathetically insecure—she added, "You're her boyfriend."

Annoyance shadowed his face. "For the last time, I'm not. Sabrina and I like to spend time together. Having me around boosts her profile, and when I need a date who's not going to cause a scandal, she's my first choice. We're friends. Old friends."

"All the more reason for you to have mentioned her hair."

"I couldn't. Blame it on my mom—she raised me to always be polite to a lady. Never to point out her faults."

"It doesn't seem to work that way with me."

He rubbed his chin. "You're right, there's some kind of mutant instinct at play where you're concerned." He splayed his hands on the table, his fingers strong, capable. "I still think you were mean not to tell Sabrina."

"You were mean, too."

"We were both mean," he said.

The awful thing was, Bethany enjoyed the

comfort of that shared failing. She buried her face in her hands. "I can't believe I've sunk to your level."

"Or I've come up to yours," he suggested helpfully.

She glared. "I would *never* have been that selfish before I met you."

He shook his head sadly. "I'm just glad Ben's too young to understand how you've fallen."

She sighed in agreement. "You're probably a better role model for him than I am right now."

He reared back. "That's going a bit far."

"I'm paid to look after him," she pointed out. "You've been spending two hours a day with him without fail, and you've been great with him."

"I had to be blackmailed into it," he reminded her.

"There is that," she said, relieved.

He folded his arms across the powerful chest that she realized she'd seen naked more often than clothed. A smile played on those firm lips. "You really think I'm great with Ben?"

"Occasionally," Bethany said, because he didn't need a bigger ego.

He surprised her by looking thoughtful instead of pleased with himself. So she added honestly, "I might even have misjudged your commitment to the foundation."

"Is that so?"

"At first I thought you didn't take it seriously,

that you enjoyed the social aspects and didn't care about the people you help."

"What's changed your mind?" he said cautiously.

"You've worked so hard on publicity, all those media interviews you've done the last couple of weeks. You're becoming almost as boring on the subject of family issues as I am about kidneys."

"No way," he said, shocked.

She smiled. "And there's nothing in it for you, you're doing it all for the foundation. I…admire that."

Tyler shifted in his seat. "Let me guess, this is a ploy to get me to listen to your Kidneys 101 lecture." He sure as hell hoped it was—the last thing he wanted was Bethany seeing him as some kind of hero.

Naturally, she wasn't able to pass up the opportunity.

"I'll keep this lecture short," she said, "out of deference to your attention span for any subject other than yourself."

She didn't seem to be able to pass up the chance to have a dig at him either, Tyler thought, amused. Her foot brushed his under the table, gaining her his full attention.

"How would you feel if Ben had kidney disease? If, unless the doctors were able to learn more about his condition, that disease would kill him?"

Pain slammed through Tyler, winding him. Was she trying to break some bad news? "He's not sick, is he?"

She shook her head. "That's the situation my patients and their families are in."

Tyler regrouped his emotions. "That was a low tactic," he said coldly. "Don't do it again."

She looked down her nose at him, unrepentant. "I've said all I wanted to say. Think about it."

TYLER DIDN'T THINK about kids with kidney disease that night, not once. But he did think about Bethany.

She'd sneaked into his mind subtly, infuriatingly, at first only with the odd stray, usually negative, thought, but now she'd launched a full-scale invasion of his mental space.

There was no reason for it, Tyler thought as he stared unseeing at the computer screen on his desk the next morning. Except, maybe, that by not telling him much about herself, she'd intrigued him enough to make him want to know more.

Many of the women Tyler dated were Atlanta socialites whose families he'd known for years, their pedigrees a matter of public record. And as most women were keen to talk about themselves, he usually ended up knowing way more than he ever wanted to about them.

What did he know about Bethany?

That she was prickly and defensive about her work, yet ready to laugh at her own expense about anything else. That she was small-minded enough not to tell Sabrina about the gunk in her hair, yet compassionate to the point of self-sacrifice for sick kids. That she attacked Tyler's ego with all guns blazing, yet she lavished tenderness on Ben. That she kissed like a dream.

Get a grip. Tyler hauled his wandering mind back to the facts he knew about Dr. Bethany Hart. She'd studied medicine at the Medical College of Georgia. She worked at Children's Healthcare of Atlanta, on the Emory University campus. He cast around for more hard facts. He had no idea about former boyfriends, lovers…and decided ignorance was much better for his peace of mind. He knew she had parents in Madison, a brother, and a sister who'd died. Of kidney disease.

Which must have been a big deal, big enough to set the course of her life. Yet she'd never mentioned it again, not even when she was haranguing Tyler for money. He needed to find out more.

OLIVIA HAD GIVEN the cardiologist his marching orders. He was showing alarming signs of thinking long-term, and she'd resolved she wouldn't get engaged again until she found a man who would love her above all else.

Of course, she'd made the mistake before of thinking she'd found such a man—seven times—but she was starting to realize that was because she'd been looking at the wrong kind of man. She dated men who liked to be seen with a beautiful woman, one who fit right into their expensive homes and wealthy lifestyles.

She needed a man who would care more about her than he did about life's accoutrements. A man like Silas, who was not only incredibly attractive but also a physics professor at Georgia State, who thought deeply about things and, more important, cared deeply. Yet who still had a reassuringly large fortune, to judge by his house, his car.

Olivia couldn't think why she hadn't dated a man like him before.

The things she didn't like about Silas—his dress sense, his droning on about frogs, his tendency to stare into space saying nothing—could be fixed in a jiffy.

He arrived at her place at six on Wednesday night, right on time.

"Hello, Olivia." He stepped into her home without looking left or right, no curiosity about her environment discernible.

But as she led him through the house, she felt his eyes on her back, on her hips as they moved in her slim-cut black velvet skirt, as surely as if they'd been his hands, and was glad she'd dressed up.

It was more than he'd done. Although his plaid shirt looked clean, his jeans had the beginnings of a hole in one knee and his overcoat was as disreputable as ever.

But—she hugged the knowledge to herself,

didn't betray by so much as a smile that she'd noticed—Silas had shaved.

In place of that rough stubble was smooth male skin that tempted Olivia to reach out and touch.

Instead, she wrapped her hands around a hundred-dollar bottle of merlot and offered him a glass.

He accepted, to her relief. She'd worried his eco-warrior attitude might extend to most of life's pleasures, though the Maserati had afforded her some hope.

Since this was supposed to be a business meeting, she steered him to the dining room table. Silas opened his battered briefcase—his battered *Gucci* briefcase—and withdrew a rough outline for his pitch, along with some of the background material.

He spread the documents across the table and invited Olivia to take a look. He stood next to her, explaining, in his sexy voice, which photos, charts and statistical information he considered most useful.

It had to be the contrast between those polished vowels and his rough appearance that made Olivia's insides curl in on themselves with excitement. He left her short of breath, long on giddy anticipation.

As she gave him her views on the presentation and what he should be covering, it was impossible to tell if she had the same impact on him. Once or twice, she thought she saw him glancing at her legs when she moved and the slit at the side of her dress parted. And his gaze rested on her cleavage for several seconds as she leaned over the table to look

at the state map that showed the location of the red
spotted tree frog's habitats.

If only she could be certain he was actually thinking
about her cleavage, rather than those blasted frogs.

She poured him a second glass of wine, but when
it was only half-full he reached out, covered her
hand with his and tilted the bottle upright.

"No more for me."

His fingers interlaced with hers around the bottle—
his thick and roughened, hers pale, pink-tipped.

Olivia couldn't drag her gaze away from the
contrast. She sensed him looking down at her, and
a strange shyness stopped her from looking back,
even though she longed to show him how much
she liked him.

Then his hand twisted, broke the contact, and he
took the bottle from her. He stood it on the table,
moved away so there were several feet of space
between them, and she wondered if she'd imagined
the whole charged moment.

She cleared her throat. "How did you get interested in the frog?"

"Through my wife," he said.

Her stomach caved in. "You—you're married?"
Everything changed in the blink of an eye, leaving
her feeling naive and very foolish.

"Widowed," he said. "Anna died two years ago."

"I'm sorry," she said, ashamed of the relief she
felt. "Was she sick?"

He shook his head. "She had an accident out at the frog sanctuary she'd established—the preservation of the red-spotted tree frog was her life's work. She slipped and fell at the edge of a pond. Hit her head on a rock and drowned."

"Silas, that's awful." Olivia swallowed. "Was she a scientist too?"

"A biologist."

"She must have been smart." Olivia had spent her three years in college organizing sorority parties. She'd passed one exam, more or less by accident. She'd quit before they threw her out.

"Anna was smart," he agreed. "And kind, and good." He added, almost belligerently, "I loved her very much."

"Of course you did." It was the depth of Silas's feelings that had first attracted Olivia to him. "You must have been very happy."

For the first time since they'd met, he didn't look her directly in the eye. "Before the accident, I was involved in an international physics project, which meant a lot of travel. I…neglected Anna. She was unhappy when she died." He sounded wretched.

Olivia didn't know how best to comfort him. Awkwardly, she reached for his hand, clasped it between hers.

"That's why I'm on sabbatical from Georgia State." He lifted his gaze. "I'm taking a year out to secure the future of the Anna Grant Frog Sanctuary."

Olivia knew she absolutely should not feel jealous of a woman she'd never met, a woman who'd died tragically. "It's a beautiful gesture," she managed to say.

His mouth twisted. "It's better than nothing. Though my kids don't see it that way."

"You have kids?"

"A son and a daughter, Paul and Jemma. But," he said heavily, "they don't speak to me. They haven't forgiven me for upsetting their mother. I don't blame them."

He looked so remorseful, Olivia wanted to shake him. She couldn't believe Anna had been unhappy. Not with a husband who loved her enough to take over her cause after her death.

Silas moved around the table, gathering his papers. "Thank you for your help tonight, I appreciate it."

"Would you like to stay for dinner? It's just leftovers." Actually, it was a freshly cooked chicken-and-mushroom casserole.

He looked at her, looked away. "I don't think so." He sounded distant, distracted again.

She followed him out to the entryway, where he took his coat off the hook, pulled it on. He shoved his hands into its pockets.

Olivia said, "Silas, do you ever have that coat cleaned?"

He looked down at her in surprise. "Not much

point. I go out to the frog sanctuary fairly regularly, just to think about things, and I often end up with a frog or two in my pocket."

She shuddered.

A beat-up Chevy truck sat outside her front door, alerting her neighbors to his presence. She'd have to say she was interviewing a new gardener. She wondered why Silas hadn't brought the Maserati. Hopefully, of course, he had no idea she knew of its existence.

As he climbed into the truck, he said, "Can we do this again? Maybe at my place on Saturday morning? I should have a clearer idea of this presentation by then. We could start on the Power-Point."

"Of course." Olivia's heart skipped and her mouth developed the irrepressible curve of a sixteen-year-old with a crush. "Uh, what's your address?"

The corners of his mouth moved in the tiniest smile. "I haven't moved since Friday night."

Drat.

BETHANY'S BROTHER, Ryan, arrived at Tyler's house at five o'clock on Friday.

She hugged him, delighted to see his awkward, angular face.

"Nice place," he said with a fifteen-year-old's casual interest as he looked around Tyler's open-plan living and dining room.

"Nice enough," she agreed. "Come and mee Ben." The baby was in his high chair, and she se Ryan to feeding him while she made a start on th hamburgers she'd planned for their meal.

An hour later, they were just sitting down to ea when Tyler walked into the kitchen.

Bethany's knife clattered onto her plate. "Wha are you doing here?"

"I live here." He headed for Ryan, who'd stoo and was wiping his mouth with his napkin. "I'n Tyler Warrington, you must be Bethany's brother."

"Ryan," Ryan agreed. He shook hands with Tyle

"I thought you had a concert," Bethany persisted

Tyler said to Ryan, "This must be what it's lik to be married. So glad I never took the plunge."

She glared. "Unfortunately, marriage doe require one to think of someone other than oneself I doubt you're suited to it."

"I always thought it was for people who'd run ou of ideas," Tyler returned.

Ryan was glancing from one to the other, lookin slightly shocked.

"Sorry, Ryan," Tyler said, "your sister is such a interesting conversationalist, I sometimes forge my manners."

"Sometimes…" Bethany muttered. More loudly she said, "There are extra hamburgers if you'd lik some."

Tyler loaded up a plate with burger and salad

hen joined them. Between mouthfuls, he asked Ryan a few questions, eventually eliciting the information that Ryan was on a weekend away from his boarding school near Atlanta.

"Why do you go to boarding school?" Tyler asked. "Aren't there good schools in Madison?"

Ryan's mouth turned sullen. "Mom and Dad don't want me around."

Bethany got over her surprise that Tyler had remembered her hometown and tried to forestall a conversation that could only give him too much information. "That's not true," she scolded Ryan. To Tyler, she said, "Mom hasn't been well for a long time. I boarded through most of high school, and now Ryan's doing the same."

Ryan made a gagging noise. "You don't believe that crap any more than I do. They sent me to an elementary boarding school when I was eight. They'd have sent me to boarding preschool if they could."

"Ryan…" Bethany sent Tyler a helpless look, pleading with him to drop the subject.

Tyler didn't even consider complying. When had she ever paid the slightest attention to his requests that she drop the subject of her work? "What exactly is wrong with your mom?"

"Nothing," Ben said. "I get on her nerves and so does Bethany. So does anyone who's not Melanie."

Bethany closed her eyes, evidently giving up the fight.

"You were only a baby when Melanie died, weren'
you?" Ryan hadn't been much older than Ben.

Some of the resentment drained out of Ryan a
Tyler's reasonable tone. He sagged back in hi
chair, nodded. "I don't remember her, I only eve
saw photos."

"Do you look like her?" There was a clear resem
blance between Ryan and Bethany, in the russe
color of their hair and in the shape of their faces
though Ryan had brown eyes.

"Some," the boy said. He fidgeted with his fork
flipping it between his fingers. "I never really knev
Mom and Dad, not the way they were befor
Melanie got sick. They probably used to be okay.'

"Melanie had a rare blood type that made ;
kidney transplant almost impossible," Bethany said
"Dad had the same blood type, but he couldn'
donate because he had only one kidney." Seeing
Tyler's shock, she said, "A single kidney isn't tha
unusual—most people born that way never realiz
they don't have two. Anyway, Mom and Dad hac
some very stressful years." To Ryan, she added
"But they love you. And me."

"They loved Melanie more." Ryan's tone was so
flat, even Bethany didn't argue further. She threw
Tyler a glance that said, *Thanks a lot.*

Tyler felt an out-of-character obligation to repai
the damage. He tried to steer the conversation inti
safer waters. "What brings you here, Ryan?"

Ryan looked at his sister, dropped his gaze, then muttered, "I ran away from school."

"You *what?*" Bethany jumped to her feet.

"I hate it there," Ryan said. "If you're no good at sports, no one likes you. And then you get bullied."

"You're being bullied?" Her face whitened.

Her brother nodded abruptly, as if he was ashamed.

"Have you told Mom and Dad?"

He waved a hand at her. "I tried, but they said I should tell the teachers."

Tyler knew that wasn't a solution any teenage boy would welcome. "Maybe your parents could talk to the principal, in confidence."

"They'd have to care first," Ryan said.

Bethany held up a hand. "They do care. And right now, I need to phone the school and tell them you're with me. You'd better hope they haven't already called Mom."

"They won't know I'm gone," Ryan said. "I had a pass into town and I'm not due back until ten."

He was right—when Bethany spoke to the housemaster, Ryan's absence hadn't yet been noticed. That put the man at a disadvantage, and Bethany was able to insist she keep her brother for the weekend. When she suggested she would tell her parents she'd invited Ryan to stay, the man agreed with obvious relief.

Ryan grinned when she told him the news. She warned him sternly, "But Sunday night, you're going back to school, no arguments."

She felt awful when his elation evaporated.

"Will you talk to Mom and Dad about the bullying for me?" he begged.

Bethany didn't want to say yes. Her relationship with her parents was fragile enough that she didn't want to risk damaging it. She didn't want to put another brick in the wall that separated them from her.

"I'll try," she told Ryan discouragingly. Tyler shot her a surprised look.

It was all very well for him. He had a mother who doted on his every word. He'd never had to earn his parents' love.

He'd never disappointed his parents the way she'd disappointed hers.

CHAPTER ELEVEN

TYLER DECIDED on Monday morning that he needed to stop thinking about Bethany as a woman, turn the clock back to those days he'd thought of her as nothing more than a pediatrician and a pain in the butt.

He shouldn't have invited her and Ryan to Zoo Atlanta with him and Ben on Saturday. He'd justified it to himself on the basis she could help with Ben at the zoo, but instead, he'd just had a good time with her. He'd compounded his error by taking Bethany and Ryan to Mom's for lunch on Sunday, which had produced speaking glances from the family.

From now on, he would take less interest in her body, because that was what kept him making overtures to her, and more interest in her work—guaranteed to turn him off big-time. Which meant he had to make a great personal sacrifice, and start learning about kidney disease.

Bethany was the last person he wanted to talk to on the subject. Any whiff of interest on his part and he'd never hear the end of it. Not only that, she'd assume the foundation was going to extend her research grant, and if that didn't happen, she'd be devastated.

He called Olivia into his office and asked her to find out who the main research teams were in pediatric kidney disease. She cocked her head, inquiring. But Tyler turned back to his computer screen, so after a moment she left to do as he'd asked, tutting under her breath.

Two hours later, Tyler placed a call to Dr. Robert Harvey at Toronto's Hospital for Sick Children.

The doctor was patient and courteous in explaining kidney disease and the main areas of research. Among those, Tyler recognized Bethany's area of specialty—overcoming antibody barriers to kidney transplants.

"It's a very exciting area that several research teams, including ours, are following up," the doctor said. He made a whistling sound through his teeth. "Like everyone, we're limited by our funding as to what we can do." He paused. "What would be our chances of a grant from the Warrington Foundation?"

Alarms clanged in Tyler's head. "Anyone in North America can apply," he said cautiously. "You can use the application form on our Web site, or format your own application, and from there we'll contact you if we think it's worth your pitching to us."

He ended the call with a far greater understanding of the issues surrounding pediatric kidney disease…and with a fervent hope that Dr. Harvey wouldn't apply for funds.

THREE DAYS LATER a FedEx package arrived from Toronto.

Dr. Harvey must have stayed up all night, judging from the comprehensiveness of the material enclosed in support of his application. The foundation would have to take it seriously. Tyler told Olivia to contact the doctor and invite him to pitch at the next PhilStrat meeting.

"Another kidney project?" she said.

"Yep."

"But it's against the foundation's policy to fund more than one project in a specific area."

"You don't say."

She sucked in a breath, but didn't comment further. Now that he thought about it, Olivia hadn't been butting into his affairs much lately.

"How's your romance with Frog Guy?" he asked.

She sniffed. "It's not a romance, it's a working relationship."

"Bad luck," Tyler said. Then he realized her situation was similar to his with Bethany. The difference, he told himself, was that he wasn't looking for more than a working relationship.

BETHANY'S CONSCIENCE, aided by Ben's erratic sleep patterns, was keeping her awake at night. It was definitely her conscience, not thoughts of Tyler sleeping across the hall, so she asked Tyler to invite Sabrina for lunch on Saturday.

Sabrina's acceptance of the invitation, coming as it did from Bethany rather than Tyler, said a lot about her graciousness. Bethany was determined to make amends.

The sooner she said what had to be said the better. As they enjoyed a glass of wine with hors d'oeuvres in the kitchen before lunch, she announced, "I owe you an apology."

Sabrina's perfectly shaped eyebrows rose. "You do?"

Tyler stopped stirring the pumpkin soup Bethany had on the stove and came to listen. Bethany wasn't sure she wanted an audience.

"That day, when you had cereal in your hair." She blushed at the memory. "I'm so ashamed I didn't tell you. I was… relieved you could mess up like the rest of us. I was jealous," she said honestly, "that you're so beautiful and so put together. And I'm really sorry."

Tyler had an odd look on his face. Sabrina stared. *Great, I made a complete idiot of myself.*

Sabrina started to laugh. It didn't sound malicious, and Bethany couldn't help smiling. "Glad you find my base emotions so amusing."

"I knew you felt bad," Sabrina said. "You were so sweet the way you never told Jake that I made coq au vin for Ben, which I later mentioned to a friend of mine who's a nurse and she hasn't stopped laughing since."

"You made coq au vin for a baby?" Tyler said, aghast.

Sabrina raised her wineglass to him in ironic salute. "As if you would have known it was a dumb idea... But, Bethany, I do appreciate your apology. When I saw that stuff in my hair I couldn't figure out why you wouldn't have said something, and then I wondered if maybe you thought I wanted Tyler and you were in love with him—"

"No!" The horrified cry came from both Bethany and Tyler.

"But now, well, let's forget all that and just be friends."

"I'd love to," Bethany said. There was an awkward silence, then Tyler said, "What the heck," and kissed both of them. Typical of him to turn the situation to his advantage, Bethany thought, even as she noted that he lingered a lot longer on her lips than he did on Sabrina's.

"We must have lunch one day next week," Sabrina said. "I'll be in Washington, D.C., on Monday and Tuesday, briefing Senator Bates about the peace initiatives in Kurdistan. But any other day is fine."

Which gave Bethany another chance to feel like a worm, just in case she needed it.

While they were eating the pumpkin soup, along with the bread Bethany had made in Tyler's bread machine, Sabrina offered to visit some of the kidney kids Bethany worked with. Bethany jumped on the invitation, and they agreed on the following Thursday.

After lunch, Bethany and Tyler stood on the porch to wave Sabrina off. As soon as her car turned out of the driveway, Bethany smacked Tyler on the arm.

He grabbed her hand, held it in place. "What was that for?"

"Why didn't you tell me she really does work for world peace? You knew I thought that was a crock of beauty-queen babble."

His gaze alighted on her fingers, crumpling the crisp cotton of his sleeve. Then he looked right at her. "I didn't want to spoil your illusion that unless you wear odd clothes and beg for money you're a shallow, worthless person."

Bethany drew a sharp breath. Was that how she came across? Worse, was that what she believed deep inside? She pressed a fist to her mouth, gnawed on a knuckle.

Tyler shook his head, exasperated yet amused. "If it makes you feel any better, it's only peace in Southwest Asia."

Oh, yeah, she felt much better.

OLIVIA AND SILAS had had several more meetings, but they'd all, for one reason or another, ended up taking place at Olivia's house. Today, finally, she got to go the big Federal-style house on Armada.

The cynical side of Olivia couldn't think why she was excited about visiting a man who was so devastated by his wife's death that he'd dedicated his life to saving her precious tree frog.

Ironic that when she at last found a man who knew how to love a woman above everything else, he'd already given that love away.

The foolish, romantic side of her wondered if it was possible to love that way twice. Because if he loved her, she could definitely love him back.

But she still had no idea how he felt about her.

She'd dressed to impress regardless, in a knee-length green skirt that showed her shapely calves, and a lighter green blouse, classy and just the tiniest bit transparent.

Silas opened the door before she got there. A different plaid shirt today, this one blue and gray, worn with faded jeans that looked almost normal. Apart from the fact that he was barefoot, he could have been a dressed-down version of any man she knew.

Then he said, "Good evening, Olivia," and the words brushed her skin like a hot summer breeze, and she knew he was a man apart.

Inside, the house was as beautiful as the exterior promised. Her gaze flitted around the paneled entryway, up the wide, curving staircase to high ceilings as she followed Silas into an enormous living room.

She gasped.

Every wall was plastered with posters of frogs, aerial photographs of wetlands, charts showing population statistics. The coffee table bore several stacks of papers, and more covered the sideboard along the far wall.

"May I take your coat?" Silas asked.

She shrugged out of her ivory wool peacoat. When his fingers touched her shoulders, Olivia shivered.

He frowned. "I guess I forgot to put the heating on." A pause. "I'll do that now."

When he returned, Olivia was reading one of the red-spotted tree frog fact sheets on the wall, still trying to feel the passion that Silas did. Still failing. She turned, and found Silas right behind her. Up close, he was so big she longed to lean into him.

His thick lashes made his eyes his best feature, she thought. Or maybe that was his mouth, with that thinnish top lip and full bottom lip. She'd never paid much attention to the tiny details of a man's face before. She was more a pocketbook girl, she liked to evaluate her dates' material assets.

Silas cleared his throat. "Perhaps it would be best," he said, "if I just kissed you and got it over with."

That's how deranged this man made her—she thought he'd just said something about kissing her. "Excuse me?"

"I can't stop thinking about kissing you—" he spoke faster than she knew he could "—and don't tell me you can, because I can see you can't."

"I—I—"

"I haven't kissed another woman since Anna. Haven't wanted to, until I met you." He'd slowed down again and he sounded so subdued, not at all enthusiastic, that Olivia just stared at him, mute, wondering if she was hearing right.

"How long since you kissed a man?" he asked with about as much energy as if he was asking if she thought it might rain.

"A couple of weeks." Now she wished she hadn't gone tongue-to-tongue with the cardiologist.

His craggy eyebrows shot up. "Any good?"

"I beg your pardon?"

"Was it any good?"

"Not really," she admitted.

He humphed. "We'd better give it a try."

"Surely some enthusiasm would be appropriate," she said.

Then his arms closed around her and she was incapable of speech, just filled with relief that at last it was happening.

His kiss was at once tender and rough, seeking and taking. Olivia opened to his firm, warm lips, pressed herself against him. She should be alarmed at how wanton he made her feel.

His large hands roamed her curves, making

Olivia, taller than most of her friends, feel delicate. He was strong enough that he could probably sweep her up in his arms, carry her upstairs.

Then the kiss was over, as suddenly as it had started. Silas moved away from her, and she grabbed hold of the back of the couch for support. He looked pleased and annoyed at the same time.

"You're a good-looking woman," he said.

She nodded.

"Did you ever get married?"

"No," she said discouragingly.

"Why not?"

"Not for lack of offers," she said tartly, and pushed herself off the couch, steadier now.

"Never thought it was." Silas leaned against the sideboard, his gray eyes inquiring.

"I've been engaged seven times," she admitted.

His laugh cracked the air. "Just altar shy, huh?"

"Perhaps." She busied herself with tucking in her blouse, which had come away from her skirt.

His eyes followed her movements. "What was wrong with those men?"

Her hands paused. "Maybe there was something wrong with me."

He looked skeptical.

"They were good men," she said. "But any man I married would need to prove he'll always put me first."

"Selfish," he commented.

"I suppose I am. My parents led very busy lives, separate from each other and from me."

"I've heard of them." Her family had been prominent Atlanta benefactors.

"Nothing I did, good or bad, got their attention for more than a few minutes." She didn't want him to see how that hurt, so she fixed her gaze on the one piece of non-frog-related paraphernalia in the room. A silver-framed photo of a smiling, dark-haired woman, a child seated either side of her. This must be Anna. Olivia's focus blurred. "I hated that I could never be sure my parents loved me. I want a man who loves me so much he proves it every day, by choosing me above everything."

"Hard for any man to measure up."

You could. Olivia pushed her hair behind her ears. "I'm lonely, Silas. I have friends, I have a lot of fun, but I've always been lonely, every day of my life. But at least I know what to expect and can live my life around it. I'm terrified of marrying someone and having it not last, and I'll have forgotten how to survive on my own."

"Sometimes you have to take a risk."

She shivered, hugged her arms around her, turned slightly so she couldn't see that photo of Anna. "Finding someone, knowing that love, then ending up lonely again, would be worse than never knowing it at all."

"Chicken," he said. "I miss Anna every day, I'd

give anything to have her back. But I'll never wish I hadn't loved her."

Olivia swallowed a salty lump in her throat.

His brow creased. "So you never met a man you loved enough to take the risk?"

"Never."

The wheezy sound from the back of his throat was a laugh. "You want a man who loves you enough to take a risk on you, but you don't want to give him the same."

She stepped back. "That's not true."

He didn't say anything, and Olivia considered the subject dropped. They moved into work mode: she busied herself with reading his presentation, made a few comments and suggestions, then refused his invitation to stay for supper.

"Come back tomorrow," he said as he showed her out the front door.

Silas watched her leave, driving that toy car of hers too fast down the driveway. Today he'd been to the deli for the first time in years, to buy the fancy foods he knew Olivia would like. He'd hoped she would stay; a small part of him wanted her never to leave.

Maybe, like her, he was lonely. Yet while he missed Anna, he didn't hate being on his own. Olivia was a special temptation. The taste of her, the feel of her in his arms, had been sweeter than anything he could remember.

He ran his knuckles across his mouth, fancied he could still feel her lips on his.

If Olivia knew the truth, that kiss would never have happened.

THE TYLER WARRINGTON publicity machine was an unstoppable beast. Tyler had only to decide he would come along on Sabrina's visit to the kidney ward, and his PR team swung into action. They had no trouble lining up a group of journalists to accompany him: Atlanta's favorite playboy was now Atlanta's favorite daddy.

Bethany had to assume all this publicity was doing the foundation some good, though she'd never fully understood the link between media coverage and its ability to boost the foundation's work. But it was nice to think that needy people were benefiting.

Sabrina looked stunning in a pale blue wool wrap dress and decked out in her Miss Georgia crown and sash. To Bethany's mind, Tyler was equally gorgeous in his black suit, pale gray shirt, and black-and-gray tie threaded with silver.

First on the agenda was a tour of the ward. The kids were ecstatic to see Miss Georgia, and so were their fathers. The mothers took more interest in Tyler, and Bethany saw a couple of appreciative glances from women she knew to be happily married.

"Tyler, this is Molly." She introduced him to a

ten-year-old who was waiting for a transplant, and gave him a brief rundown of the girl's condition.

In less than a minute he'd charmed Molly out of her anxiety-induced moodiness.

That set the pattern for the rest of the visit. With every child, he requested details of his or her condition, first from the patient, then supplementing those shyly given but often painfully honest replies with technical information from Bethany. Then he'd chat until the child was relaxed and smiling. For a guy who never thought about anyone other than himself, he did a great job.

Bethany couldn't stop the hope that bubbled up inside her. Tyler was taking an interest in her work—if this visit convinced him to spend more of the foundation's money, the last month would have been worthwhile.

It already was worthwhile, she realized as, having introduced Tyler to a young boy who'd recently had surgery, she stepped back to let the man work his magic. Regardless of the outcome for her research, it had been a pleasure to look after Ben. She'd made a new friend in Sabrina. And then there was Tyler.

The man who'd argued with her, flirted with her, kissed her.

The man who was starting to mean something to her.

Not that.

"Bethany, how did Jason's surgery go?" Tyler called her attention back to the moment.

She bustled forward. "He's doing great."

It was almost an hour before they left the ward. One of the nurses came to "borrow" Ben to show her colleagues, while Sabrina and Tyler hosted an informal question-and-answer session with the media. A crowd of spectators gathered, among them Susan Warrington, presumably here to watch Tyler at work.

Tyler, well briefed as always, talked about sick kids and the strain illness put on families, and how the foundation was here to support families.

One of the reporters asked if he had a particular interest in kidney disease. Tyler grabbed Bethany's hand, tugged her forward.

"This is Dr. Bethany Hart. Her research into antibody production is funded by the Warrington Foundation. The foundation is committed long term to supporting advances in understanding and treating pediatric kidney disorders."

To the journalists it might have been just a quotable quote. But Bethany's ears latched on to the words *long term*.

Tyler must plan to renew her funding. What else could he mean? Of course, she wasn't rash enough to whip out her cell phone and call her parents—she'd wait until she knew exactly how much she was getting. But she had to struggle not to break into a skip.

One of the reporters asked for an update on Ben. Tyler described Ben's latest development with an accuracy that surprised Bethany—he must have been reading those books.

The crowd had questions about Ben, too. Tyler fielded queries about his sleeping and eating habits with aplomb. When he said he only had time for one more question, a teenage girl with blond dreadlocks raised her hand.

"Do you think the baby would rather be with his mother?" she asked. She sounded distressed on Ben's behalf, and Bethany wondered if maybe she'd been fostered herself.

Dismay flashed across Tyler's face, as if the thought of Ben's mother hadn't occurred to him in a while. Bethany took that as a good sign. A sign that he couldn't easily relinquish Ben, because he was fond of him.

When Tyler didn't answer, she stepped forward and said carefully, "I don't think Ben is consciously upset that he doesn't have his mom. But I'm sure he has a bond with her that he doesn't with anyone else." The girl nodded doubtfully. Mindful of the listening media and the chance to reach out to Ben's mother, Bethany added, "We would love for his mom to come forward, for her sake as well as his."

Deliberately, she shut down the voice that warned it wouldn't be easy to hand Ben back. Then shut down her own speculation as to what Ben's mother's reappearance would do to Tyler, to her and to their relationship.

AFTERWARD, THEY moved into the staff cafeteria for a coffee get-together with some of the nurses.

At Tyler's invitation, his mother joined them in the cafeteria, along with his brother, Max, who arrived just as they were on the move. Susan hugged Bethany in greeting.

"Nice to see you." Bethany hugged her back. "You too, Max."

"Darling," Susan addressed her older son, "shouldn't you be at work signing the multimillion-dollar contracts that are going to support me into my old age?"

"And miss out on seeing Tyler being fawned over by all these nurses?" Max protested mildly.

"He *is* rather popular." Fondly, Susan watched Tyler charming the half-dozen nurses clustered around him.

"Tyler did a wonderful job with the media," Bethany said. "He's so good at getting to the essentials of an issue and putting it in terms anyone can understand."

It wasn't her job to make sure Tyler's family appreciated him, but she couldn't help herself.

Susan and Max gave polite agreement, but didn't show any interest in continuing to discuss Tyler's accomplishments. But Bethany's words had carried to the man himself, and he turned to look at her.

She met his gaze...then she winked at him. Tyler laughed out loud, and excused himself from the nurses.

"Don't you know that winking at someone can ruin their concentration?" he complained as he reached her.

"You're a pro," she reminded him with a smile. "Nothing I do could hurt you."

"Maybe not." His gaze turned brooding. "Come out for lunch with me after this. Mom can take Ben back to her place." He sent his mother a questioning look. Susan nodded.

Bethany shrugged. "I guess lunch would be fine."

Tyler grinned. To judge by Bethany's lack of enthusiasm, you'd think she wasn't hot for him. He knew better. "I'll find Ben, and we'll hand him over to Mom."

The nurse who'd taken Ben originally no longer had him. She pointed Tyler in the direction of a group of nurses. Several of them held babies. He groaned inwardly. Not this again.

"Ladies, how are you?" He edged into the circle with a smile and hoped someone would offer him Ben. They returned his greeting and politely tried to involve him in their conversation.

Tyler replied to a question while he surreptitiously checked out the babies.

Then he said to the nurse on his left, "May I take Ben now?" And held his breath.

Maybe she replied right away, but to Tyler it felt like hours.

"He's so cute," the woman said as she handed Ben over.

"He is," Tyler agreed mechanically, barely processing her words through his relief. He hugged Ben to him—*hey, pardner, we did it!*—and headed back to Bethany, who was now chatting to a doctor she evidently knew.

"Why the goofy grin?" she asked.

"I got the right baby." He recounted what had happened.

"I told you you're bonding with him," she said in her superior tone.

"I'm not bonding," Tyler growled. But his heart wasn't in it.

The familiar unmistakable aroma wafted from Ben's diaper.

"I'll change him before we give him to Susan," Bethany said.

Tyler went with her. In the corridor, they found a parent-and-child bathroom.

"You don't get any less stinky as you get older," she told Ben as she wiped him clean.

He said something that might have been "Ah goo."

"Goo indeed," she said severely as she bundled the mess into a plastic bag. "He's been saying that sort of thing for a couple of weeks," she told Tyler, "which suggests he's four months old."

Ben batted her face with his little hand. When she'd fixed the new diaper in place, she spent a couple of minutes playing peekaboo, a game that involved Bethany holding a receiving blanket between her and Ben. She slowly lowered the blanket, and when Ben saw her eyes and started to smile, she said, "Peekaboo," and blew a raspberry on his bare tummy, which had Ben squirming and laughing.

"Can anyone play?" Tyler asked.

"Sure." She offered him the blanket.

"I wanted Ben's part," he said.

"Don't be silly." But her eyes wandered over him, and Tyler would bet she was thinking about what she could do to him naked, just as, increasingly, he was thinking that about her. It had to happen soon.

CHAPTER TWELVE

TYLER WAS AWARE he'd gotten carried away during today's informal press conference. He'd talked to half a dozen sick kids, and the next minute he was committing the foundation to long-term support of kidney disease. His usual strategy of noninvolvement—or as Bethany would say, non-caring—suddenly made a whole lot of sense.

He knew exactly what Bethany would be thinking after this morning's visit.

He couldn't let her.

He took her to Magritte, one of Atlanta's most expensive restaurants. When the maître d' helped Bethany out of the coat she'd worn all the way around the hospital, it turned out she'd actually dressed sexy today, though he doubted she knew that. Skinny black pants emphasized the length of her legs, and her faded green scoop-necked T-shirt had a shabby-chic, shrunk-in-the-wash look that sat a half inch above the waistband of her pants and enticingly low on her breasts.

Bethany looked around at the restaurant's soaring ceilings, the chandeliers, the plush banquette seating.

Her interest in her surroundings meant she didn't notice the curious appraisal of several male diners, all accompanied by much more glamorously, elegantly dressed women. Tyler found himself taking her hand possessively as the maître d' led them to the table that would be unavailable to most people arriving without a reservation.

"This place is incredible," Bethany said after the waiter had handed them menus and poured water into their glasses. She scanned the leather-bound menu. "So are the prices."

Tyler held up a hand. "I don't want to know how many kidney transplants you could do for the price of the lobster entrée."

She feigned disappointment. "You're so shallow."

They ordered their food and two glasses of wine. Tyler sat back, watched her from beneath lowered lids. "Do you realize this is the first time we've been out on our own, without Ben?"

Bethany spread her fingers on the banquette's taupe microsuede. "We'll probably have nothing to say to each other."

"Probably," he agreed.

Then he asked her a question about one of the less friendly doctors he'd met today, and that led to a conversation about people with Napoleon complexes.

The time flew until the waiter arrived with their appetizers.

Tyler watched Bethany savor her tomato-and-basil soup with grilled prawns. He found it oddly satisfying to observe her enjoying herself. *That's because if she's enjoying herself, she's not nagging me.*

"Thanks for sticking up for me with Mom and Max today," he said.

She put down her spoon. "I only told the truth."

"You had to see the truth first," he said. "My family has never gotten beyond the playing around I used to do."

"*Used* to?"

He laughed. "Used to do a lot more. The foundation is big business these days, I have to take it seriously. But I doubt Max will ever see that."

"His jealousy won't let him," Bethany agreed.

Tyler choked on his water. "Max isn't jealous of me."

"Of course he is." She took a ladylike sip of her wine.

"Why?"

She sighed as if he was too dense for words. "Because you're Susan's favorite."

He recoiled. "Garbage."

Bethany put down her wineglass, leaned in. "Tyler, your mom hangs on your every word and dismisses most of what Max says, unless it's about the business."

"Mom thinks of me as someone to help out at afternoon tea," he said.

"That's because you're her precious boy." Bethany grinned at his revulsion. "She adores you. I'm not saying she doesn't love Max, but you're the one she dotes on."

It was true, Tyler realized. His mom was much more indulgent toward him than she was to Max. "And you think Max sees that?"

The bitter edge to her laugh reminded Tyler what her brother had said about his and Bethany's parents loving Melanie the most. "Believe me, he sees it. And believe me when I tell you that if you said this to your mom, she wouldn't accept it and she'd be hurt."

"I won't say anything." Tyler sat back for the waiter to deliver his entrée.

They ate in silence for a few minutes. Then Bethany said, "Tyler, about the foundation's support for kidney kids." She put down her cutlery, fixed him with a searching look. "Was that just heat-of-the-moment stuff to impress the journalists? Or did you mean it?"

He'd been expecting the question, and he had his answer ready. "I didn't intend to say it, but now that I have, I'll stick with my word."

She shook her head, her smile tremulous. "I can't believe it."

He reached across the table, laid his hand on hers. The warm heat of her skin felt like home—he couldn't have drawn back if he'd tried. "Bethany, it's not as simple as you think. I want you to pitch to the PhilStrat Committee again, for however much money you need. The next meeting is in two weeks, does that give you enough time?"

Her eyes shone. "It's fine. Better than fine, it's wonderful."

Now came the difficult part. "I need to tell you I've had an application from another research team in the same field—from the Hospital for Sick Children in Toronto."

Bethany opened her mouth, then closed it again. She chewed her lip. "I'd have thought the Warrington Foundation was off their radar, I wonder how they—" She shook her head. "Of course, Sick Kids has a great kidney team," she said abstractedly. "But, Tyler, I am going to do such a great job of my pitch, you won't recognize it."

The excitement in her face softened him inside in a way he didn't recognize. But he couldn't afford to go easy on her. "You'll need to." He lifted his hand from hers. "You know, Bethany, this isn't all my decision. The committee decides who gets the funds."

"Of course," she said quickly. "But I know I can do a great job, and as an incumbent project, I must have some advantage."

That was true. It was easier for someone who already had funding to get more than to break in from scratch. The other truth was, although the decisions were made by committee, Tyler had the casting vote. He couldn't even claim a conflict of interest; the foundation's charter stipulated that applications from Warrington Group employees and related parties were to be encouraged. One big happy family…he groaned inwardly.

As they ate their entrées, chatting about everything and nothing, Tyler realized he hadn't had so much fun in a long time. It wasn't his usual kind of fun. In fact, it was so suspiciously close to *good clean fun* that it had him wanting to hightail it out of here and seduce a pastor's daughter.

The thought slammed home that the only woman he wanted to seduce was Bethany.

OLIVIA HAD SPENT almost every evening with Silas since that first time he'd kissed her. Ostensibly, it was to help with his presentation, but every day their kisses grew more heated. They started the second she walked in the door, occurred at regular intervals through the evening, and severely delayed her departure at the end.

They ate together most nights and, on weekends, they had whole days to revel in each other's company. With Silas's lack of interest in small talk, those were quiet days—but Olivia found she didn't miss talking about food, books, mutual acquaintances. On the occasions Silas had something to say, it was serious. At first she had to stretch her mind to accommodate the conversation and found herself praying it would be over before she made a fool of herself. But Silas's patience meant she never felt under pressure, and somehow they always connected. Olivia had never talked so little yet felt as if she'd said so much.

When she was with Silas, nothing existed except the two of them. And the frogs.

They didn't go any further than those kisses and increasingly intimate touches. Physically, Olivia was frustrated. Emotionally, she was almost willing to wait. Silas had lost his wife, he had some irrational sense of guilt over whether she'd been happy or not. He wouldn't rush past those obstacles, but ultimately he'd get there. And then…

For the first time, Olivia had none of those doubts about whether a man could love her enough. Once Silas made up his mind to move on from his old life, he would be hers, for always. And then, she would love him back.

In the meantime, she made maximum space for him in her life. She'd bowed out of her book club meeting, a friend's daughter's bridal shower and a bachelorette party for an acquaintance embarking on her third marriage. But when she tried to cancel dinner with Susan Warrington, things got sticky.

"Who is it?" Susan demanded. "I know you're seeing someone."

"What did Tyler say?"

"You told *Tyler* and you didn't tell me?"

Drat, she'd given herself away. "I'm…interested in a man who's pitching to the foundation."

"A doctor?" Susan asked excitedly. "What charity is he with?"

"He's a professor, actually. Physics. His name is Silas."

"I want you both here for dinner on Friday," Susan ordered.

Olivia tried not to reveal her alarm in her voice. "We're not really dating."

"I'll invite Tyler and Bethany. You can tell Silas it's a chance to get to know Tyler before he pitches." Susan's tone held the implacability that compelled even her two strong sons to accede to her demands. Olivia didn't stand a chance. "If you won't invite him, I'll have Tyler do it."

Olivia could just imagine Tyler's response to that. "I'll invite him," she said. "But, Susan…"

"Yes, sweetie?" Susan was nice as pie now that she had her own way.

"Silas isn't the kind of man I usually date. He's not very sociable."

Silence. "I'm sure we can draw him out," Susan had finally said.

OLIVIA WARNED Silas the evening at Susan's might not be to his liking.

"Take a risk," he told her, smiling.

"I'm not afraid," she lied. "I just thought you might not enjoy it."

"I'll risk it," he said with gentle irony.

Olivia picked him up from his house because she couldn't guarantee that he'd bring the Maserati rather than the truck. By the time they got to Susan's, the others were already there.

Silas and Tyler had never met before. They appraised each other in the way strong men do—the handshakes were overly firm, the greetings were respectful but not too friendly. Both appeared to be reserving judgment.

Olivia tried to see Silas through Tyler's and Susan's eyes…and quailed. He'd made an effort, but it wouldn't be obvious to anyone else. His chinos were wrinkled, his white shirt was missing a button. He fell far short of the sartorial standard set by Tyler, impeccable in dark pants and ironed shirt.

Susan looked mystified from the moment Silas walked into her living room. Olivia could understand her initial reaction, but half an hour later Susan was still nibbling on her bottom lip every time Silas spoke. Admittedly, he was getting somewhat carried away in his discourse about conservation…. But couldn't Susan see he had more emotion, more depth in his little finger than all the other men they knew put together?

Bethany made a valiant effort to talk to Silas, asking him intelligent questions about frogs.

Which, perversely, annoyed Olivia, who'd never pretended a genuine interest in the red-spotted tree frog. Silas hadn't seemed to mind, but Olivia didn't need Bethany being *so* curious about the thing.

They shouldn't have come; she wasn't ready to expose her relationship to scrutiny.

They sat at the oak dining table to eat. Susan, at the head of the table, directed Olivia and Bethany to sit on either side of her. Silas and Tyler were opposite each other farther down.

The two men were engrossed in a discussion of how the foundation worked, when Susan leaned close to Olivia. "Silas is unusual, isn't he?"

Olivia nodded, though she knew Susan used the word as a euphemism. She meant *odd.*

"He's wearing sneakers," Susan said. "I'm not even sure they match."

Olivia was certain they didn't. "There are worse things than wearing sneakers to dinner."

Susan put down her silverware and hissed, "You're making a mistake, Olivia."

"Just because Silas doesn't dress well," Olivia began defensively.

"It's not just the clothes. Nothing about this makes sense."

"I like him." Though that didn't make much sense, either.

"He's the wrong man for you," Susan said. "And you know I'm always right about you and men."

It was true. Olivia normally welcomed Susan's opinions of the men she dated—her friend had excellent instincts.

"Maybe you're wrong this time."

Susan had always been the bossy one in their friendship, and she didn't like being contradicted. "Listen to me, Olivia, or you'll end up making a fool of yourself."

Too late, both women realized the men had stopped talking, and everyone had heard Susan.

Silas put his hand over Olivia's on the tabletop.

Susan blushed slightly. "I'm sorry, it was rude of me to let you hear that."

"Whereas saying it behind my back wouldn't have been?" Silas asked mildly.

Susan's color deepened. "I'm not saying you're not a nice man, Silas. I just don't think you're right for Olivia. And—" she drew a sharp breath "—I can't help wondering if you're using her to get to Tyler."

Strangely, the thought had never once occurred to Olivia. But now Susan said it, doubt pierced her on all sides. It was entirely possible that Silas was exploiting her attraction to him. She swallowed, looked at him, waited for him to say in that deep voice that he found her a "very interesting woman."

If she could just hear that sturdy, Silas-style endorsement, she would be fine.

He was staring at her. She read his mind as

clearly as if he'd spoken aloud. *Take a risk.* He wanted her to trust him—he deserved to have her trust him. But he'd never said he loved her....

"Olivia," Tyler said from across the table, and she tore her gaze from Silas, "remember those instincts we were talking about?"

It was all very well for Tyler to tell her to trust herself—he wasn't the one who stood to lose... everything.

Olivia shut her eyes, aware she was at a crossroads. She knew Susan's intentions were pure. Others would say far worse. If she thought they had no future, now was the time to end it.

Silas still cupped her hand. Olivia turned hers over, so their palms met. "Silas," she said, "will you come to the Biedermeyers' ball with me next week?"

Susan looked shocked. Stu and Margie Biedermeyer were staunchly correct. Tyler gave Olivia a thumbs-up.

"Yes," Silas said.

Usually Olivia loved that he either said yes or no, no conditions, no questions, no procrastination. But her invitation was a significant milestone, and she'd have liked him to acknowledge that. But this was Silas, the man she'd decided to take on trust.

SILAS DIDN'T SAY anything about her decision on the drive home. But he did tell her he had met the

Biedermeyers. In fact, as they talked about Atlanta society, the kind of thing they never talked about, she learned that Silas knew many of her friends. She'd been aware his family had had plenty of money—which was how he lived in this beautiful home on an academic salary—but she hadn't realized how far their circles overlapped with hers.

Olivia felt as if she was being rewarded for her brave decision. All she had to do now was make sure Silas was presentable on the big night.

"Silas...sweetheart," she said, as she drove through his automatic gates, "would you mind if I choose something for you to wear to the ball?"

"Sure. Do you want to take a look at what I've got?" He gestured toward the house.

She'd only been in his bedroom once, when he'd given her a tour of the place. She'd admired the cherrywood four-poster, the beautiful silk taffeta drapes. She had a feeling she wouldn't admire the contents of his closet.

"If you don't mind," she said, "I might find something...somewhere else."

The look he gave her was long, harder than she expected, and Olivia felt her face grow warm. But his kiss good-night was as thrilling, as powerful, as demanding, as always.

TWO DAYS LATER, Tyler and the rest of the Warrington Foundation's Philanthropic Strategy committee heard this month's six shortlisted applications for funding.

Silas turned up in an impeccably cut navy suit, pale blue lawn shirt and a red striped tie. Tyler had to admit that his case for the preservation of the red-spotted tree frog hit all the right buttons and was as professionally prepared as any pitch could be.

Next up came the team from Toronto's Hospital for Sick Children. It would have been hard to find a bunch of more dedicated and able medics. Their presentation was fluent, comprehensive, compelling.

"Those guys are good," Jake, who'd sat in as Warrington Construction's observer on the committee, said afterward. He slid a glance at Tyler. "How's the cute kidney doctor going to stack up?"

"She'll be fine," Tyler said shortly, and prayed it was true.

Bethany had refused to let him hear her presentation ahead of time, even though he'd offered to coach her. He'd had to be content with asking Olivia to schedule Bethany's pitch for two o'clock, right after lunch. The team would be fresh, and if she arrived early, she could chat to the committee less formally before she began her presentation. He figured it might relax her. Bethany had been wary of being too relaxed, so he wasn't sure if she would get there ahead of time or not.

By ten to two, he'd given up on her early arrival. At five to two, she stepped into the foundation's boardroom. She bore no resemblance to the woman in the ill-fitting suit who'd pitched a year ago.

She wore a dress Tyler had never seen—copper-colored wool crepe, high waisted to emphasize her bust, then slim fitting to her knees. Her heels were higher than normal, making her calves look even more slender. Bronze lipstick made her mouth shimmer beneath that pert nose, and those blue eyes were mesmerizing beneath lashes that had been lengthened by mascara.

She looked calm and confident, except for her white-knuckled grip on the folder tucked under her arm.

Tyler had planned to treat her like any other candidate. But he couldn't keep away from her.

He reached her almost before she made it over the threshold. He stood close so no one would overhear, and said, "You look incredible."

Her cheeks colored prettily. "I asked Sabrina to help me choose a new outfit when we had lunch yesterday."

New perfume, too, he guessed. She smelled of peaches and honeysuckle; instinctively he moved closer. "You should have told me you could look like this," he murmured.

"Because looks are so important?" Humor lit her eyes. "I was afraid you might not be able to control yourself."

His body tightened. "You're probably right."

Behind them, people were starting to sit down and Tyler heard water glasses being topped up, the shuffle of papers. It was time to start.

Certain no one could see, he touched a hand to her cheek. "Good luck, Peaches."

She didn't need luck. Tyler silently cheered her as she smiled a greeting at the committee, introduced herself and her work, and launched into a polished presentation.

Tyler tossed in insightful and intelligent questions that allowed her to show off her knowledge. He could see her confidence grow by the minute as his colleagues took their lead from him and gave her their full attention. She didn't stumble once, and her presentation hit every one of the foundation's criteria.

It was hard to believe this was the same Bethany Hart he'd listened to a year ago.

When she left the meeting, Tyler could tell she was walking on air. He watched her go, the swing of her behind in her new dress. And knew he had to make one of the toughest decisions of his life.

BETHANY KEPT the promise she'd made her brother. She told Tyler she needed a day off on Saturday to visit her parents.

"What am I supposed to do with Ben for a whole day?" he demanded.

"The same as you do for two hours, only more."

He frowned at her as she folded Ben's clean laundry. "Ben and I will come with you."

"No, you won't." She started in on her own laundry. "Find your own family freak show. I need to talk to Mom and Dad about Ryan."

"I assume you'll be driving there in the car I bought you?"

He'd bought her a Honda Accord to take Ben around town. "Are you saying because you bought the car you get to go everywhere with me?" she said. "Because I need to make a trip to the store to buy diapers."

"I'm merely suggesting I might be able to help." Tyler eyed the panties she was folding with interest.

"You can't," she said with absolute certainty as she stuffed the panties beneath Ben's rompers. "Besides, you don't know how to help if it doesn't involve signing a check." Not that she actually believed that these days, but it wouldn't pay to let him see that.

"I'm coming with you," he said stubbornly.

It occurred to her he might be planning an extravagant gesture—announcing in front of her parents that the foundation would renew her funding. But that was the stuff of dreams. More likely, he didn't want to change diapers for a whole day.

Of course, there was a faint chance Mom and Dad might be more reasonable with a stranger present.

"Okay," she said, "you can come."

"PRETTY PLACE," Tyler said as they drove past the antebellum houses that made Madison one of the state's tourist attractions.

"Yep," Bethany said glumly.

"Wasn't it the only town around here that Sherman didn't burn down in the Civil War?"

"Yep." Her gloom seemed to deepen.

Where was the intrepid battler who never hesitated to come out fighting? "Your parents can't be that bad," he told her. "You just need to stand up to them."

Her lips flattened. "Thanks for that useful tip."

That's what a guy got for trying to help.

Bethany's parents lived in a quiet cul-de-sac. From the way Bethany dragged her feet up the cobbled path to the front door of the Arts and Crafts–style home, you'd think she was on her way to an execution. Her own.

She pushed open the door, called out a greeting. After a moment's stifling silence, her parents came into the hallway.

Mrs. Hart had the same coloring as Bethany and her brother, but unlike her daughter she enhanced it with well-chosen clothes. She was still pretty, with big, tragic eyes. Her husband was tall and spare, and one long arm curled protectively around his wife's shoulders.

Bethany kissed her parents. "Mom, Dad, meet Tyler Warrington. Tyler, these are my parents,

Joanne and David Hart. And this is Ben." Her parents made a perfunctory fuss over the baby.

Tyler shook hands with her parents, while Bethany carried Ben, asleep in his car seat, to a bedroom.

They sat down to coffee in a living room dominated by photos of a girl who looked like Bethany but wasn't. She was pretty; Bethany was prettier. Melanie Hart had had serious eyes, a thin frame and a mouth that looked as if it might quiver. There was a lot of her mother in her.

The conversation focused on incidentals for all of fifteen minutes. Then Bethany put her mug down on the coffee table and said, "Mom, Dad, I'm here about Ryan."

"What's wrong?" Her mother started to flap and flutter. "Did something happen? Why didn't the school call me?"

"It's nothing," Bethany soothed her. Then she said firmly, "No, it's not nothing, it's important. Ryan's being bullied."

David tsked. "Not this again." He took his wife's hand in his. "Your mother and I have spoken to Ryan. We concluded he doesn't like being away from home, and that's led him to exaggerate a couple of minor incidents in his own mind."

"He's upset," Bethany countered. "I think you should talk to the principal."

"It's not true," her father insisted.

"Maybe he needs to come home and go to a local

school. He's not as independent as I was," Bethany said. "I think he's lonely."

Joanne's hands tightened on the arm of her chair. "You know I'm not strong enough to have him here, Bethany." Her reproachful look suggested Bethany was unspeakably cruel to even suggest it.

"Your mother hasn't been well lately," David said.

From what Tyler remembered Ryan saying, Joanne hadn't been well for some time. He wondered exactly what the matter was.

"How about we talk about something else," David said to Tyler. "I saw in the paper the other day that the Warrington Foundation is committed to supporting kidney patients—that's great news."

Tyler made a noncommittal reply. He couldn't see anywhere this conversation could head that wouldn't be a problem for Bethany.

"Does that mean you'll renew Bethany's funding?"

Bingo.

"Dad, I pitched to the foundation yesterday, but I won't know the outcome for a while." Bethany slid an apologetic glance at Tyler. "And it's not just Tyler's decision."

Both her parents looked suspicious, and rightly so, Tyler thought.

"Dear," her mom said, "did you make sure these people know exactly what you can achieve with that money?"

There followed an interrogation and an impromptu—and totally useless—coaching session, that had Bethany tying herself in knots.

When Tyler couldn't stand it any longer, he said, "Ryan seems a nice kid." Why not exchange one touchy subject for another?

There was a brief pause while the combatants adjusted.

"You've obviously done a great job bringing him up," Tyler said to fill the silence. "But I think Bethany's right. He's lonely."

One good thing about speaking so plainly, he wore out his welcome fast. Bethany's parents were stiff and suspicious, no matter how deeply he drew on his reserves of charm. When Tyler told Bethany it was time they headed home, her folks didn't argue.

Back in the BMW, Bethany sat hugging herself, despite the car's excellent heating system.

"Thanks for your support back there," she said as they hit the freeway.

"I did more harm than good," he said ruefully.

"It was nice to have someone on my side." She sounded almost shy.

"Did your mom ever take you shopping for clothes?" he asked.

She blinked at the change of direction. "Not after Mel died."

"You need to dress a lot better than you do."

She bristled. "My clothes are none of your business."

"You looked fantastic at yesterday's pitch. I realized the crap you normally wear is a sign of a lack of self-respect."

"That's idiotic." Her eyes flashed. "My work is very important."

"I know you respect your work," he said. "But you're more than your research, Bethany. Having met your parents, I can see why maybe you don't know that, but trust me, it's true. You're smart, kind, determined—you're as persistent as a damn leech." She started, and he said, "That's a compliment, by the way. If you don't know where to find that self-respect inside yourself, then start building it on the outside. Dress properly, show everyone how beautiful you are, and then you might start to realize you're just as incredible on the inside."

No one had ever said anything so blunt, so personal, so insightful to her before.

Bethany dropped her chin to her chest before Tyler could see the shock in her face. Her hair swung forward, concealing the unexpected, illogical tears that scored hot, salty trails down her cheeks.

"Bethany?" A hand touched her hair, and she shied away. "Peaches, I'm sorry, I didn't mean to upset you."

Sorry she was so pathetic? Sorry to have held up

a reality check that threatened to unbalance her? Or sorry because he'd already figured out what Bethany had only just realized: that sometime in the last few weeks she'd added Tyler to the list of people she loved and who didn't love her back.

CHAPTER THIRTEEN

BY THE TIME they got back to Atlanta, Ben was grumpy, Bethany subdued and Tyler edgy in a way he didn't recognize, but it felt vaguely like a storm was brewing.

"What exactly is the problem with your mom's health?" he asked Bethany as he dished up the Chinese takeout they'd bought on the way home. Thankfully, she'd recovered from that little upset in the car before he'd even figured out what he'd said to cause it.

Kneeling on the rug, she buttoned Ben's rocket-and-teddy pajamas. "In my professional opinion, she's suffered severe depression since Melanie died.. In fact, since Melanie first got ill."

"Have you told her that?"

"I have, but she's of a generation that sees depression as weakness."

"So instead she wallows in it, and drives her other children away because she can't cope."

Bethany tsked. "If you knew how long, how hard, Mom and Dad fought for Melanie's survival you might be more sympathetic. Mom had Melanie when she was thirty-two. She and Dad had been trying for a baby for ten years. Mel was their miracle."

"So your mom was…how old when she had Ryan?"

"Forty-five. Another miracle, though I'm not sure they saw it that way. By the time Melanie died, I think Mom and Dad had exhausted their stock of parental emotions."

"And you were the miracle in the middle." The words slipped out. Tyler wasn't even sure what he meant by them, but he knew they sounded…serious. He hurried on. "Your folks are pretty tough on you about your work."

She smiled distractedly, and he guessed she was trying to unravel that crap he'd blurted about miracles. "I made the mistake of saying right after Melanie died that when I grew up I'd become a doctor and make sure other kids didn't die, too. It gave them something to hold on to, and they started saving for me to go to medical school."

"A mistake?" He latched on to the word. "You think you made a mistake in your choice of career?"

"I—" She looked confused. "Of course not. I love my work. The mistake was letting Mom and Dad get so hung up on it." She shrugged. "I can understand they don't want other parents to go through what they did with Melanie. They have high expectations of me."

He handed her a pair of chopsticks and sat down on a stool at the island. "Whereas my family would be amazed if I achieved anything."

Bethany smiled, happy to move the conversation away from herself. Tyler's comment had been made without rancor, and she knew he was mindful of what she'd told him at the restaurant the other day about his mother and Max.

She lunged at a mouthful of chop suey that was about to slide off her chopsticks, slurped it into her mouth.

"Nothing like a well-mannered woman to turn a guy on," he said.

She slurped louder with the next bite, just to make it clear she wasn't trying to turn him on. And she wasn't. After that moment of illumination earlier, she'd pushed the realization that she loved Tyler out of her mind. There was a danger she might inadvertently give her feelings away before she decided what to do about loving him.

Were her feelings something to bury, to forget about? Or something to pin her hopes on?

She couldn't explain why she loved him—apart from the fact that he was great with Ben even when he didn't want to be…that no one could make her angrier or make her laugh more…that in little more than a month he knew her better than anyone else did… Okay, maybe there were a few reasons to love him. But he didn't love her, she knew that, and she couldn't think of a single reason why he would.

AFTER DINNER Bethany sat on the couch with her knitting. She seemed to have lost half a row, because this section was definitely wonky. Or maybe it was a tension problem. The tension in the wool, not in her. Tyler sprawled next to her with a book, which meant she had to divide her concentration between her stitches and trying not to notice the solid length of him, the hard line of his jaw, the dark wave of his hair.

Clearly, she wasn't succeeding.

"What are you knitting?"

"A sweater." A fleeting glance satisfied her craving for the sight of him. For now.

"Are you sure you have the size right? It looks too small."

"This is a sleeve." Already, she wanted to look at him again. She focused on her work.

"You look good in those jeans."

"Thanks." Sabrina had helped Bethany with a couple of other purchases, made at an outlet center. The jeans sat low on her hips and hugged her derriere.

Tyler tweaked her knitting, which made her look at him. "Are you going to wear this sweater with those jeans?" he asked.

"Not after what you said today," she admitted reluctantly.

He smirked. "Good. Because that thing you're knitting now is the worst yet."

He was right. She jammed the knitting down between the sofa cushions, out of his sight and hers. "I don't know why so many women like you."

"Don't you?" he said softly.

The air between them thrummed with awareness—Bethany couldn't think how she'd ever had the gall to deny it existed.

"You're too quiet tonight," he said. "I'm used to you jabbering at me until I can't take it anymore." An odd tenderness belied the blunt words.

"I'm surprised you're here then, rather than out on a date," she said, breathless.

"Me too. But since I am…" Tyler leaned toward her. Then: "Ouch." He'd put a hand down on the exposed tip of a knitting needle. He tugged the whole mess out and tossed it to the floor.

"Hey," Bethany protested as she saw a bunch of stitches unravel.

He grasped the hem of her body-hugging cerise skinny rib. "I'll buy you a new sweater, better than anything you could knit in a dozen lifetimes, if I get to take this one off."

"What?" Instinctively, she put her hands over his to prevent any upward movement.

His eyes gleamed with laughter, but also with unmistakable heat. He might not love her, but he wanted her. Bethany's heart beat faster under her sweater.

She dropped her hands and said slowly, "Okay."

Her agreement obviously surprised him, and for a moment he didn't move. Bethany swallowed, threw him the most challenging look she could muster, then raised her arms above her head.

Her boldness elicited a hum of appreciation from Tyler. His eyes held hers, intense, glittering, as he lifted her sweater. It wasn't until he pulled it over her face that the eye contact was broken.

"Damn."

Inside her cerise cocoon, Bethany heard the curse. She giggled. Tyler tugged the sweater over her head in one sharp movement. "Very funny," he said.

"I don't know what you mean." Innocently, she folded her arms beneath her breasts—over her turquoise stretch cotton tank.

"I could have sworn you didn't have anything on under this thing." He waved the cerise sweater in her face. "I would have bet money on it."

"You did bet money," she pointed out. "You owe me a new sweater."

Tyler lost interest in the bet, his gaze arrested by the way that figure-hugging tank molded to Bethany's generous curves.

All the way to Madison and back, the whole time he'd been in her parents' house, he'd wanted her. It made no sense, he couldn't remember ever feeling so *hot* for such an extended period.

"Now, if you've had your fun…" She took the sweater from him, and he realized she was about to put it back on.

Not going to happen. In one seamless movement reminiscent of his glory days in college football, he tossed the sweater to the floor, hauled Bethany into his arms and kissed her.

First, a quick kiss that did an effective job of silencing her automatic protest. When that reminded him of the ambrosia he'd found on her lips before, he went back for more.

Their last kiss had been incendiary. This one was hotter, needier, a conflagration.

Bethany's passion kindled under Tyler's instant heat, and she responded with something embarrassingly close to desperation. Her hands found his shoulders, clutched, then moved up and around, burrowing into his dark hair.

The pressure of her fingers against Tyler's scalp drew a groan from him, and he plunged into her mouth, his tongue seeking her warmth.

Bethany explored his mouth with the same searching thoroughness, with a hunger so great she couldn't imagine it ever being satisfied.

When he broke away, a cry of protest sprang to her lips. But he trailed a path with his mouth, with his tongue, until he found her earlobe.

He nibbled, sending darts of pleasure through her so she quaked with longing.

Tyler moved down to her neck, nuzzled the frantic pulse. Against her skin, he murmured, "I've been wanting to do this for a long, long time."

"How—how long?" That couldn't be her voice, all throaty and raw.

He lifted his head, and his eyes blazed into hers. "If I said since the day you first pitched to the foundation, would that sound tacky and unprofessional?"

"Totally," she breathed, more turned on than she'd have thought possible.

Turned on not just by the mouth that kissed her and by the hands that lifted her derriere to pull her closer against him, but by his sense of humor, by the laughter they'd shared in getting to this point.

This is love, she thought, and the knowledge that he didn't love her back—yet—didn't hurt the way it had earlier.

Because she'd felt and seen the tenderness that warred with the outright desire in his kiss, in his eyes. She knew this was about more than sex for him. Just as she knew he loved Ben, even though he hadn't figured it out yet.

"Tyler." She tugged his head back down to her, kissed him again. Restless, she pressed herself into him.

Tyler wanted to make love with Bethany more than he could remember wanting anything else. Ever. That she wanted the same thing made this moment perfect.

His hands slipped beneath the stretchy fabric of her tank, found the warm skin of her waist. She shivered at the contact, her whole body brushing against him until he thought he might explode.

Easy, he warned himself. If this perfect moment was to be as incredible for Bethany, he couldn't rush it.

And he did want it to be incredible for her. She was the most giving person he knew, she deserved his best.

He took her mouth again, and was stunned to find that his sensual pleasure was increased by the strength of his desire to give to her.

He wanted to put his mouth to the softness of her waist, her stomach, to make her shiver again.

He slid down her, grazing her curves with his hands, pushed her tank up.

"You're so beautiful." He pressed a kiss to her navel, and her hips jerked in instinctive demand. He unsnapped those sexy jeans, tugged them down a little, then pulled away so he could see more of her. Oh, yes, he could take his time right here.

His tongue traced the bottom of her rib cage, then moved lower to the soft roundness of her stomach. Bethany writhed, then giggled, as he found a ticklish spot. He kissed her there until she yelped, a sexy, frustrated sound. Tyler moved on, discovered two tiny scars, one just to the right of her navel, the other way over to the left. He kissed one, then the other.

"What happened here?" The tip of his tongue probed one of the scars. "A knitting accident?"

She half gasped, half laughed, soft and breathy. "Keyhole surgery."

"Poor baby." He used the excuse to kiss both scars again. "Anything major?"

She stilled. "I, uh, had a nephrectomy."

He chuckled. Even in the throes of lovemaking, she was an egghead doctor. "Are you going to tell me what that is, or do we have to play Twenty Questions?"

"It's…a kidney removal."

"What?" The haze of desire had Tyler befuddled, but it was dissipating fast. He lifted his head to stare at her. "You had kidney disease, as well as your sister?"

"I donated a kidney to Melanie." Bethany's fingers kneaded his shoulders, and she squirmed against him. "Tyler, can we get back to where we were?"

"How old were you?" he demanded.

She sighed. "Thirteen, does it matter?"

Does it matter? *You bet it does.* Tyler sat up, raked a hand through his hair. "That's got to be illegal, for a child to give away a kidney."

With an exasperated huff, she scrambled into a sitting position. "Okay, we can have this conversation, but then I want to get back to what we were doing." She'd left her jeans unsnapped, and Tyler fought to keep his eyes on her face.

"In the USA you have to be eighteen to donate an organ, but in England they'll use a younger donor in exceptional circumstances," she said. "Melanie's rare blood type meant she was highly unlikely to find a match from the general donor pool, and she had no chance of survival without a transplant. I was a perfect match. Our doctor here in the States put us in touch with a private surgeon in London—he considered our situation exceptional enough to allow me to donate."

Fury rose within Tyler. "Your parents made you do it."

"Of course they didn't," she said, shocked. "I wanted to. We all wanted Mel to get better."

"What happened?" he asked.

"The surgery was initially successful. But T cell–mediated responses were generated to the transplanted organ and Melanie suffered acute rejection a week later." Bethany spoke as if reading from a medical report. Then her calm fractured, leaving still-raw pain exposed. "It shouldn't have happened, but it did. And she died."

"So it was all for nothing," Tyler said flatly.

Bethany nodded. She couldn't begin to express the despair she'd felt when Melanie's body had rejected the transplant.

"You think it was your fault," he said.

She stuck her nose in the air. "I know perfectly well it was not my fault."

"You know it wasn't, but you think it was," he said.

Bethany scowled at him, but Tyler barely noticed. He was shaken to the core.

Two minutes ago he'd been congratulating himself on his generosity in wanting to show her a good time in bed. Bethany had trumped that feeble gesture by revealing she'd given away a kidney, a part of herself, when she was just a kid. At an age when Tyler had been so self-absorbed he'd barely known anyone else existed.

Bethany would say he was still that way.

For the first time, it occurred to him she was right. Because he couldn't imagine making the decision she'd made, then or now. And even if he admitted to himself that he could be—should be—a more giving person, he knew he didn't want to give that much.

Her selflessness terrified him.

He eased away from her. Saw understanding, then hurt, flash in her eyes.

"We're not going to pick up where we left off?" Her flippancy sounded forced.

Tyler shook his head. Without looking down, he refastened her jeans. His fingers brushed her abdomen—*near those scars*—and she quivered.

"I don't get to be your first one-kidney lover?" She might have made that a quip, but he read the pleading in her eyes, and it scared him even more.

"You and I are very different people, Bethany."

He didn't need to tell her that—she'd never believed he was one of the good guys. "This—" he waved a hand to encompass her tousled hair, her swollen lips, the skewed straps of her tank "—would mean nothing to me."

And everything to her. He could see that now could only be thankful he'd seen it in time.

CHAPTER FOURTEEN

OLIVIA HAD TAKEN a taxi to Silas's house, and from there they would go to the ball.

"You look gorgeous," he told her. She smiled. It was by his standards a flowery compliment, one he would have been incapable of a few weeks ago.

She leaned forward slightly in her red silk dress so that it showed off her breasts. Which had Silas pulling her into his arms for one of those exquisitely thorough kisses, while his hands checked out exactly how well that dress fit her.

But they were due at the Biedermeyers' at eight, so Olivia broke off the kiss. She picked up the suit carrier that had fallen to the floor when he'd taken her in his arms. "I brought your clothes."

She'd spent a lot of money on him, but he didn't need to know that, and going by how little he knew about fashion, he'd never guess. "Let me show you." She started to unzip the bag.

His hand closed over hers on the zipper. "Why don't I just go put these on."

That took some of the fun out of it, but she didn't argue.

She wandered into the living room. And found it transformed. The frog paraphernalia was gone, leaving the deep cream walls bare, except for five striking modern-art canvases that Silas must have stowed while he worked on the frog project. The coffee table and the sideboard bore nothing but the gleam of polish, and the scent of wax hung in the air.

What did this mean? Confusion churned into hope. Olivia told herself to stay calm, but her fingers shook as she repaired her lipstick in the gilt-edged mirror above the mantelpiece.

Silas rejoined her just fifteen minutes later.

"You look wonderful," Olivia exclaimed, knowing her excitement wasn't attributable solely to the perfect fit of the tuxedo, the delicious contrast the white shirt provided against his healthy skin tone. His bow tie sat exactly as it should, tied from scratch by Silas. She'd expected to have to help him.

He wore the cuff links she'd tucked into the pocket of the tuxedo jacket. Gold with a very discreet diamond stud. Freshly shaved, he was every inch the debonair kind of man any woman would be proud to be seen with.

She put her hands on his arms, went up on tiptoe to kiss him. His kiss felt reserved.

"Is something wrong?" She hadn't left the price tag on the tuxedo, had she?

"I don't want to ruin your lipstick."

My, he was turning into quite the gentleman. Olivia couldn't contain her curiosity another moment. "Silas, what happened to everything?" She waved at the bare walls.

He looked around the room as if, like her, he was seeing it for the first time. "I packed it all up after the pitch to the foundation."

"Why?"

"It's time," he said slowly, "to move forward."

It was what she'd been waiting for, but Olivia hadn't expected the flood of joy that left her feeling as if she was floating.

Silas grabbed her hand, as if to anchor her. "Let's go."

IT TURNED OUT Silas knew around half the people at the Spring Fling, which was held at the Biedermeyers' country estate just out of town.

Olivia loved having him on her arm, loved the widening of her friends' eyes as they took in her handsome escort. Silas was the best-looking man there—and the best dressed.

He got quieter as she chatted gaily to as many people as she could. She suspected he was overwhelmed—hardly surprising, given there must have been five hundred people at the ball. Early on, they met up with Charlie Gooding, who was apparently an old friend of Silas's.

The two men shook hands, clapped each other on the back. Charlie kissed Olivia's cheek. "I couldn't believe it when Silas told me you and he are an item," he said. "Never thought you'd go for a dull dog like him."

Silas had told people about her? She darted a glance at him. He was looking at her with mingled amusement and…surely not disappointment?

She took his hand in hers, and stepped forward to kiss him, right there in front of Charlie. There, that should prove… whatever it was that needed proving.

Silas smiled so tenderly it made her want to cry. Then he leaned down and his lips skimmed her ear.

"I love you, Olivia," he murmured.

He straightened again. "Before you answer that," he said, so calmly that if she hadn't seen that blaze of emotion in his eyes, she'd have thought she'd imagined those words, "we need to talk."

"You two look far too cozy compared with all us married folks," Charlie complained. "I insist you dance with me, Olivia."

Before she had a chance to tell Silas she loved him back, Charlie tugged her onto the dance floor. She threw Silas a beseeching look over her shoulder, but he just smiled his usual imperturbable smile.

She didn't see him again for half an hour, by which time he was talking to Mary-Jane Dayton. Olivia loved that Silas was the kind of man who'd never give her any reason to be jealous when he spoke to another woman. Then she realized he looked upset.

She hurried over to him. "Hello, sweetheart." Concerned by his pallor, she laced her fingers through his. He squeezed her hand, but the gaze he turned on her was troubled.

"I just heard that you and Silas are together," Mary-Jane said.

Olivia nodded.

"Silas's wife was my best friend."

Olivia hadn't thought about the fact that if Silas knew some of her friends, his late wife, Anna, would have known them too. "I'm sorry, you must miss her."

"Apparently more than he does." Mary-Jane brushed a tear from her eye with an angry swipe.

Olivia drew in a sharp breath. Silas pulled her hand against his chest. "Excuse us, Mary-Jane, but Olivia and I have things to talk about."

That was what he'd said earlier. Olivia had envisaged declarations of love, plans for the future. Now, a chill blew down her spine.

They left immediately, drove to Olivia's house. Silas didn't talk, but he kept one hand on her thigh the entire journey. As if he was trying to make her stay.

"Silas," she said as she snapped on the lights in her living room, "you're worrying me."

He didn't take her in his arms, as she wished he would. His hands hung at his sides, his fingers loose and open.

"Olivia," he said slowly, "I lied to you. I didn't tell you the truth."

"About Anna," she guessed.

He nodded. "This will hurt you, and I'm sorry." He closed his eyes, as if he couldn't bear to witness her reaction. "Olivia, I cheated on her."

A knife of pain stabbed her, deep, deep. "No."

"Just once—just one night. But Anna found out."

"No," she said again. She groped behind her for the sofa, and collapsed onto it.

Silas stayed where he was. "She was devastated, nothing I said could convince her how sorry I was. After one of our arguments, she left to visit the frog sanctuary, said she had to get away."

Olivia moaned. "That's when she fell."

"It was my fault," he said.

If he thought she would disagree, he was wrong. An ache seized Olivia's chest, spread through her until she wanted to double over.

"The kids blamed me for her death, that's why they don't speak to me."

Olivia blamed him, too. "You should have told me." She would *never* have let herself feel anything for a cheater.

Two steps brought him to the sofa. He hunkered down, took her hands. "I'm asking you to forgive me, to love me back, the way I love you. *No matter what.*"

This isn't fair. "You know," she said shakily, "you know I can't."

He nodded, as if he had indeed known, and she felt a stab of irrational resentment that he thought so little of her.

"You need to leave now," she said.

BETHANY AVOIDED TYLER for two days. At the start of their time together he'd managed to slip in and out of the house without encountering her; now she became a master of the same art.

It wasn't that difficult. Given that he didn't want to see her any more than she wanted to see him.

His rejection the other night had hurt so much, he'd been convinced she would wake up the next morning to find her love for him had disappeared.

Instead, she'd woken numb. And when the numbness wore off, the love was still there. So strong that Bethany found herself trying to understand his reaction, which she was certain wasn't physical repulsion at the thought of her having only one kidney.

He was scared, she'd concluded. It had taken her a couple of days to realize that, but now, as she sat stirring her coffee in Tyler's kitchen at ten o'clock on Tuesday morning, she was convinced she had it right.

Tyler was afraid that loving her might mean he

had to make some grand sacrifice—not a physical sacrifice, like a kidney, but something in his life or his nature he didn't want to change. And he didn't know if he could do it.

Bethany added a third spoonful of sugar to her coffee—she hadn't felt like eating much, and was maintaining her energy with regular doses of syrup and caffeine. She tossed the spoon into the sink.

"Scaredy-cat," she said out loud.

Because no one knew what sacrifice they were capable of making until the need arose. She hadn't started out intending to give Melanie her kidney, but when they'd reached the stage where that was the only option, she hadn't thought twice.

Not true. She remembered several nights lying awake, wondering what would happen if she ever got really sick and needed that kidney back. But in the daytime, the fears receded, and when she made her decision—on her own, unpressured by Mom and Dad—it hadn't felt like a huge sacrifice.

She held her coffee mug up to her face, cupped in her hands, and let the steam warm her.

Tyler had never been tested, so it was no wonder he didn't trust himself to do the right thing.

WHEN TYLER'S BMW M6 roared up to the house an hour later, an illogical hope kicked Bethany's pulse into overdrive. He'd never come home during the day before.

But any thought that he might be here to put things right between them was dispelled by the grim set of his face when he strode into the kitchen, where Bethany, uncharacteristically inactive, still sat.

"Where's Ben?" he asked.

"Having his morning nap." Ben had at last settled into a routine of two major naps a day, which made Bethany's life easier.

Tyler stopped in front of her, hands fisted carelessly in the pockets of his suit pants. "Ben's mother has come forward."

Whatever she'd expected, it wasn't that. "How? Who is she?"

"She's been watching the coverage in the media. The investigator says she can't bear to be without him any longer."

Of course she couldn't, Bethany thought. Ben was so precious. The poor woman must have been in desperate straits to give him up in the first place.

"Social services will want to talk to her," she said. "*I* want to talk to her. We can't give Ben back unless we're sure she's able to care for him." Not that she or Tyler would have any say in the matter once the authorities took over.

For once, Tyler didn't question her emphasis on caring. "I already told the investigator to set up a meeting for us at her home, so we can check out the environment Ben will be going into. Then if it's appropriate we can help with social services." He sounded like an expert on child custody.

"And if everything's all right," Bethany said, "Ben will go back to her." And Bethany would go back to work. She reminded herself she needed to do that, tried to feel enthusiastic.

A tiny pause. "It's not our decision. But she is his mother."

He was right, but Bethany couldn't find it in herself to be glad. She would miss that little boy so much…she'd fallen in love with him every bit as much as she'd fallen in love with Tyler. Her love for Ben was an entirely separate thing, and yet it made her love for Tyler more meaningful.

Which it shouldn't, because Ben wasn't Tyler's child any more than he was hers.

"How will you feel," she asked, "about giving him back?"

His eyebrows drew together. "This isn't about how I feel. Ben should be with his mother."

She'd lifted a hand, intending to comfort him with a pat on the shoulder. Now she let it fall back to her side. "Thanks for coming to tell me in person," she said awkwardly.

He tipped his head back, scanned the rack of gleaming pans suspended from the ceiling above the counter. "That's not the only reason I'm here."

Now he would talk about the other night.

When he lowered his gaze to hers, his eyes were

as unyielding as flint, his *GQ* cheekbones thrown into sharp relief by the severe slash of his mouth.

Bethany gulped.

"The PhilStrat Committee met first thing this morning to finalize its recommendations." He spoke fast, without expression. "We agreed your pitch was excellent…but Toronto's was better. We're giving them the money."

She felt a pit open up somewhere inside her, hope gushing out, draining away. "No."

Bethany clamped down with her teeth so hard on her lower lip, Tyler thought she might draw blood. She breathed in, out, in, out as she battled to contain her emotions.

Just as, in the end, she'd contained them the other night. He knew he'd hurt her, had been grateful for her restraint. Now he had hurt her again.

He told himself it was a good idea to reinforce the message that he was a selfish jerk.

"The committee—" her voice was scratchy, she cleared her throat "—how does the vote work?"

He knew what she was asking. If he'd voted for her but been outnumbered. He thought about lying. But why leave her with any illusions? He'd recognized when he first met her that Bethany had a rare courage, though he'd had no idea just how rare. He would honor that courage by having the guts to tell her the truth.

"It was unanimous."

She flinched, and he knew he couldn't leave it there. Maybe he could never be the man she needed, but he didn't want her to hate him. "The Toronto team does amazing work. Their presentation convinced me they're the best people to achieve your goal."

She swayed on her stool. "You know how hard I've worked for this, how much it means."

"That's assuming," he continued, as if she hadn't spoken, "your goal is to save those children. Not just to assuage your guilt over Melanie's death."

Her chin snapped up as if he'd hit her with an uppercut. "How dare you."

"Bethany, my decision was in the best interest of kids with kidney disease." He watched as the inevitable inarticulateness overtook her, and she clammed up, red-faced, mouth tight, shoulders shaking with emotion.

"I imagine you don't want to be around me right now, so I'll stay at Mom's place tonight," he said. "Shall I take Ben?"

Bethany found her voice, but it was thick, water-logged. "All his stuff is here, best leave him with me."

He nodded, scooped up his car keys from the counter. "I'll pick you up tomorrow afternoon for the visit to Ben's mother." When he reached the kitchen doorway, he stopped. Without turning around, he said, "Bethany…I'm going to miss the little guy."

"I don't believe you," she choked.

NEXT MORNING, Tyler got some news he'd been waiting for. One of the scheduled guests had canceled out of the *Marlene Black Show,* a live TV program based in Atlanta but syndicated all over the United States. The show, a mix of hard news and magazine-format stories, was one of the most respected in the country. This was the media breakthrough Tyler need to clinch the job in Washington, D.C.

The timing would be tight, but he could do the interview before they went to see Ben's mother.

STILL SO ANGRY she hadn't been able to talk to Tyler, Bethany stood by as talk show host Marlene Black introduced herself to him. Bethany sneered when he said he'd been a fan of Marlene's for a long time, but no one was looking at her. Predictably, when Tyler turned that smile of his on Marlene, her voice grew more animated, her eyes brighter.

"I'll introduce the segment, then we'll cut away to the footage of the mother leaving the baby at your office," she said. "Then, Tyler, I'll talk to you about the baby." She turned to Bethany. "Maybe I'll ask you about the baby's health and development."

She signaled to one of the crew to attach a microphone to Bethany.

"But I don't want—" Bethany said.

"Actually, Marlene, I'd rather we spent as much time as possible talking about how the foundation helps parents and children," Tyler said. "Do you think we could do that?" He gave her a smile so hot, Bethany half expected the woman to combust. Dammit, he was such a manipulator.

"Absolutely," Marlene breathed, and laid a hand on Tyler's arm. "I think the work you do is wonderful."

"If you think that's wonderful, you should see him naked," Bethany said snarkily. Because that's what the woman *meant*, Bethany would bet her entire research budget on it.

Tyler choked. Marlene whisked her hand off his arm faster than the speed of light.

"Not that I have," Bethany said chattily, "but his secretary assures me it's an impressive sight." Olivia hadn't used that exact word when she'd mentioned seeing Tyler naked as a baby, but Bethany was extrapolating.

"Uh…" Marlene darted a confused glance at Tyler.

"Let's just stick to business, shall we?" He glared at Bethany. "I'll hold Ben for the start of the interview, then I'll pass him to you before he starts crying or puking."

That's right, duck out of the hard yards, she fumed.

After his introduction Tyler handed Ben over to

Bethany. He presented a compassionate yet authoritative persona to the camera as he talked about how rewarding his time with the baby had been.

The interviewer still looked wary every time she caught Bethany's eye. Then the woman said, "We're going to talk to pediatrician Bethany Hart about Ben's health and development."

What? If this was Marlene's idea of revenge for that comment Bethany had made earlier... But the camera was on her, so she made sure she was the consummate pediatric professional as she gave her expert opinion.

She'd thought she was doing pretty well, but then, from the corner of her eye, she saw Tyler glance at his watch. Just the way he had when she'd bored him with her pitch. No doubt he was counting the seconds until he could get all the attention back on himself and his precious foundation. Until he could forget Ben's existence.

"How did you come to get involved with young Ben?" Marlene asked her.

"I've been fortunate to have my research into childhood kidney disease funded by the generosity of Tyler Warrington and the Warrington Foundation," she said.

She caught Tyler's surprised, pleased look. Good, she had his full attention. "Or should I say, it used to be funded," she amended. "Unfortunately the foundation hasn't renewed its grant, so if I want to make real progress in the battle against childhood kidney disease, I need to look elsewhere." She sensed rather than saw Tyler's shock. *Take that, Mr. Hotshot Philanthropist.*

"If I get more money," Bethany said, "I know my work can make a difference." At first, she talked fast, not wanting to give Marlene any chance to break in. Then she realized the presenter had eased back in her chair and, beyond chipping in with the occasional "uh-huh," was going to let her say her piece. She slowed her pace, made sure she got across several important points about childhood kidney disease and the importance of securing extra research funds. She talked for what felt like two whole minutes.

By the time the cameras went off them and the ad break kicked in, Tyler was ready to explode. Thanks to Bethany's hijack, he'd barely gotten a word in, and this was his last chance to impress Washington. She'd hitched a ride on his wagon, then proceeded to shove him off it!

"Thanks for letting me say so much about my research," she was saying now as she shook Marlene's hand while Tyler stood fuming to one side.

The other woman's mouth twisted in a wry smile. "I didn't have much choice, after you made it plain you doubted my professionalism."

"Oh." Bethany blushed—and so she damn well should, Tyler thought. "Sorry about that."

"I'm just glad you didn't say it on air." A giggle softened the talk-show host's sophistication and made her look a lot more attractive, though Bethany was the prettier of the two. "It would've livened the segment up if you had."

Yeah, and hadn't it needed livening up, with Bethany going on about kidney disease.

"If you two have finished your girl talk," Tyler said with a smoothness that didn't entirely hide his fury, "we have a baby here who needs his lunch."

Bethany's face held a hint of gloating and a whole lot of "since when do you care about the baby?" And, dammit, she still looked pretty. She said goodbye to Marlene and headed for the door, her hips swinging beneath a soft turquoise skirt he'd never seen before, her high-heeled shoes drawing his attention to her slim ankles. Tyler picked up Ben in his car seat and followed her.

Ben was tired—overtired—and on the way home he started to squall. Bethany turned around in her seat and tried to soothe him, but nothing worked. When the din got so loud Tyler couldn't concentrate on driving, he pulled over.

"You'd better get in the back and give him a bottle, or something," he snapped.

She did as he suggested, and it seemed to calm Ben. Tyler pulled out into traffic again, but within a minute Ben was pulling away from the bottle, crying angrily.

"I think he's teething, he's been extra drooly the past few days."

Huh, she managed to speak civilly enough when it was about Ben. In the rearview mirror, Tyler saw her lean over to drop a kiss on the baby's head. Then she began to sing: "Tom, Tom, the piper's son, stole a pig and away did run. The pig was eat and Tom was beat, and Tom ran crying down the street."

Her voice was so soft, Tyler had to strain to hear the words. He grunted sour disapproval. "I can't believe you think a rhyme about juvenile delinquency and child abuse is fit for a baby's ears."

"Shut up," she said with an anger that shocked him.

CHAPTER FIFTEEN

BETHANY DECIDED they shouldn't take Ben with them to see his mother. Having him there could make the meeting too emotional. Tyler was in full agreement.

When she thought about the options available to Ben and his mom, none of them included Bethany having any ongoing responsibility for the little boy. Nor Tyler. Though Tyler hadn't yet told social services about the woman coming forward. Inevitably, she would be investigated, possibly charged by the police. If she loved Ben and could look after him, if her abandonment had been a moment's desperation, prison would be a terrible outcome. Tyler might need to offer his lawyer's assistance to keep mother and baby together.

Bethany wished she could feel happier for Ben as they walked up the path of the shabby but clean white clapboard house in Clayton County.

The woman who answered the doorbell was older than Bethany expected. Tall, skinny—as she'd appeared in the security footage—with a child

Bethany judged to be about two years old perched on her hip.

"Alice James?" Tyler said.

She looked eagerly past Bethany and Tyler. "Where's Davey?"

That must be Ben's real name.

Tyler introduced himself and Bethany. He said with that charming smile that could sell sand to a Bedouin, "Before we return your son to you, we want to be sure you have everything you need to look after him." Bethany assumed he hadn't mentioned the inevitable involvement of the authorities in this process because he didn't want to alarm her.

She looked suspicious. "He's my baby, he should be here with me."

"Ms. James, we need to understand why you left Ben, and how your circumstances have changed so that you now feel able to have him back," Bethany said.

Tears welled up in the woman's eyes. "I'll never forgive myself for leaving my baby." She buried her face against the toddler's neck.

Tyler put an arm across her shoulders and shepherded her inside. As they followed her down a hallway that smelled of boiled vegetables, Bethany glanced up at Tyler. He was frowning, his eyes on Ben's mother's back. Alice led them into a small living room, furnished with a worn green couch, a set of nested tables and not much else. In a corner, two more children, identical twins, were playing. Bethany judged them to be around four years old.

They sat on the couch, and Bethany invited the woman to talk about her family. Seemed there was no man around, and Alice, understandably, was too busy looking after the kids to go out to work.

"Tell us about…Davey," Tyler said.

She drew a deep breath. "He was born October fifteenth." That fit with Bethany's conclusions about Ben's age. "I had him here at home, with the midwife. It all went very easily. I'm used to it." She sniffed. "He was a lovely baby, right from the start. Quiet, not a screamer like my other kids." She picked up a piece of paper from the topmost of the nested tables. "Here's his birth certificate."

Bethany scanned the document. Davey Dwayne James, born October fifteenth to Alice Catherine James. Father: Joseph Stanners. Bethany wondered if Mr. Stanners knew he had a child.

"I'm on my own, and it all got too much." Alice's voice wobbled. "The kids had ear infections, they were all so sick, I couldn't cope. I thought, why am I doing this, when I'm such a bad mother? I saw a couple of articles about you in the newspaper—" she nodded to Tyler "—and you seemed so nice, I thought you'd be a good person to have Davey."

That lamentable piece of logic aside, Bethany found herself feeling sorry for the woman.

His eyes fixed on Alice, Tyler said, "Tell us about the day you left him at my office."

She buried her face in her hands. "I asked my neighbor to look after the other kids—she was rude about it, she always is, but she said she'd mind them for a couple of hours. I put Davey in the bag—"

"What color was the bag?" Tyler asked.

Bethany stared at him. Surely he didn't doubt the poor woman's story?

Alice blinked. "Green. It was one I had from high school. It's all faded from the sun."

"What were you wearing that day?"

Alice described her clothing, which matched what they'd seen on the security tape. "I was afraid someone would recognize my scarf, so I threw that and the hat away." She fixed him with an accusing look. "Don't you believe I'm Davey's mother?"

Tyler hesitated. "We were expecting someone younger."

That started her crying again. "I'm only twenty-six, but I look ten years older and that's because of all these kids."

"You don't look a day over twenty-five," Tyler said politely.

Alice managed a watery smile.

Then he said, "You must be proud of your kids, they're all so cute."

That dried Alice's eyes. He continued, "But while I may be biased, I think Davey's the cutest of the lot." He turned to Bethany. "We're really going to miss the little guy, aren't we, hon?" He clamped a hand down on her knee, gave it a shake.

Hon? And what was with the knee groping? His eyes were steely, so she didn't argue. "We sure are."

"I can't wait to have him home," Alice confessed. "I've missed him so much."

"He's adorable," Tyler said. "He's going to have hair like yours."

Alice touched a hand to her wavy blond locks, thin like the rest of her. "I think you're right."

Tyler studied her face. "He has your eyes, too." The other woman flushed.

"He's all-round a great kid," Tyler said. "You can already tell he's got so much personality, that birthmark is never going to bother him." He squeezed Bethany's knee, choking the question she would have blurted.

"N-no," Alice agreed uncertainly. "I guess not."

"I mean, right now it's pretty big," Tyler said. "But hardly anyone gets to see his chest, and we're so used to it already, we barely notice it." He turned to Bethany. "You're pretty sure it's going to fade, right, hon?"

"I—yes." Bethany dredged her memories of medical school. "Most strawberry birthmarks disappear by the time the child is ten years old."

"Did the doctors say much about it to you?" Tyler asked Alice.

The woman had turned white. "I haven't taken him to a doctor yet."

Bethany let slip a cry of shock. Tyler stood, tugged her to her feet. "I don't know what your game is, Ms. James, but I know for sure you're not that baby's mother."

Alice clutched the hem of Tyler's jacket. "I knew he doesn't have a birthmark, you had me confused. Please," she said as she began to cry, "I was a surrogate for another couple, I gave my Davey away. But I can't stop thinking about him, I need him. I need a baby."

BETHANY WEPT on the way home. The tears started as a trickle of moisture and overflowed into a river.

"How did you know?" she sobbed to Tyler after he'd gotten off his cell phone from the police and social services. He'd also acted on what seemed a very natural instinct after what they'd just been through, and called his mom to check that Ben was okay.

He kept his eyes on the road. "It was her shoulders."

Bethany stared at him, confused.

"She had broader shoulders than the woman on the tape," he said.

"You remember that?"

"When it comes to women's figures, I have excellent recall." He was half joking, but Bethany couldn't summon a smile.

"I can't believe someone would try that. I can't believe I believed her."

"If anyone else turns up, we'll insist on DNA tests."

She reached over, put her hand over his on the steering wheel. "Tyler, I can't thank you enough."

He glanced briefly at her. "If we hadn't figured it out, social services would have. I didn't want to lose Ben, so I was looking for obstacles. I lucked out big-time."

Bethany wasn't so sure social services would have seen through the woman. But she focused on his other words. "You didn't want Ben to leave?"

He ignored her. "Bethany, things aren't going well between you and me—" understatement of the decade "—but for Ben's sake, please don't quit before we find his real mom." His hands tightened on the wheel. "I'm sick at the thought of how vulnerable he is. I don't trust anyone else to look after him. Apart from me and you."

He pulled in to his mother's driveway, and Bethany breathed easier knowing Ben was safe just a few yards away.

"What if we don't find his mom anytime soon?" she asked. "I can't stay forever."

He switched off the engine. "I don't know, I can't think that far ahead right now." He ran a hand down his face. "Bethany, please, just…stay."

He only wanted her for Ben.

"I'll stay," she said.

BETHANY AND TYLER fell into an uneasy truce. It was hard for Bethany to remain spitting mad at him after he'd saved Ben from that woman.

Ben thrived in blissful ignorance of his narrow escape; Tyler went to work as normal, though he phoned several times each day to check on Ben. Bethany started applying for jobs.

She should be talking to other research teams, submitting applications to funding organizations, but she was so tired of talking, thinking, living kidney research that she couldn't face it. She told herself she'd find a six-month hospital contract, then revisit the research options. But some of the jobs she applied for were permanent positions.

SOMETHING'S WRONG with Ben. Bethany sat bolt upright in bed. The clock on her nightstand said six forty-five; it was Monday morning. She threw the covers aside, raced out of her room—and bumped right into Tyler.

"Did you get up to see to Ben in the night?" he demanded.

"No, did you?" Without waiting for a reply, she charged down the hall. Tyler was on her heels, and when she came to a stop in the nursery doorway, he bumped into her. He steadied her with his hands on his shoulders.

They both stared at Ben, lying there with his eyes

closed, his thumb in his mouth, his cheeks moving rhythmically as he sucked.

"He's asleep." Tyler whispered the obvious.

"He slept through the night," Bethany murmured. "The first time."

By unspoken mutual agreement, they backed out of the doorway.

Now Bethany realized she was wearing only her skimpy MCG T-shirt. Tyler had noticed too, and his eyes darkened as he stared down at her.

"Bethany." He reached out, smoothed her tousled hair.

She stepped back. "Don't," she said. "Not unless you're going to say something I want to hear."

He held her gaze for a long moment. Downstairs, the phone rang. "I'll get that," he said.

Bethany went to put on her robe before she headed downstairs to make coffee. Tyler was in the kitchen, talking on the phone. It seemed to her he was standing at attention.

He listened for the next few minutes, occasionally agreeing with whoever he was talking to, sometimes asking brief questions such as, "How soon?" and "When will you announce it?" At one stage he said, "Sir, I'm honored." The call ended with thanks on Tyler's part.

He was grinning from ear to ear as he said to Bethany, "That was the secretary of health and human services, calling on his way to catch a flight to London. Looks like I have a new job."

She listened, first in bemusement, then in growing outrage as he told her about a think tank in Washington, D.C., set up to help families. Tyler had been invited to chair it, and it was obvious the invitation wasn't a surprise.

"You knew you were up for the job." She interrupted his monologue.

"I heard a rumor," he corrected. He poured coffee into two mugs, pushed one across the island to her.

Bethany ignored it. "That's why you wanted to keep Ben, why you did all those interviews. Ben gave you a positive association with parents and kids."

Tyler stirred sugar into his coffee, said nothing.

"None of those interviews were to help the foundation," she said. "They were all about you. Only you."

"They did help the foundation," he said coolly.

Her lip curled. "Will you move to Washington?"

"It's a full-time job."

"Who'll run the foundation?"

"The foundation was never going to be the rest of my life," he said. "I have several very competent executives, one of them will step up to the plate."

"But you're the best." She knew that now.

He shrugged.

"You used Ben," Bethany said. "And now you're abandoning him and the foundation."

"I'll admit I did keep Ben at first because of the job," he said. "But I've grown very fond of him. I won't leave before he's settled, either with his mom or a long-term foster placement."

She snorted.

His eyes narrowed. "You can't talk about using Ben. You used him to get to me."

"I cared about him from the start."

"Really?" He launched a hard, accusing look at her. "It suited you to look after Ben. If this job had been an obstacle to your precious research, you never would have done it."

Tyler knew he was right, and it seemed Bethany did too, because her eyes widened, then she clammed up and stormed out of the room. *Good.*

He wandered into the living room, threw himself onto a couch and thought about his new job. He should be thrilled at the prospect.

But he wasn't enjoying the moment as much as he should, and that was Bethany's fault.

TYLER WAS LATE for work, and since Olivia had a policy of not starting work before him, she had time to attend to some personal correspondence. Such as her astronomical credit-card bills. Three major shopping sprees had resulted in four new pairs of shoes and a beaded evening purse in a shade of purple she wouldn't be seen carrying. Then there was the Venetian-glass vase to complement her collection, a new dinner set and an antique brass candlestick.

Silas would hate it all.

Good.

Bad.

She loved the man. She wasn't supposed to fall in love with him until she knew he would always put her first, and she could no longer be certain of that. But she loved him anyway. It was going to make life complicated. Much more complicated than she liked it to be.

Olivia pulled the telephone directory out of her desk and began searching for the numbers she needed.

With luck, she could make her calls and skip out of the office before Tyler got here.

STILL REELING from Tyler's news, Bethany took Ben on a visit to Susan that she'd arranged earlier in the week. But she was in no mood to be sociable, and it seemed Susan hadn't heard about the D.C. appointment yet, so conversation was difficult. The visit didn't last long.

On the way back, she drove past Emory University and it reminded her it had been a while since she'd visited the pediatric kidney patients. Last time she'd visited, Tyler had gone with her.

The thought soured in her mouth and she tried to recall some of the more pleasant memories of that day. The pervasive cheerfulness among the kids after Tyler talked to them. The fun they'd had with the nurses afterward. That teenage girl who'd asked if Ben would rather be with his mom, making Tyler aware of how much he would miss Ben when he left.

Bethany froze. Ahead of her the red light turned green. The driver behind honked his horn. Still, she didn't move.

That girl, the teenager…she was Ben's mother. Her build—her shoulders—fit with the young woman on the video, and she'd been so upset about Ben's feelings. Not exactly conclusive evidence, Bethany knew, but the hunch she had about this was almost overwhelming.

Bethany pulled ahead, prompted by the mounting din behind her. She broke a personal rule by pulling out her cell phone while she was driving to call Tyler.

"I've found Ben's mother," she said. "I know it's her."

BETHANY AND TYLER arrived at the hospital at one. Bethany described the girl to the senior receptionist, a woman whom she knew slightly, and asked if she was a regular visitor to the hospital. The girl's blond dreadlocks were sufficient for the receptionist to identify her.

"That'll be Kylie Carter. She visits her mom— Nancy Carter, stomach cancer—every day."

"Is she here now?" Tyler asked.

The nurse nodded. "She comes while her younger siblings are in school. Ward ten, room 203."

When they found the right room, they stopped outside. Bethany said, "I'll ask her to come out, in case her mom doesn't know she had a baby."

"She may not have," Tyler said. "This is a very long shot." He sounded almost as if he hoped Bethany was wrong.

The girl—Kylie—looked up at Bethany's entrance. Her face paled, then reddened.

"Excuse me, Mrs. Carter," Bethany said to her mother, thin and pale in the bed. "I'm Dr. Bethany Hart, I'd like a word with your daughter."

The mother waved weakly. Kylie sprang out of the vinyl visitor's chair and followed Bethany. When she saw Tyler in the corridor, her shoulders slumped and she burst into tears, looking more like a baby herself than someone who'd given birth.

Bethany wrapped her arms around the girl. "It's okay, sweetie, we want to help you."

After a minute the storm of tears subsided. Kylie pulled away from Bethany, her shoulders squared in defiance, but her limbs trembling. "Wh-where's my baby?"

"He's with my mother," Tyler said. "Just for a few hours."

"Are you going to report me to the cops? Because my mom is really sick, and if she hears about this she might—"

"We want to help you," Bethany said again. An inquiry at the nurses' station gave them access to an empty room. Kylie sat on the bed, Bethany beside her.

"Tell us about Ben," Tyler said.

"I called him Jordan," Kylie said. "I didn't want to put his name in the note because there were people who would've known he was mine. But Ben's nice too."

"When was he born?" Bethany asked.

"October twelfth. At a clinic in Houston."

"Was anyone with you?"

"One of the nuns I'd been staying with—they have a home for single mothers." Kylie gave a mighty sniff. "My boyfriend, Marcus, left me right before that."

"How did you end up in Houston?" Tyler asked.

"Mom was really mad when I got pregnant. She did the same thing—that's how she ended up with me—and she wanted me to be different. I was sixteen and Marcus was nineteen. Mom complained to the police about statutory rape and got social services involved. I loved Marcus, so we ran away."

Bethany gripped her hand, squeezed it. The girl must have been terrified, giving birth with no one she loved at hand.

"When did you come back to Atlanta?" Tyler said. "And why did you give Ben away?"

Her lip quivered. "I called home, I was so lonely.

The kids told me Mom was sick and there was no one to look after them. I wanted to come back, but I knew I couldn't look after Ben as well as the kids and Mom. I saw your picture in the newspaper, you looked nice and kind."

He made a stifled sound.

"I told Mom I'd had a late miscarriage." She hung her head. "How is Jordan—Ben?"

"He slept through the night for the first time last night," Bethany said. "Maybe he knew we were about to find his mommy."

Tears sprang to Kylie's eyes again. "I miss him so much. But I can't look after him. I can't work, not with Mom to visit and the other kids to look after, and there's no money and no time."

"We can fix that," Tyler said.

SOON THEY WOULD KNOW for sure if Kylie was Ben's mother—she'd taken a DNA test. But Tyler's instinct told him she was the real deal. His lawyer, Malcolm Farthing, came to the office for a meeting two days after they'd found Kylie.

"You know, Tyler, if you want to keep this baby, you could contest the mother."

Keep Ben? Tyler half rose from his chair, then gripped the arms, forced himself to sit down again, to say without excitement, "He's Kylie's child."

"Whom she abandoned," Malcolm said smoothly, "with a request that you adopt the boy. She didn't come forward, you and Dr. Hart tracked her down. It appears she's in no position to raise the child herself, she doesn't have any extended family who can support her…" He shuffled his papers. "Fact is, if we're thinking about what's best for the baby, there's every chance Ben will be better off with you. You can afford the best child care, he'll never want for anything—"

"And I love him," Tyler said sharply.

Malcolm pursed his lips. "That, too."

Tyler pictured a scenario where he kept Ben and they had their own little family. Him and Ben and— not Bethany, but eventually, maybe someday, a woman he wanted to marry. A woman who was selfless, but not too selfless. He had trouble conjuring that, so he pushed the thought aside.

But Kylie…she was Ben's mother. She was desperate. Brave. Was it right to take a child from his mother?

Caring wasn't about money… Bethany and Ben had shown him that. Yet the lawyer was right, Tyler's wealth would ensure Ben had security. And Tyler didn't want to lose Ben.

He thought about it so long without speaking that Malcolm glanced at his watch and cleared his throat.

"You're right," Tyler said. "Money talks."

CHAPTER SIXTEEN

IT TOOK an appallingly short time—almost no time at all—for the arrangements to be made.

By ten o'clock Thursday morning, the removal guys had packaged up most of the nursery's contents and started on the trip across town to Kylie's home.

Tyler, holding Ben, sat down in the armchair that was one of the few furnishings that remained in the room. He was due to deliver Ben to Kylie in an hour. He couldn't imagine how empty the house would feel. Bethany would move out, too, of course. Yesterday she'd attended a job interview at Piedmont Hospital for a full-time resident position.

He shifted in the seat. Maybe it was the transition from upright to half lying down, but Ben started to whimper. Tyler felt like doing the same.

"Hush, baby." He ran a finger down Ben's cheek.

He'd seen Bethany do that with calming effect, but now Ben's whine turned into something nearer a wail. Tyler jiggled the baby on his shoulder, but Ben squalled louder.

It was about now that Bethany would start to sing. Tyler managed a "la-la-la" under his breath. Ben's cries approached a shriek.

Bethany had said he was teething, and his cheeks had two bright red patches, so Tyler assumed the poor kid was in pain. He didn't want Ben's last memory of his time with Tyler to be full of pain. He knew Ben didn't have that kind of memory, but still… He sighed. How could he ever have thought it would be easy to give Ben back?

Reluctantly, rustily, he began to sing.

"Twinkle, twinkle, little star…"

Ben's eyes unscrunched.

"How I wonder what you are."

Was it his imagination, or was Ben quieting?

"Up above the world so high, like a diamond in the sky…"

At least this rhyme bore some resemblance to reality, Tyler told himself. Not like some of Bethany's ditties about cows jumping over the moon, or farmers' wives cutting off mice's tails.

"Twinkle, twinkle, little star, how I wonder what you are."

Ben's distress had wound down to a quiet sobbing. By the time Tyler sang the song through once again, the baby had stuck his thumb in his mouth and was watching Tyler with big eyes.

Tyler studied the little boy in his arms until he couldn't see for the haze in front of his eyes.

"You're my little star, kid." He blinked, but somehow a drop of moisture escaped and landed on Ben's arm. Tyler brushed it away with his thumb.

"Tyler?" Bethany's voice from the doorway made him jump a mile high.

"What do you want?" he said roughly, not looking at her.

"I, uh, thought I heard singing." She came into the room, pretty in that copper-colored dress Sabrina had helped her buy.

He cleared his throat. "I don't think so. Ben sure wasn't singing."

She looked at him, at his possessive hold on Ben, at his face, which was no doubt red and possibly even damp. She put a hand on his shoulder and squeezed sympathetically. "Bonded, huh?"

What was the point of denying, to himself or to her, the overwhelming love he felt for Ben? He looked up at Bethany, met her eyes for what felt like the first moment of honesty between them in a long while. "Superglue."

WITH THE ATMOSPHERE still so strained between her and Tyler in the lead-up to Ben's departure, Bethany had asked Susan for the details of Tyler's arrangements for Kylie and Ben.

Susan had told her that Tyler had paid for Kylie's mom, Nancy, to move into a private room in the hospital, where she could have her family around her. The doctors had started another round of chemotherapy—Nancy wanted to try every last option—but they were predicting she'd need hospice care in another couple of months. Tyler had promised Kylie he'd pay for that, too.

He'd paid off the mortgage on the family's home—Susan assured Bethany it was a laughably small amount for him—and with the help of a guidance counselor worked with Kylie to devise a plan for her to finish high school at a school that catered to single moms by providing on-site child care. Tyler would fund an after-school sitter for the other kids so Kylie and Ben could visit Nancy each day. He'd met with social services to make sure Kylie wasn't in any trouble, and that they would keep an eye on the family. It wouldn't be easy for Kylie, but the girl seemed determined to succeed.

For a guy who didn't like to do more than sign checks, it was an impressive effort.

With Ben gone, there was nothing to keep Bethany at Tyler's house. After he left to take Ben to his new home, she started packing. She hadn't finished by the time he got back.

He showed up in the doorway of her room, took in the sight of her suitcase, the pile of clothes on the bed. "You're going back to your apartment?"

She nodded. "I need to visit my parents for a couple of days, too. I still haven't told them I didn't get the foundation's money, and I owe them some kind of explanation as to why I haven't bothered to find an alternative source of funds."

"*They* owe you," he said. "They owe you years of love."

Bethany dropped her chin to her chest, didn't want to engage in talk of love with him, when he didn't love her. She rummaged in her pocket. "I found Ben gumming this a couple of days ago."

She held it out to him. His silver pen. His bemused frown as he turned the object over between his fingers suggested he'd forgotten its existence.

"So Ben had it all along, huh?"

"I haven't seen it before... He may have just found it tucked in a fold of his stroller."

Tyler clicked the nib down, then up again. "Was he enjoying it? I could give it back to him—you said he needs hard things to gum while he's teething."

"A twelve-hundred-dollar pen would be overkill." When he looked as if he was about to argue, she added, "The pen isn't child safe, it's sharp and it might have small parts he could choke on."

Tyler shoved it into his pocket as if he never wanted to see it again. Did he remember how horrified he'd been when she'd lost it?

She stacked a pile of clothes in the suitcase. Then took most of them out again, dropped them on the floor.

"Why did you do that?"

"You're right, I do have awful clothes. I'm going to get rid of them. All of them."

"Peaches, I'm a hundred percent in favor of you going without clothes, but I'm not sure Atlanta is ready for it."

The *Peaches* made her eyes sting, but it was so nice to have him talk to her in that light, teasing, Tyler voice that she let herself laugh. "I have the things I bought with Sabrina, and she said she has a couple more to pass on to me. Anything of hers will be so tasteful, even I can't go wrong."

He nodded, but it seemed he wasn't really listening. "What happened about the job at Piedmont?"

"It's mine if I want it."

"That's great."

"I'm not sure I do. I still want to get back into research, and there's always a possibility of—" she concentrated on zipping up her half-empty case "—Toronto."

"You don't mean that," he said dangerously.

"What's it to you if I go to Toronto?" she challenged him. Tyler's eyes shot daggers, but he didn't reply.

She hefted the case off the bed. "Okay, I'm done."

They both knew it was more than her packing that was done. *I'm done living with you. I'm done laughing with you, crying over you. I'm done waiting for you to love me back.*

We're done.

He carried her case downstairs. The cab she'd ordered was waiting. Bethany halted beside it, gave him one last chance to ask her to stay.

"Thanks," he said, "for all you did for Ben."

Dammit, that was all he planned to say. How could he be so dense?

"It hurt you horribly to give Ben back," she said. Susan had told her Tyler's lawyer had suggested he keep the baby—Bethany knew how tempted he must have been. She could hardly bear to think of not seeing Ben again herself, was deliberately *not* thinking about it. It would be just as bad for Tyler.

He shook his head impatiently.

"You gave up something infinitely precious because it was the right thing, the unselfish thing, to do," she persisted.

"That wasn't it at all," he growled.

Beneath his words, Bethany saw the truth. Tyler had made a huge sacrifice. But it had hurt too much. He didn't want to risk that hurt again.

She had no answer to that.

As if he saw her concession of defeat, he opened the taxi door, waited for her to get in. Then he shut it firmly, finally.

She was out of Tyler Warrington's life as surely as if she'd never been in it.

TYLER HAD EXPECTED to miss Ben horribly, and he did. What he hadn't expected was that nothing would feel right without Bethany. Not even aspects of his life where she'd barely been involved—work and social events. And lunch with Mom on Sunday had been so flat, the whole family had noticed.

A part of him had wanted to ask Bethany to stay. But for what? She'd been the mother of "his" child the last couple of months—of course he felt some attachment to her. But now Ben was gone, there was nothing between them.

Apart from an all-consuming desire to take her to bed. *I'll get over that.*

Talking to her was a lot of fun, too. He couldn't think of a single conversation that wasn't better for having it with Bethany. And, of course, she was pretty sharp when it came to interpreting his family.

And what about when he went to visit Ben, which Kylie had promised he could do? If Bethany came, they could talk about what Ben was up to, share their memories of his time with them.

Dammit, the new appreciation of life he'd experienced recently came from sharing everything with Bethany. Garnering her disapproval, teasing her, making her laugh against her will. Being driven crazy with desire for her.

He remembered the day they'd disgraced themselves, both too cowardly to tell Sabrina she had cereal in her hair. Those midnight rendezvous in the nursery with Ben. The night he'd nearly made love to her.

She'd been gone five days and his home had gone back to being just a house.

He reminded himself he hadn't liked having her constantly judging him. With his next breath, he admitted it had been strangely comforting to know she saw his faults and…liked him anyway.

He loved that she wasn't Little Miss Perfect, either. Not just her truly awful clothes, which he acknowledged with a twinge of regret might be a thing of the past, but the way she assumed the worst of him, even as she manipulated him to her own ends. She made him laugh, some of the outrageous accusations she leveled at him.

She made him laugh, full stop.

Right now, he didn't feel like laughing at all.

"I DIDN'T GET the funding." Bethany was beyond sugarcoating the news for her parents.

Her mother's face crumpled. "Oh, Bethany." Not sympathy. Accusation.

"I'm still trying other organizations." Okay, maybe she wasn't beyond sugarcoating.

Her father let out a whistling breath between his teeth, his eyes on his wife. He shook his head but didn't say anything.

Bethany saw how worried he was for her mom.

Suddenly, she was sick of bearing the brunt of the responsibility for making something out of Melanie's death.

"It wasn't my fault," she said.

"I'm sure you did your best," her father said heavily. "I suppose that foundation has a lot of people asking for money."

"I mean," Bethany said, "it wasn't my fault Melanie died."

Her mother flinched, and her dad's gaze turned reproachful.

"No one's ever blamed you," he said.

"Not out loud," Bethany admitted. "But you've said it in the way you don't love me, the way you don't love Ryan, because neither of us could save Melanie."

Her mom's fists clenched in her lap. "That's not true, we do love you."

"Then you loved Melanie the best, and I guess someone has to be loved the best, so that's all right." The words poured out of Bethany in a torrent. "But it's not fair to take it out on us. It's not fair to duck out of life because the one you loved most has gone. Give us a chance, Mom, Dad. Get some help to get better, and give me and Ryan a chance to be part of a real family—or say goodbye to us both."

ADMITTING HE WAS WRONG didn't come easily to Tyler. But if he was going to be a better person, that was what he'd have to do. He couldn't afford to screw things up with Bethany, so he decided to practice on his brother.

He found Max with Jake, poring over architectural plans for a new condo development.

Max looked pleased to see him, and Tyler realized he felt the same. "Can we talk?" he asked.

Max waved him to a seat. "Go ahead."

"It's kind of private." Tyler looked at Jake, who got to his feet.

"Sit down," Max told their cousin lazily. "Tyler probably just wants to show off about his new job."

Jake sank down again.

"Mom told you," Tyler said.

Max nodded. After a moment, he said, "Congratulations." He stood, offered Tyler his hand. "Getting this think-tank job—it's a big deal. You've done well, Tyler."

"Not bad for a guy who couldn't hold down a job in his own family's business," Tyler agreed. So much for admitting he was wrong—it was harder than he'd thought. "I didn't mean that," he said. "I'm here to say you did the right thing firing me."

Max protested, but not too hard. Tyler grinned. "I could have done the marketing job well, but I didn't. I was coasting, and you knew it."

Max lifted one shoulder. "I could have given you another chance. I pushed you out as fast as I could."

"I was pretty mad," Tyler said. "And hurt that Mom took your side, like she always does when it comes to the business."

"She takes your side with everything else," Max said gruffly.

Tyler nodded. "That's the other thing I'm here to say. Mom loves you just as much as she loves me."

Jake groaned. "Do I have to listen to this?"

"Whatever it is you're trying to do—" Max shifted in his chair "—you don't have to. I've always known you're Mom's favorite." The words came out in a rush, as if he'd been holding them in for a long time, then his jaw slackened.

"I don't see it," Tyler said frankly. "But Bethany tells me it's true, and I believe her."

Max looked shocked at the acknowledgment, then maddened. Perhaps he'd been hoping Tyler would say Max was wrong about Mom. Oops. Maybe this wasn't such a smart idea. Tyler tried a lighter approach. "I know it annoys you when Mom wants me rather than you to charm the old ladies—"

"It doesn't annoy me," Max said, visibly annoyed. The temperature in the room seemed to have gone up a couple of notches.

"You guys have got this all wrong." Jake's laconic interruption arrested the tension. Tyler sat back, looked at his cousin. "There's only one favorite in your mom's life, and that's Mitzy."

Tyler laughed first, then Max joined in. Tyler sent his brother a look that requested a truce, and received a not-unfriendly shrug in reply.

"If your visit here is a prelude to any kind of

heart-to-heart with Bethany," Max said with uncanny fraternal acuity, "you might want to plan what you're going to say a little better."

Tyler grinned. Okay, so he hadn't made the best job of hashing things out with Max. But surely they could move forward from here.

"What's happening with the cute kidney doctor?" Jake asked. "Is she available?"

"Never to you," Tyler said.

OLIVIA PARKED out front of Silas's house and wished she was a less selfish, nobler woman. One who wanted what was best for Silas, instead of just worrying about how miserable she was without him.

She got out of the car, pulled her sable coat tighter around her.

He must have seen her coming, for he opened the door as she stepped onto the porch. The sight of him filling the door frame set her stomach fluttering.

The hope in his eyes told her she was doing the right thing.

"You're not the only one who has something to confess," she said before she even stepped inside.

He took her hands in his, tugged her over the threshold. "Tell me, my love."

No wariness, no sign that he would allow anything she'd done to change the way he felt about her.

"I want you to know that I'm selfish, shallow and demanding."

He smiled, and he seemed almost boyish. "Those are the things I love most about you."

That couldn't be true. Slightly less confidently, she said, "I was so worried about what my friends would think of you, I didn't tell them about you. I wouldn't have taken you to that ball if you hadn't let me choose your clothes."

He chuckled. "I could have slapped you for that."

She gaped. "You knew?"

He shrugged. "I love you," he said, "no matter what."

"I'm not willing to take second place. Not to Anna, not to those frogs. Not to anything, not ever."

"You'll always come first," he said.

Tears sprang to her eyes, because this was where she still couldn't be certain. "How do I know you mean it?"

He dropped a kiss on her lips, one so sweet that she almost caved right then and there. Then he led her to the living room, pushed her gently onto a sofa and sat down next to her.

"You know that the Warrington Foundation gave me the money for the frogs," he said.

She nodded.

"I've wound up my involvement, organized the trust to run without me." He kissed her hand. "I've made my peace in here—" he touched Olivia's hand to his chest "—with Anna. I loved her. I did something stupid, something terrible. I have to live with the consequences."

"Which brings me to my next confession." She drew a deep breath. "Silas, I visited your children."

His jaw dropped.

"I know it was forward of me, but I had to tell Jemma and Paul what a wonderful man you are. I told them you'd made a mistake and they had to forgive you." She said proudly, "Paul seemed ready to talk to you. Jemma might be a tougher nut to crack, but I told her I'd keep calling, keep visiting, until she agreed."

"Darling." He pulled her into his arms, kissed her tenderly. "You're amazing."

When he looked at her like that, Olivia *felt* amazing.

Silas knuckled his eyes. "I love you, Olivia, but I understand you might not truly believe that until I'm ninety-nine and no longer capable of saying it. But I'll be in the bed next to yours in the nursing home and inside I'll be saying I told you so."

She laughed and then she cried and then she kissed him with all the passion, all the love, she had. "I love you, too. No matter what. And that means I'm going to take the risk. I want to be with you always."

He kissed her so hard she couldn't breathe. "I know it's only a tiny risk," she assured him.

"Infinitesimal." He kissed her again, did incredible things to her mouth with his tongue.

When the kiss ended, she sighed against his chest. "Does this mean we're engaged?"

"Hell, no!"

His vehemence startled her. "But you said—"

He hauled her back into his arms. "I love you too much to get engaged and have you change your mind."

"I won't," she protested. "Silas, I've never felt like this before, not for any of my fiancés."

"Darling, I know I told you to take a risk, but I'm not as brave as you. We're not getting engaged, we're getting married." He kissed the tip of her nose. "Today."

"Silas!"

He looked at his watch. "It's a four-hour drive to Nashville, where there's no waiting period, no blood test. We can have a license by three o'clock and be married by four."

"But I want a proper wedding with a five-thousand-dollar dress and hundreds of guests."

"Too bad." He stood, fished in his pocket for his car keys. "We can do the big event later—after we're married. I'm not going to risk losing you, Olivia." He pulled her to her feet, silenced any further protests with a kiss.

Olivia followed him out the door, happier than she'd known it was possible to be. She might be about to marry a man who was wearing jeans with holes in them and nonmatching sneakers, but she would travel to her wedding in a Maserati.

TYLER HAD CALLED Bethany and asked her to come to his house. "It's urgent," he said. Then he hung up.

Heedless of the extravagance, she took a cab. It could be a crisis, something to do with Ben. Even if it wasn't, she was desperate enough to see Tyler again that she wanted to get there as fast as possible.

When the taxi pulled up outside his house, Tyler stood in the doorway, waiting. Tall, gorgeous, the man she loved. And yet, not the same man.

This Tyler looked as if he didn't have a designer suit to his name. He wore baggy sweatpants, a ratty T-shirt that couldn't have belonged to him—he must have wrestled it off some homeless guy—and his feet were bare. His hair was rumpled, not in a sexy way—though she found it sexy anyway. He looked as if he hadn't slept in a couple of nights.

"Bethany." His gaze skimmed her new outfit, a wrap dress in green wool, her curves, her hair. "You look fantastic." He sounded hungry. For her?

Bethany's stomach lurched in response, and she put a hand to it. "What's so urgent?"

She followed him into the house and realized it felt more like home than anywhere else in the world.

"I have something for you." He led the way to the dining room. On the antique wooden table sat a familiar, faded green duffel bag, incongruous in the luxury of the room.

"Another baby?" she said stupidly.

He smiled, a grim movement of the lips. "No, but that's not to say I didn't think about using that ploy, before I hit on the rather obvious idea of giving you money."

She lost the end of that sentence in her focus on the first part. "A ploy to what?"

He picked up the bag, tossed it to her.

Bethany caught it. At first glance, she thought it was empty. Then she saw a small rectangle of paper. She pulled it out, dropped the bag on the carpet so she could examine her find.

"It's—Tyler, it's a check for a hundred thousand dollars." Made out to her.

"It's your research money," Tyler said.

"But you said the foundation won't fund two projects in the same field."

"This check isn't from the foundation."

She glanced down at the slip of paper. The account name swam in front of her. "This is your personal check."

He nodded. "I wish your dream wasn't to sacrifice yourself on the altar of your sister's memory, but it is, so I'm damn well going to help you climb up there. Then I'm going to hang around until you're ready to get down again."

"I don't understand," she said.

"I want you to come to Washington with me. There's a team there working in the same field. I spoke to the doctor in charge and he'd welcome another fully funded researcher on board."

She knew the team he meant—they were top-notch. "You said Toronto were the best people to do the work."

"It's your dream," he said again. "I can't say it makes a lot of sense to me, and I sure can't say I'm happy about it. But if we're going to get married I don't want to spend the rest of my life being nagged by you about your kidney research." He pulled her into a loose embrace. "Besides, I've met my in-laws, and you know what they're like about this kidney stuff."

She put a hand to his chest. "Did you say *get married?*"

He sighed. "I can't see any way around it. You're not likely to stay with me if I keep dating other women, are you?"

"I'd kill you if you even *thought* about dating other women," she said. "Tyler, you don't need a babysitter, you don't need female companionship, you don't need a woman to tell you you're wonderful—"

"It would be too damn bad if I did, with you around," he interrupted.

"So why are you even talking about me and marriage in the same breath?"

"Why do you think?" He smiled so tenderly, so

lovingly, it took her breath away. "I love you, Bethany."

She couldn't speak.

"Here, I'll show you." He let go of her so he could reach into his back pocket. He pulled out his wallet, produced his driver's license. "Look." He pointed to the small print.

It said Tyler was registered as an organ donor.

Laughter welled within Bethany, bubbled over.

"Hey," he protested. "I just signed up to give away some of the best parts of me when I die."

"And this is proof that you love me?" she teased, seeing the way his mind was working and loving him even more.

"These guys have to wait until I'm dead." He stuffed the license back in his wallet, tossed it onto the dining table. "But you—" he took her in his arms again "—you get all of me right now. You want a kidney, it's yours." His eyes darkened. "And you already have my heart."

"Oh." It was hardly expressive of what she felt, but it seemed sufficient for Tyler to claim her mouth in a scorching kiss.

Bethany let her lips, her tongue, say what she needed to. When Tyler pulled away, he was shaking. He held her close, his chin resting on her head.

"I know you're way too good for me," he said. "Too kind, too nice."

"Too smart," she inserted.

"I don't think so," he said smugly. "If you were at all smart, you'd have figured out by now that I'm crazy about you, and you'd have worked out some way to take advantage of my pitiful state."

Bethany had never seen anyone less deserving of pity.

"But even though you're all of those things and I don't deserve you," he said, serious now, "I love you too much to let a better man have you. Be mine, Bethany, for always."

She swallowed an instantaneous *yes*. "Are you sure this isn't because you miss Ben? Because you associate me with him, which makes you emotionally vulnerable to me?"

"That's what I've been telling myself the last week," he said. "I do miss Ben, like crazy. But the way I feel about you is…well, it's all about you." He looked into her eyes. "Bethany, put me out of my misery. Do you love me?"

"For someone who knows a lot about women, you're pretty dumb," she said. "Of course I love you, you idiot."

He shook his head at his own stupidity. "I don't know how I didn't figure that out, given those endearments you lavish on me." He put a finger under her chin, tilted it. "I can't wait to get you into bed."

"Yes, please," she said.

"We'll get married," he said. "We'll have children."

"Yes, please," she said happily.

Tyler's face clouded. "It would be great if we still had Ben, wouldn't it? But we can get started on those kids right away, if you want."

"We might have one sooner than you think," Bethany said. "I told my parents I plan to invite Ryan to live with me. That means with you." She held her breath and watched him process that.

"Uh, great." He thought some more, then said firmly, "You're right, it's a great idea. We'd better start checking out schools. Day schools, no more boarding."

Selfish playboy Tyler Warrington was taking on her brother, just like that? He was putty in her hands—the power almost made Bethany dizzy.

"There's something I have to do," she said, "and I really hate to do it."

"It doesn't involve kidneys, does it?"

"Sort of." She picked up the check she'd dropped on the table. She tore it in half.

"But—"

She put a finger to his lips, smiled when he kissed it. "Tyler, you made the right decision giving that money to Toronto. I hadn't realized I don't even like doing research. I like working with kids—I was getting more satisfaction out of my E.R. work than anything else."

He kissed her. "So that's what you want to do? Be an E.R. doctor?"

She shook her head. "I've seen an awful lot of

illness in my life. I want to treat sick kids, but I also want to see healthy kids, help them stay that way. I want to work in a private practice, with lower-income families—you'll have to subsidize me with your fabulous wealth, of course."

"Of course."

"I want to help them make the most of what they're doing right, treat them when they're going wrong."

He nuzzled her neck, sending shivers through her. "That sounds flexible enough for us to fit our own children in somewhere along the line."

Bethany nodded. "Though in some ways I'll always feel as if Ben was our first child."

"Me too." He gazed down into her eyes. "He brought us together."

"I love you, Tyler."

His kiss was thorough, demanding, rapturous. Bethany wanted it to last forever.

From a distance, she heard the doorbell.

Tyler broke off the kiss to say, "Ignore it," then he kissed her again.

But the bell rang again, and again, and again. Finally he released her.

"Dammit," he growled as he strode to the door. "If it's those religious nuts in the white robes, they can go to hell."

"With your reputation, I daresay that's where they think you're going," Bethany pointed out.

He yanked the door open.

"Kylie." All heat was gone from his voice.

Bethany came out into the entryway. Kylie stood on the doorstep, Ben in his stroller in front of her. He'd grown, even in a week, and he was more adorable than ever.

"Come in." Tyler picked up the front of the stroller and lifted it over the doorstep.

Kylie's smile was tremulous but happy. "I've brought him home. To you."

EPILOGUE

JUST WHEN TYLER thought he couldn't get any happier…he did.

He and Bethany—his sexy, gorgeous, adorable wife—had Ben back in their home, and the adoption would be through any day now.

Kylie was as excited about it as they were—she loved her son, but she was certain she wasn't ready to be a mother.

She needed to focus on her own family, on her mom, whose life had been blessedly extended, but who wouldn't last much longer now. Some time in the future, Kylie wanted to go to college, then get a job working with kids. One day, she'd told them, she wanted to get married, have a family of her own, do it all properly this time.

But for now, she wanted to be an aunt to Ben, and a much-loved member of the extended Warrington family. Just like Ryan, and just like Silas and Olivia, the unlikeliest couple Tyler had ever known—and, next to him and Bethany, the happiest.

With Ben and Kylie in their lives, Tyler and

Bethany hadn't been able to move to Washington—he'd had to pass on the think-tank job. But that was okay, Tyler was full of ideas for the Warrington Foundation—he'd talked them through with Max, and the new direction they'd set had him excited about his work.

Best of all, he had Bethany. Just looking at her made him want to laugh out loud—then kiss her senseless. He couldn't wait to spend the rest of his life with her, with their family.

Who'd have thought caring could be so much fun?

* * * * *

Enjoy a sneak preview of
MATCHMAKING WITH A MISSION
by B.J. Daniels,
part of the **WHITEHORSE, MONTANA**
miniseries.
Available from Harlequin Intrigue
in April 2008.

Nate Dempsey has returned to Whitehorse to uncover the truth about his past…

Nate sensed someone watching the house and looked out in surprise to see a woman astride a paint horse just on the other side of the fence. He quickly stepped back from the filthy second-floor window, although he doubted she could have seen him. Only a little of the June sun pierced the dirty glass to glow on the dust-coated floor at his feet as he waited a few heartbeats before he looked out again.

The place was so isolated he hadn't expected to see another soul. Like the front yard, the dirt road was waist-high with weeds. When he'd broken the lock on the back door, he'd had to kick aside a pile of rotten leaves that had blown in from last fall.

As he sneaked a look, he saw that she was still there, staring at the house in a way that unnerved him. He shielded his eyes from the glare of the sun off the dirty window and studied her, taking in her head of long blond hair that feathered out in the breeze from under her Western straw hat.

She wore a tan canvas jacket, jeans and boots. But it was the way she sat astride the brown-and-white horse that nudged the memory.

He felt a chill as he realized he'd seen her before. In that very spot. She'd been just a kid then. A kid on a pretty paint horse. Not this one—the markings were different. Anyway, it couldn't have been the same horse, considering the last time he had seen her was more than twenty years ago. That horse would be dead by now.

His mind argued it probably wasn't even the same girl. But he knew better. It was the way she sat the horse, so at home in a saddle and secure in her world on the other side of that fence.

To the boy he'd been, she and her horse had represented freedom, a freedom he'd known he would never have—even after he escaped this house.

Nate saw her shift in the saddle, and for a moment he feared she planned to dismount and come toward the house. With Ellis Harper in his grave, there would be little to keep her away.

To his relief, she reined her horse around and rode back the way she'd come.

As he watched her ride away, he thought about the way she'd stared at the house—today and years ago. While the smartest thing she could do was to stay clear of this house, he had a feeling she'd be back.

Finding out her name should prove easy, since he figured she must live close by. As for her interest in Harper House… He would just have to make sure it didn't become a problem.

* * * * *

Be sure to look for
MATCHMAKING WITH A MISSION
and other suspenseful
Harlequin Intrigue stories,
available in April 2008
wherever books are sold.

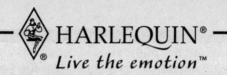

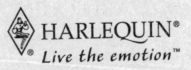

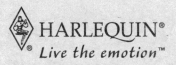

Harlequin® Historical
Historical Romantic Adventure!

*Imagine a time of chivalrous
knights and unconventional ladies,
roguish rakes and impetuous
heiresses, rugged cowboys
and spirited frontierswomen—
these rich and vivid tales will
capture your imagination!*

*Harlequin Historical . . .
they're too good to miss!*

HHDIR06